I0654953

THE
GANGERS

Michael Yates

Nettle Books

Published 2016 by Nettle Books, Yorkshire

nettlebooks@hotmail.co.uk
©2016 Michael Yates
ISBN: 978-0-9561513-9-1
Classification: Fiction

Dedicated to
DICK SULLIVAN, CRESSIDA DOWNING
and GRACE THIELE

This book has had a long gestation. The idea dawned as far back as 1983 when I wrote a piece for the *Sheffield Star* based on the brilliant history book *Navvyman* by Mr Sullivan. That was the start of my interest in the Navvy culture and legacy. But I didn't do the work until 2010. In 2012, I sent a synopsis and three chapters to Ms Downing. She gave me advice and encouragement; and I acted on that. Then in 2015 Ms Thiele, who was working for publishers Aurora Metro, asked to see the full manuscript and responded that she "absolutely loved" it. But things didn't work out.

It's now 2016. And *The Gangers* are once more digging the gullies and driving the nails. At last.

Contents

Prologue: Busumbi, Southern Africa, 1868...........5

Part One: Mollie Proudlove...............…...9

Part Two: Moleskin Jimmy..............................83

Part Three: Sergeant Joseph..........................160

Epilogue: Busumbi, Southern Africa, 1868.........252

Prologue: Busumbi, Southern Africa, 1868

THE ZULU JUMPED TO HIS FEET and there was suddenly a long curved knife in his hand. In an instant, he slashed at the sergeant and the sergeant's blood spurted on the sand.

The sergeant fell. The Zulu jumped on him, poised to deal the death blow.

A HALF HOUR previous, Sergeant Joseph and Corporal Briscoe had been lying atop the ridge. The corporal was philosophising.

"It is the usual trouble," said the corporal. He had been loading his Snider-Enfield rifle. Now he put up a hand to shield his eyes from the sun and studied carefully the escarpment ahead.

"Pish!" said the sergeant, "It is indeed the usual trouble. It is the hot blood of young men that makes for all the trouble in the world, ye ken. Every season they come of age, rape the women and steal the cows and we pursue them." He spoke with an Edinburgh accent that had been somewhat subdued by his constant dealings with Englishmen. Now he turned and gazed steadily at his companion. "It is the endless cycle, Phil. Let us be grateful. Otherwise we would have no duty to perform for our proud Queen Empress and her handsome German Consort. And no pay at the end of the month."

The corporal and the sergeant were on guard. They lay prone on the narrow ridge above a depression where their company of less than a dozen had bivouacked. They were stripped to the waist, partly from the intense heat of day, partly because their browned flesh made less of a target for snipers than their standard issue red tunics. The sergeant was a tall, broadly built man at the start of middle age, who scratched now at his dark moustache from which sweat steadily dripped. The corporal was as tall as the sergeant, but younger, clean shaven and more boyish in build. Both still wore their pith helmets but had rubbed sand into the brilliant whiteness.

"The usual trouble," said the corporal, "is that we have an officer who is a fool."

"That too is the usual trouble. This one is a numpty, no doubt about it. But if the officers could truly fight, why would the government need to pay *us*?"

"And a scout who is a traitor. That young Zulu has almost certainly murdered the older one."

"Yes. That too. I agree."

"But the lieutenant continues to trust him."

"Yes, he does. I offer no argument."

They lapsed into silence. They were two professionals who had come to an impasse. But in a while Moyles and Ferguson came up to relieve them and they slid down the sandy incline to join the others.

"Look at him," said the corporal.

"You mean Bekhi?"

The tall young Zulu was squatting by his bedroll smoking a cigarette. He was naked except for a loincloth and a necklace of rhino horn. He did not look towards them.

The corporal sighed. "This is no life, Lorenzo. I am going to leave it."

"How can you consider such a thing? Where else will you find such boisterous companions, witty conversation and generous monthly stipend?" They had come now to where their own bedrolls lay, and they sat and rolled cigarettes from their shared tobacco tin.

"Oh, and I have a confession. I have a sweetheart," said the corporal and grinned shyly.

"Well done, mon. And is she Zulu or Herero?"

"She is English, and we have been writing for six months. Now I plan to visit her. I thought to keep it a secret until my leave was due…"

"You do right not to share your sweetheart with these vulgar galoots."

"… but I can hold it inside myself no longer. Here. I have a portrait." He produced a small sepia photograph from his tunic on the ground.

The sergeant took it and grinned. A young lady dressed in a white, frilly blouse and long, dark skirt was standing in the typically stiff posture that the camera operators were wont to induce. She had fine bone structure, fair hair that fell in curls down her shoulders, and a nose which was probably not too large, though the angle made it difficult to be certain. "She is a beauty," said the sergeant, "What is her name?"

"Her name is my secret!" said the corporal. "All lovers must have secrets! But I can tell you she has a brother who is looking for a partner in his business enterprise."

"Which is?"

"He owns a tavern in the north of England."

"Then it will of a certainty be a good match! Your young lady is blessed on two counts."

"So you may see how eager I am to end this excursion successfully."

"You mean with your life and body parts intact?"

"I mean that the Zulu is leading us into an ambush and everyone knows it except the lieutenant."

The sergeant sighed. "Well then, we must act decisively…" He handed back the photograph. "…for the sake of your future bride."

THE TWO OF THEM ROSE and picked up their rifles. The sergeant picked up a length of rope. They walked across to where the Zulu was now lying down, apparently asleep. "We

7

will take him," said the sergeant, "and we will bind him and we will make him tell us the truth."

When they reached Bekhi, the sergeant kicked him and he awoke.

"You," said the sergeant in the Zulu language, "are a traitor and a murderer. You have killed the scout we knew and trusted. You plan to lead us into ambush."

"No!" shouted the Zulu in English and jumped up into a squatting position.

"Yes!" said the sergeant, also in English. And the shout of "yes!" was taken up by four or five others who had come up behind him.

"You will not bind me," said Bekhi in the Zulu language.

"I *will* bind you!" said the sergeant in the Zulu language. He unwound the rope and displayed it taut between his fists.

"Yes!" shouted the soldiers around them.

And the Zulu leapt to his feet.

KERRRRAAAKKKKKK!!! The corporal fired his rifle. The force of the bullet sent the Zulu hurtling backwards some ten feet or more. He did not cry out. The soldiers rushed across to him. "He is dead," confirmed Pvt Horswell, who had himself been hit by a bullet only two months previous.

The sergeant got to his feet and staunched his own blood with the first tunic offered. "It will not harm the colour," he said. And of the Zulu: "He would not be bound. Let that be a lesson for us all!" And to the corporal: "You have saved my life, young bridegroom!"

PART ONE: MOLLIE PROUDLOVE

Chapter 1

ALL OF A SUDDEN Mollie Proudlove was struck by the unexpected sight.

She was lying, waiting, her school satchel under her head, hidden behind the third rowan tree along the pathway to Dovecote, where the woodland met the River Ribble on its way through its Yorkshire haunts.

She was waiting, with that strange mixture of boredom and anticipation, for her schoolmate Christopher Truss to find her: boredom because he was taking so long, he *always* took so long; anticipation that eventually – she knew – he *would* find her among the green toothy leaves and the bright red berries and there *would* be the usual squeals and wrestles and tickles. It had already become one of those enjoyable events in her 12-year-old life that she recognised but could not properly explain.

And all of a sudden she was struck by the sound and then the sight of the stranger. He came down over the ridge, alongside the beck, riding a tall spirited grey which snorted as he held it in check.

She knew enough about horses not to call it white. She knew that people who knew about horses would call it grey, and Mollie was always quick to call things as she knew other people called them. And she could see how tall it was – more than a foot higher than her own four feet six inches, though people who knew about horses would measure it in hands. They would call it, oh, 17 hands or more. From that first glance she always thought of it as a *steed*, a warrior's horse, as the kind of horse Alexander might have ridden into Persepolis at the head of his cheering hordes or Caesar might have mounted to cross the Rubicon and claim the dominions of Rome.

She watched the stranger, careful not to give herself away, careful not to give Christopher Truss an easy time with their game of hide-and-go-seek. It was not merely the rowan that protected her from the stranger's gaze; she had chosen also a patch of rhododendrons to shield her from Christopher's eagerness. Not that she had made things *too* hard for him; that would never do.

She could see the man was also tall, perhaps also 17 hands, and that he rode the horse in straight-backed fashion – partly, she knew, because he had to keep steady control as he brought it down the steepness; partly, she guessed, because this would anyway be the way he habitually carried himself. Like a warrior indeed! Like a soldier! She had seen only a few soldiers in her young life, but their memory had remained with her.

As he came closer – he could be no more than five yards away by now – she could make out his clothes, his limbs, his face. The clothes were not workaday riding clothes. How would she describe them to her father? They were (she listed them in detail for she was a person who loved lists) a black bowler hat, pulled low over the man's brow as though he were uncomfortable with it; a dark brown frock coat, rather longer than was fashionable with her father and the local men; a linen shirt which might once have been white, topped by a red-and-black-spotted kerchief; and blue corduroy trousers stuffed into black leather riding boots.

She was mystified as to why a grown man who could afford a good proud horse should dress with such – she searched for the word – *nonchalance.* Yes, that was the word. From the French. Meaning *with unconcern or indifference.* She would describe him as such when she related the incident later. She would say: "Father, I have seen today a nonchalant stranger astride a grey horse." And her father, the Reverend Eli Proudlove, would praise her alertness and her vocabulary.

It was her father, an intense but tender man, who pressed on her the need for learning new words and for constant reading, whether it were the novels of Mr Dickens (though he thought some scenes from *Oliver Twist* were unnecessarily vulgar) or *The Times* newspaper, over which, at the moment, he was poring regularly with mixed feelings as he read of the incursions of the Prussian army into Papist Paris.

"Well," he would say, "is this not a fitting end for the ambitions of the Bonapartes who have laid waste our civilisation this past 70 years, bringing low the hopes of the multitude and the slaughter of so many? Not to mention disillusion to such great minds as Mr Wordsworth." Then he would add: "The Hun are no better, of course, and potentially more threatening to our interests."

The stranger's body – she could now see – was broad about the shoulder and he was also big-chested. And she realised his legs, which were obscured by the angle of her vision, would certainly need to be long and muscular to suit such a *steed*.

She sighed at the incompleteness of her description, wondering again how she would report him. Contemplating the face, she saw it was lean and lined and surprisingly brown; the long nose broken; the eyes screwed up against the strong sun of early July; the mouth set hard as he guided the horse; a heavy dark moustache covered that mouth and a bluish stubble coloured his jaw. Overall it was not unpleasing, though it was nothing like the clean-shaven, pinkly handsome face of the young Mr Shollitoe, her father's sandy-haired curate, whom she had often contemplated at length over the teacups.

She tried to think of the right word for the stranger's face. Perhaps another word from the French. But no. For the moment, it defeated her. It was just *not* a French face. Then she thought: *dangereux*. But that was not a word she could take back to her father. No, not really.

"AAAAAGGGGHHH!" CHRISTOPHER TRUSS screamed out as he fell upon her. And Mollie squealed as she always did. And they began once more the amicable struggle. But then the stranger's horse reared and whinnied and pawed the earth. And the stranger shouted: *"Hola!* Hold! Hold, Snowbird!" and turned the horse, and backed it, and stroked it, and reined it in and brought it under control, though now it stood fretfully. And the stranger called out into the trees: "Who's there? Show yourself!"

Christopher held his breath and lay back, suddenly overwhelmed. "Hush," he said softly, "Appen e can't see where we are." He was still carrying his own satchel over his shoulder and his left hand fiddled nervously with the buckle.

"You!" she whispered back fiercely, "I don't know why you always make such a kerfuffle. Can you not be quiet now and then? Are boys *never* quiet?"

"It was you," he said, "it was you as much as me."

"Who's there? Show yourself!" called the stranger again.

And Mollie knew straightway she had to obey the man. They had frightened his horse. They had committed a trespass, though it had been unintended. They had put themselves in the wrong. The only thing now was to do the Christian thing – make full confession and ask forgiveness. That was what her father would say. In any case, there was no harm done. Not really. The horse was alarmed but the man had calmed it. And because it was a big, handsome horse, she would like to see it at closer quarters and perhaps stroke it.

She jumped to her feet, brushed the twigs and grass from her calf-length calico dress and navy blue pinafore, picked up her satchel, took a deep breath and strode out onto the rock-strewn path.

"Sir," she said confidently, standing as close as she felt was safe to the horse's head, "I am sorry to have frightened your animal." She struggled to make her voice as

13

loud as contrition would permit. "I truly regret your inconvenience. I trust you will accept my apology."

The horse shied again. The stranger quieted him again, saying: "Snowbird, Snowbird," in the calm, subdued way a father might settle a baby, then he studied Mollie for a further minute while she counted out the seconds in her head.

"There's yet another," said the man, "*thee* is not the only chick in the nest." He spoke slowly, quietly, with a Scotch accent, what her father would call a *burr*, a voice as brown as his face.

"Yes," she agreed, "but I am the older by ten weeks and must therefore be held to blame."

"Now where's the other barmpot got to?" The man stared hard at the rowan as though the force of his gaze might pierce its bark or at least set the leaves a-shaking. Mollie wondered at the effect on Christopher. Would he break and run? Had he already done so? She asked herself, not for the first time, what she saw in his friendship.

"Lassie, ye have a sweetheart, I think," said the stranger, "who is nae man enough to show himself." He grinned, showing large white teeth, though a trifle tobacco-stained.

"I have *not!*" Mollie felt herself redden. This time, she realised, she had raised her voice well above the accepted level. She took another deep breath. She thought of Susanna defending herself before the Elders of Israel. "Sir," she said, "I do not have a sweetheart, nor do I desire one. Why would you think such a thing?"

"Firstly," said the stranger, "I think it because I *cannae* imagine a young lassie like thysen, fair in the tint of your hair and fair in the eyes of men, should fail to have a sweetheart…"

"I do *not!*" she heard herself say.

"...and second because I cannot divine a better explanation as to why you appear from the undergrowth with grass in your hair."

Mollie let a hand stray to her head, then caught herself. "I have no grass in my hair!"

"No," he said, and laughed. "But you have given yourself away, child!" And as he laughed, the blessed horse – Mollie never said *damn* – whinnied again, as though joining in.

"Now," said the stranger, "what is your name?"

She considered whether she should give it. After all, an innocent young person such as herself might have every right to refuse, even to a grown-up. But what would an innocent person have to fear from having their name known? She would show herself unafraid.

"I am Mary Proudlove, daughter of the vicar of the parish of St Agnes in Padstone in the county of Yorkshire."

"Then we are well met, Mary." He raised his hat, revealing thick hair, parted and slicked down flat, long at the back and sides, the colour of his moustache. "For you are the daughter of the very man I seek. Will you take me to him?"

She hesitated and he caught her mood. "Let us forget this bit of blether, Mary. I dinnae seek to trouble your father about you and your young man skittishing my horse, so have no worry on that account. No, I am come to ask your father's help. Already I have written to him, now I show my person. I am Lorenzo Joseph."

He spoke his name as if she might have known it, but she did not. "I have not heard my father speak of you. But I am pleased to meet you, Mr Joseph," she said. For a moment she wondered if she should curtsey but thought it would appear an affectation.

"*Sergeant* Joseph," he said.

Then he *was* a soldier! And the realisation took her back suddenly to that day last autumn when… "Do you come

15

about the *other* soldier? Do you come about Corporal Briscoe, the man who died?"

"The man who was killed," said Sergeant Joseph. "Yes, Mary, that is the thing I come about. Are we near to the vicarage? Will you ride up with me and be my guide?" He held out his hand. "You and Snowbird have already met. Now you can be better acquainted."

She hesitated for a moment, wondering at the temper of the horse, whether it were still skittish, wondering also if riding in the grip of the tall brown sergeant might be an immodest thing to do, something her father would chide her for.

She said: "Thank you, Sergeant Joseph. Yes, I *will* ride up with you." And she flung her satchel towards him so he had to move quickly to catch it. Then she took his hand and let him pull her up in front of him and settle his arms around her to keep her from falling. But she quickly made sure the skirt of her dress was properly pulled down.

And she hoped that Christopher Truss was still in the rhododendrons behind the rowan and watching her ride away on Sergeant Joseph's Snowbird. She patted its flank to show Christopher she had no fear.

Chapter 2

THE REVEREND ELI PROUDLOVE was sitting in the drawing room of the vicarage, conversing with Lord Holtby about the morality of commerce.

His Lordship, who owned two collieries – one near Ribblehead, the other just outside Sheffield – seemed much interested in the clergyman's views on business procedures, in particular his attitude to the alarming growth of workers' combinations, through which miners and others strove to negotiate wages and conditions by way of a single collective leadership.

The Rev Proudlove acknowledged the basic decency of the English worker and lauded his industry and honesty. But he also believed, as he knew did His Lordship, that a man could not be the servant of two masters.

"A man who sells his labour must be bound by contract, and, as with all of us, whatever our station, he must take heed of what is prudent and beneficial to society as a whole. A labourer is worthy of his hire. But a rampant rise in wages would see us all in the poorhouse! And who would be the better for that?"

The vicar was of medium height, with a medium shade of brown in his medium-cut hair and a duck-egg sort of blue in his eyes. He was a man who took care in his dress, but the grey sack coat he wore with his clerical collar had seen much younger days. In contrast, Lord Holtby wore a newish bright blue coat with velvet lapel, a shirt with a wing collar, a red silk cravat, and a brown waistcoat over his large stomach, across which ran a silver watch-chain.

"But he never bothers to look at the time," said Mrs Tordoff, the vicar's housekeeper and cook. And it was true.

The drawing room was an elegant but sparsely furnished room in an elegant but sparsely furnished house occupied by the Proudlove household – the vicar, his

17

daughter, his curate, his cook and his housemaid – but belonging wholly to His Lordship, patron of the living of the stone-built 14th century church of St Agnes. The house was a mixture of timber and stone, and boasted – in addition to the book-lined drawing room – a much larger dining room, also book-lined; a study, also book-lined; five bedrooms, all light and airy for they were blessed with large sash windows; and in the basement a well-appointed kitchen; and behind the house an actual water closet, still a novelty among some of their neighbours.

The men sat at a small teak table, on two of the four pink-upholstered chairs which had been a wedding present to the Proudloves 14 years ago. They drank afternoon tea from Mr Proudlove's china cups – another wedding present, from which there had been only two breakages. (And one of these, the sugar bowl handle, had been glued back so carefully as for the break to be undetectable beneath the elegant gold-leaf pattern.) The only other piece of furniture in the room was the upright pianoforte, currently in need of tuning.

It was a weekly ritual for the two men to take tea together; and Mrs Tordoff always supplied slices of cake – either Jamaican ginger or a rich sultana. It was known that Lord Holtby had a sweet tooth.

As the vicar's patron, Lord Holtby gave every appearance of a man who took his responsibilities seriously. Also, it appeared, he got on well with the erudite and well-mannered Mr Proudlove, who knew his place and also succeeded in being popular with the congregation.

His Lordship nodded approval at the vicar's remark on wages. His Lordship acknowledged that he himself also admired – indeed, *loved* – the English working man. Had he not set with a will to bring a Christian compassion to his own dealings with his workers? Why yes, he had. His miners lived in clean, wholesome, brick terraces within walking distance of the pithead, with a water tap to wash away the coaldust and

18

those new-fangled underground sewage pipes to wash away a damn sight more than that from their backyard privvies. He apologised for his use of the word *damn*. And did they not receive part of their wage in kind? The very coal they dug was what kept them warm in winter. Was this not, in fact, a form of socialism, the working man receiving according to his need what he had produced according to his ability? In the light of this, let those radicals reconsider before indulging in their dangerous talk of revolution or whatever.

"Yes, yes," said Mr Proudlove and made a point of commenting on His Lordship's commendable familiarity with divers strains of modern thought. But he was particularly pleased that the talk had turned to coal allowance, for he himself was a beneficiary of His Lordship's favour in this matter. "Though I am not a hewer of wood nor yet a drawer of water," he sometimes added when the subject was raised.

"And of course," said His Lordship, "there are no public houses permitted within a five-mile radius of the family homes, though I surmise that, on occasion, strong drink is brought into the rooms surreptitiously, particularly at Christmas. And I intend to increase my vigilance in such matters."

"I admire," said Mr Proudlove, "your benevolence and sense of duty." He knew that His Lordship's investments and business ventures covered a multitude – and presently included the building of the Settle-Carlisle railroad which had recently decanted a tribe of navvies into a makeshift town over at Hallock Hill, a festering hole with much liquor, loose women and open sewers.

He paused to stir the sugar into his tea. "Sometimes," he said, "I believe the working man is his own worst enemy." And His Lordship again agreed.

But it was the coal allowance that Mr Proudlove returned to. "My daughter…" he said.

"Young Mary," said His Lordship.

19

"Known to friends and servants as Mollie."

"Servants can be *too* familiar."

Mr Proudlove seized on the remark. "You are very knowledgeable in such matters. In our *ménage…*" (he was now confident enough to allow himself an occasional word from the French) "…we have, as you know, the doughty Mrs Tordoff and young Lisa Mortimer as housemaid. And you must also know that Mollie currently shares a room with Lisa. And Mollie is now of that age when…" He paused. "How shall I say this…?"

"A delicate age," said His Lordship, "an age of growth and blossoming." He sighed. "I have noticed she is already a winsome little thing and I do not doubt you are contemplating her future with care. Perhaps there would be an opening for a maid in my own establishment in the near future."

"Ah. Yes." Mr Proudlove replaced the spoon in the saucer. "That is most kind. But for myself I had thought she might continue her schooling a while yet and I had considered she might proceed to a career as a governess."

"Alas, Lady Holtby and I, as you know, no longer have children of a schooling age."

It was Mrs Tordoff's opinion, well known to Mr Proudlove, that avoidance of the formidable Lady Holtby was one of the reasons His Lordship spent so much time away from High Grange, the family seat, these days; though Mr Proudlove had straightway admonished Mrs Tordoff for her lack of charity.

"I had thought to keep Mollie at home for three more years. But this is a time when sharing a room with the housemaid… Well, the relative difference in their ages does create a problem with regard to intimacy. Lisa is a good, respectable girl but…"

"Perhaps more forward than you would want your daughter to witness at this stage of her maturity."

"Exactly." Mr Proudlove screwed up his courage. "I had been considering moving Mollie into a bedroom of her own, the unused one next to mine. As you know, we employ it as an occasional guest room so there is already a bed, larger than her current one, but she will grow into that. There will be a minimum of cost: some wallpaper, a coat of paint on the skirting board. But of course, we would need to make up regularly an additional fire in her room. What cost there is lies in that direction. I wondered…"

"It is a tragedy," said His Lordship, "that the girl has no mother surviving." He put his teacup on the table.

"Indeed." Mr Proudlove's voice was pitched to suggest this was a novel thought for him, that he did not normally muse on the death from consumption of his beloved Charlotte some nine years ago.

"You should have remarried. As a Christian minister, you owe it to the community to lead by example in these matters." His Lordship hesitated. But, as Mr Proudlove knew, he was not really slow in catching a drift, and Mrs Tordoff's rich sultana had today contained a modicum of sherry. "Well then, Reverend, we shall have to increase your coal."

"That is most generous of you!"

"There are, let me see, a total of nine rooms, so I shall increase the allowance by a ninth."

Mr Proudlove quickly listed the rooms in his mind. "But we currently heat only seven rooms, so…"

"By a seventh then. Though a less generous man," His Lordship glanced at the bookshelves, "might have suggested you sell a few of these tomes to make up the difference. Such volumes are ever a magnet to dust, or so Lady Holtby tells me."

AT THAT MOMENT, the door of the drawing room crashed open and Mollie ran into the room. "Father! Father!"

21

As Mollie ran by him, Lord Holtby reached out and gripped her by the arms and swung her against his legs. "Young Mary! Mary! Let me hold you a moment! Why do you rush so headfast?" And he rubbed his cheek against hers, kissing her. She pulled away.

"Say good afternoon to His Lordship," said her father.

"Good afternoon, Your Lordship." This time she *did* choose to curtsey.

"Good afternoon to you, Mary!" Lord Holtby gave a smile and a little wave and resumed his teacup.

Mollie turned to her father. "Father, we have a visitor."

"Then why do you not let Lisa announce him as her duty requires?"

Mollie considered. "It is too exciting, father."

"So I see by your demeanour. Who is this visitor?"

At that moment Lisa appeared in the doorway. She was a tall, big-breasted, dark-haired girl, in a black dress, white pinafore and matching mob cap, who walked with some grace and confidence. She was also the daughter of Mr Proudlove's trusted verger Arthur Mortimer. She stood for a moment, then announced: "Sergeant Lorenzo Joseph. If it please you, Mr Proudlove." And suddenly Sergeant Joseph also stood in the doorway, hat in hand.

It took Mr Proudlove a moment to remember who Sergeant Joseph might be. Then he rose to his feet, walked across the room and grasped him warmly by the hand. "Sergeant, you are most welcome, though it is a sad mission on which you are occupied."

"My thanks for your welcome, sir. Sorrowful though it is, I am moved to seek a just outcome and that thought at least renders me some joy."

Mr Proudlove gestured the sergeant to take a chair. He had been impressed by the man's letter: it had been cogent and literate, more than one would normally expect from a

22

non-commissioned officer in the Queen's service, though some items of spelling could well have been improved. Remembering the nature of its content, he glanced across at Mollie.

"Now, Mollie my girl..." He saw her draw back. Whenever he called her "my girl" she knew she was about to be denied in some matter and a shadow now crossed her face. "Mollie," he repeated, "there are some subjects of conversation that are not for your tender years. You must leave the room while the sergeant and I converse."

He glanced across at Lord Holtby. "Perhaps, Your Lordship, you will remain, for I would welcome your judgement on some matters."

Then he looked across the room to Lisa. "Please take my daughter to the kitchen and ply her with lemon cordial. She will need to be recompensed for the disappointing fact that she is still a child and is now being treated as such."

Mollie turned to Sergeant Joseph. Now that he was seated, their faces were on a level. "Sergeant," she said, "I am sure we shall meet again and talk of this matter." And she held out her hand.

The sergeant smiled and took the hand briefly but firmly in his. "Miss Proudlove," he said, "I would always welcome the renewal of such an acquaintance as yours."

Mollie gave a loud and eloquent sigh, walked slowly to the doorway where Lisa still stood. Then the two of them were gone.

Chapter 3

MOLLIE RACED down the stone steps, banging her shoulder noisily against the iron railing, pulling Lisa hard until the housemaid was forced to let go of her hand. "Mollie! Mollie!" she shouted, "Stop lekking about. Stop behaving like... like..." She struggled for the right words. "...like some sort of farm animal!"

"I am *not* a farm animal!" Mollie shouted back, "Nor am I a troublesome child to be plied with cordial for the sake of my tender years!"

"No," said Lisa – without, it seemed to Mollie, much conviction.

Mollie pushed open the door to the kitchen. It slammed against the Welsh dresser, rattling the floral-decorated plates that stood on end in regiments. But Mrs Tordoff, standing at the pine table, did not look up from her rolling out of dough.

"In a paddy, are we, young madam? Well, a lot of good it will do us," said the cook. She was a plump, elderly woman with untidy salt-and-pepper hair, dressed in the usual pinafore over a faded grey muslin dress with high square neckline. Her sleeves, which flared slightly at the wrists, were now rolled well past her elbows which showed bright red against the pale skin of her powerful arms. She dipped her fingers in a bowl of flour and sprinkled the flour over the pastry board, then picked up the rolling pin once more.

Mrs Tordoff had been in the household as far back as when mother was still alive, and she had comforted Mollie in later times with stories of her own late husband, a locksmith, who had "passed over" (as she phrased it) many years before. So it was that they were friends; and Mollie normally responded well to Mrs Tordoff's rebukes. Today, however, she was in too much of a temper, though she was hard put to say why. It was not simply being shut out of the adults' conversation, for that was no novelty, and in any case she had little hope that it might prove interesting in itself; it was more in the character of Sergeant Joseph, in the fact that she had hoped to hear him speak at length whatever he had come to say, and was looking forward to the strange, warm sound of his Scotchness, of his alien *burr*.

Lisa drew a wooden chair out from under the table and sat down. Mollie slumped on the three-legged stool in front of the hearth with its black cast-iron cooking range and shiny brass fittings. She studied intently the kettle hanging over the oven, the ashpan and the revolving spit, on which they often roasted rabbits shot by Joel Truss, the sexton. She wondered briefly when Mr Truss might supply them with the next rabbit. But that only served to remind her of his son Christopher. Why did she bother with a boy like that, who hid or ran away whenever there was the slightest hint of trouble?

"And did your schooling go well today?" asked Mrs Tordoff.

"Appen it allus goes well for such a grand scholar," said Lisa, and to Mollie: "Did you use any big words to the Miss?" The Miss was Miss Brockelbank who taught the 20-or-so pupils reading, writing, arithmetic, history, geography, Christianity and nature, much as the whim moved her; she had even added pencil and paper to slate and chalk for the clever ones. And the question about "big words" from Lisa was part of a well-orchestrated banter in which the housemaid and Mollie customarily indulged.

"There are some," said Mollie in an exaggerated tone for which her father often used the Italian phrase *prima donna*, "for whom even the words *and* and *the* might well be regarded as truly gargantuan."

"Ooo-oooo-ohh!" responded Lisa in a high-pitched lilt that took exaggeration to new and heady heights. "Well, I might not have had much schooling myself, more's the pity, but I would never use *any* words – big or otherwise – to chide

25

my friends, merely on account of my ill nature. I would not make myself such a gawby."

After that, the three lapsed into silence. And it was galling to Mollie to know that inwardly they were laughing at her. After a while, however, she became restless. An idea had formed in her mind. "I have some work," she told them, "school work. I will go to our room." She nodded across at Lisa.

"Do not leave it untidy," said Lisa.

"And see thee listens for us call," said Mrs Tordoff, who sometimes lapsed into vernacular when making a point, "There's only the two of you for supper, what with Mr Shollitoe away right now. We shall eat when your father is no longer busy. We have soda bread and cold chicken."

MOLLIE RAN OUT OF THE ROOM and up the stone steps. She picked up her satchel from where she had dropped it outside the drawing room and briefly put her ear to the closed door. There was a sort of buzz from inside but the words were inaudible.

She ran up the wooden stairs to the room she shared with Lisa and deposited her satchel on her bed. Then she walked quietly across to her father's bedroom, which was directly above the drawing room, closed the door behind her, dragged the end of the wooden bedstead a foot or so from the wall and crawled on her hands and knees into the space she had made.

Within that wall, she knew, was a loose brick. It was left so when Artemis Martin, the carpenter from the village, had been called in to remove a jackdaw nest from the chimney. She had occasionally removed it for eavesdropping before, but only in what she now saw as a casual and childish fashion. This time, she considered, she had more serious intent. She pulled at a loose strip of the indigo tulip-and-willow wallpaper, folded it back, found the brick and pulled it gently out of its hole.

The first voice she heard was that of the Fat Fool, Lord Holtby. "The trail," said the Fool, "has gone cold. It is now ten months since."

"I could come no sooner," said the *Burr*, "I have been on active service…"

"Quite so, quite so."

"…and when I became more free, still there were complex arrangements, paperwork…"

"I dare say," said the Fool, "but the constable did his sworn duty to the limit that he was able."

"I do not doubt it." This was her father's voice.

"But," said the Burr, the voice slightly raised, "it did not bring us justice."

After that a brief silence. Then the offer of cigars, the routine sounds of handing round the box, the rigmarole of striking matches. Then her father again. "What action do you now propose, Sergeant?"

"To speak once more with the people involved," said the Burr, "with the constable, with the witnesses, with the young lady most of all."

"There is grave difficulty in that last course of action," said the Fool, "for the natural modesty of the lady, together with the understandable hesitancy of her family, would argue against it."

"A man is dead," said the Burr, "A man of courage."

"We are not trying to obstruct you, Sergeant Joseph." This from her father.

"Please believe us, Sergeant." The Fat Fool.

Another silence. Then her father. "Perhaps something *can* be done. We can at least attest the known facts. In a general way."

"The facts as I believe them," said the Burr, "is that a young respectable lady of the area was molested."

"So we believe." The Fool.

"Corporal Briscoe came upon the scene. He attempted to protect the young lady…"

"Oh yes," The Fool again, "Oh yes, it was bravely done, I dare say."

"*He* dared more than say!" The Burr. "Corporal Briscoe intervened. He was killed."

"Shot. Yes. Shot." The Fool again.

"And the perpetrator escaped. There appears to have been no attempt to apprehend him, no attempt at chase."

"He had a pistol." Her father. "As he had proved already."

"And afterwards?"

"And afterwards, Sergeant Joseph," said her father, "he had fled. As you acknowledge."

"Over Hallock Hill way," said the Fool, "You see, he was a navigator."

Mollie heard the footsteps on the stairs. She replaced the brick, folded down the wallpaper, pushed the end of the bed back in place and turned to the row of books on her father's mantelpiece.

"Mollie! Mollie!" Lisa's voice now. Coming from their room.

Mollie chose a book from the mantel. It was a small volume bound in olive green leather. She went over to the door, took one of the deep breaths that had become a habit today, and stepped out onto the landing. "Here I am!" she shouted. Lisa came out of their bedroom and Mollie waved the book. "I had to get a book from father's room."

"Oh?" said Lisa, ever suspicious, "and what book be that?"

"It is…" Mollie looked at the cover. "…*Dramatic Romances*. By…" She looked again. "…Robert Browning." She brushed past Lisa in the doorway and belly-flopped onto her bed. The book flew from her hand and lay open on the pillow. Lisa followed and sat across from her on the second bed, the one by the window.

Mollie said: "You tease me for my big words, Lisa. But there are words even *I* do not know. Do you know what a *navigator* is?" She was also curious about *molest*, but thought one word at a time was a more effective way to find things out.

"Navigator? Why yes, it is a man who sails a ship. He tells the ship's direction from the sun in the day and from the stars at night."

"I knew that much very well. But it cannot be all. There are navigators over Hallock Hill but there are no ships to sail."

"Oh! *That* sort of navigator. Now that's a different story, young lady. Now those men are not the sort of men you should be thinking on. Not the sort of men you should be day-dreaming about."

"I do *not* day-dream about them, Lisa. Why should I do such a thing? No, I am curious, that is all."

"And not the sort of men to be curious about neither."

Mollie sighed. "It is hard not to be curious. Do you not find it so, Lisa? I could never seriously undertake to be otherwise." She thought for a moment. She adjusted her position so she actually faced Lisa. Occasionally they would have conversations that were not about school or housework or mealtimes. Perhaps she could start one of those conversations now. "What do these navigators do?"

"They dig. And they build. First canals, now railroads. They tear down our forests and fill up our lakes with their mud and waste."

"But it cannot be a bad thing, surely, to build? My father says we live in a great age, the age of the common man."

"Well," said Lisa with a sniff, "There's some of us don't want to be so common."

29

"But we *must* have railroads, that's what father says. We must have them to hold in union the furthest reaches of our great empire. And also that we may all of us travel further afield with ease and comfort so we can visit our brothers and sisters all over the world and see and know that people everywhere are like ourselves, made in God's image."

"There's not many in Shant Town made in God's image."

"Shant Town?" Mollie changed her position again, leaning on her elbows to indicate she was paying full attention, "What is Shant Town?"

Lisa smiled, enjoying briefly her superior knowledge. "Shant Town. Shanty Town. Huts and cabins and lean-tos and hovels. Not *real* houses like respectable people know. But sties and pens and God knows what, fit only for animals, not men."

"Is that where the navigators live?"

"Live? Call it living if tha wants, my girl. But it is not living in the eyes of God. It is a drear existence of drink and blaspheming and fornication." All of a sudden, Lisa sounded old beyond her years, practically ancient beyond Mollie's.

"And are there women there also?"

"Of course there are women, though few that deserve to share the name with the rest of our tribe. Of course there are women. Else how could there be fornication?"

Mollie hesitated. She had heard the word *fornication* before in readings from the Old Testament, but she had no real idea of the meaning. She decided to consult her father's Oxford Dictionary later, rather than lose face to Lisa. Had she not, after all, already admitted to her ignorance over *navigator* and *shant*? And she had failed to pursue *molest*. She decided on another tack. "If it is so drear, this life of which you speak, why do people seek it out?"

Lisa made as if to speak, then shut her lips. She appeared nonplussed. Finally she made the effort. "Why, I expect the Enemy of Man tempts them with his falsehoods as he tempted Eve. That is something we must all remember, Mollie, that he tempts us all. Let us always make certain he does not succeed." And she rose and went out through the door as if summoned, though there had been no call from Mrs Tordoff.

Mollie gazed at the sunlight, still bright through the window. She turned over and looked at the page where Mr Browning lay open. The lines read:

"That moment she was mine, mine, fair,
Perfectly pure and good: I found
A thing to do, and all her hair
In one long yellow string I wound
Three times her little throat around
And strangled her."

Mollie read it again. Then she read the subsequent 19 lines that completed the poem, afterwards turning back to the beginning and reading it whole. A strange excitement filled her, but also a sense of guilt, a vision of Lisa saying: "We must all remember, Mollie, that he tempts us all."

And also a puzzle, a query played on her mind. How could her kindly father have such a poem in his library? But it was, she reasoned, quite well on in the book. Perhaps he had not read that far just yet.

And then came the shouts from Lisa and Mrs Tordoff and she put away her thoughts as she put away the book, back on her father's mantel in her father's room. So. Cold chicken and soda bread.

31

Chapter 4

LORD HOLTBY WAS GONE BUT Sergeant Joseph was staying the night. "We can't allow our brave soldier man to seek room at the inn," Mr Proudlove said to Mollie, "we must be Good Samaritans to those who protect us from our foes." So supper would be a little late. And it would not be merely cold chicken and soda bread after all.

He ordered Mrs Tordoff to bring out additional victuals: half a gammon joint stored in the cold part of her pantry and a jar of pickled eggs. And she boiled some potatoes. And Lisa made up the bed in the guest room, added a wash bowl, a jug of clean water from the kitchen tap and a chamber pot, and even a hand mirror so the sergeant might possibly be prompted to shave – Mollie knew that Lisa particularly approved of men who shaved regularly.

Mr Proudlove sent Mollie with word to Mr Truss's cottage to find suitable space and feed for Snowbird ("He is a beautiful horse. You will love him," Mollie told the sexton while Christopher hovered sheepishly in the background with hardly a word.)

On Mollie's return, when Mr Truss had taken the horse and its rig, her father offered to show the sergeant the amenities, escorting him to the water closet. "You will be happy to know we are a perfectly modern household," Mollie heard him say with a laugh, "You will be able to forget the privations of the field of battle at least for today."

Sergeant Joseph joined them in the dining room within the hour, sufficiently washed and groomed, his long dark hair once more combed and slicked, his linen shirt now worn without coat and kerchief so it revealed his braces and unbuttoned collar. Mollie sat opposite him at table.

Her father said Grace, and she and the sergeant joined the Amen. Then Mr Proudlove asked about the recent action seen by his guest in Southern Africa. "There is constant war between the tribes," explained the sergeant, "particularly in the area where I serve, ye ken, between the Herero and the Nama..."

"Herero and Nama," Mollie repeated the exotic names under her breath. She had seen in a book at the nearby Mechanics Institute a collection of pictures – photographs – of African warriors, their mouths wide open in battle shouts, their dark bodies apparently naked except for feathers; but their modesty protected, presumably for the sake of the Mechanics, by large oval shields.

"However," the sergeant continued, ignoring the presence of Mollie and talking cheek by jowl with her father, "the real enemy in Africa, sir, is not the Nama, the Herero nor the Ovambo, but our cousins the Germanic peoples. The African continent is already aswarm with them."

They had finished their meal by now and Lisa had cleared away the crockery. Mollie's father nodded gravely. "It is good to know the opinion of a seasoned military man like yourself. But I confess you do not surprise me. Our only solace must be that the Prussians currently have their hands full delivering a bloody nose to the French. And at least the Africas are far away. My dread is that some day the Germans will maintain a great navy which will challenge us in our own Atlantic seas."

"Our nations will always be at loggerheads, sir. It is the way of things," said the sergeant. Mollie noted he had not noticeably scraped away any part of his stubble despite the provision of the hand mirror. He went on: "It is the common talk in the NCOs' mess. Briscoe and I would speak..."

Suddenly there was a catch in his voice. To Mollie's delight, a change of mood had come over him. He had suddenly ceased to be a detached man of affairs, a commentator on the world's stage. His face grew drawn and – did Mollie imagine this? – his brown eyes seemed to water as if he were fighting back tears.

"Corporal Briscoe," he said, "saved my life."

"Oh," said Mollie, and her eyes also began to water, "he was your friend."

"Yes," said the sergeant, looking across to her at last, "my great friend, my comrade. There is a special kinship between soldiers because our very lives depend upon each other."

"Tell us how he saved your life," said Mollie firmly.

"Now, now," said her father, "I'm sure this is painful for our guest. And I am not sure I approve of young girls hearing of such…"

The sergeant raised a hand. "I shall exclude all material of a visceral nature, sir."

Visceral, thought Mollie. Another reason to consult the dictionary. She now had a significant list of new words.

"Very well," said her father, "proceed."

"WE HAD PURSUED a group of the Herero," said the sergeant, "who had been raiding along the river, stealing cattle and sometimes women, from the neighbouring tribes. These were young men, newly blooded, proving themselves to their elders. Young men, I must say, are always the most dangerous, even when the cause of their conflict is comparatively trivial.

"We were a party of ten, travelling on foot, in pursuit of the marauders. And we had our own young man – a lieutenant called Castleden, a good man but new to the Africas. The land we traversed was scrubland, in places bordering on desert. We had two Zulu scouts who kept well ahead of us, only reporting back before the sundown of each day, since a party of our size would be difficult to conceal in such a terrain and we did not wish to lose the advantage of surprise."

"Yes, yes, I see it," said Mr Proudlove, clearly excited. Mollie remained silent, staring at the sergeant,

34

waiting for each new glance as he shifted his attention back and forth between them.

"On the second day I became aware of some friction between the Zulus. One of these, Ayanda, was well known to me and I regarded him as most trustworthy. The other, who called himself Bekhi, was much younger and unknown to me. I believe he was the nephew of the older man.

"But it was obvious they were in strong disagreement. I did not like the signs. It is rare that the Zulu will reveal to a white man his true emotions or give away signs of dissent within his own people. The fact that Ayanda allowed me to see as much as I had done indicated to me the seriousness of what was happening.

"I shared my reservations with Lieutenant Castleden, but he would have none of it. *We know we are not far from our quarry*, he said, *and it would be foolish to allow ourselves to be stayed just now.* But I knew something untoward was happening and when I spoke of it to Corporal Briscoe, he agreed with me."

"What did you do?" asked Mollie's father. She could see that she was not the only one under the sergeant's spell.

"What *could* we do?" The sergeant smiled ruefully. "Were we not serving soldiers, non-commissioned officers whose obligation was to obey orders? Were we to consider mutiny for something so intangible as a mere feeling of distrust?"

"Ah," said Mollie's father, "the conflict of duty and judgement. I fully understand your dilemma."

"That night, when Bekhi returned to camp, Ayanda was not with him. And he gave us some cock-and-bull story – if you will pardon that expression in front of the child – about Ayanda staying on to observe the camp of the raiders. But I knew this could not be true. I knew there could be only one explanation for Ayanda's failure to fulfil his allotted duty..."

"He must be dead," said Mollie. She wondered whether the phrase *cock-and-bull* were an example of *visceral*.

They both looked at her. "Yes," said the sergeant, "that was what I feared."

"But who...?" began Mr Proudlove.

"Why, father, the false Zulu has betrayed his comrades and allied himself to the Herero," said Mollie, "and he has killed the true Zulu in the process. Even though the man was his uncle."

"That was my analysis," said the sergeant. Did he suddenly look at her with new respect?

"What did you do?" asked Mollie.

"I voiced my suspicions to the lieutenant but he would have none of it."

"He is a most foolish young man," said Mollie.

"*Was*," said the sergeant, then hesitated. "Though I would not besmirch the name of one who died, as it happens, very bravely."

"No, no, of course not," said Mr Proudlove.

"Do go on," said Mollie, "*please*".

"Briscoe and I spoke of this and he agreed with my opinion. We talked with the men..."

"Unbeknownst to the lieutenant," said Mollie.

"As you say, Miss Proudlove." The sergeant coughed. "The Zulu Bekhi had argued a rapid advance to the top of a nearby escarpment at which, he claimed, we should rejoin Ayanda, and from which we might glimpse the encampment of the raiders. The lieutenant agreed. But if I were right, it meant we were walking into an ambush."

"A most perilous and difficult situation," said Mr Proudlove, "Why, I am on veritable tenterhooks and I am sure my daughter is also much moved by it. On the one hand, you are duty bound to follow the orders of your commanding officer; on the other, you risk losing your whole company if you are proved right. Whatever did you do?"

"We spoke again with the lieutenant. Perhaps God moved us to greater eloquence this time, for we were able to persuade him."

"Ah," said Mr Proudlove, "It is known He moves in mysterious ways."

"So now we had a new plan. We would take and bind the Zulu Bekhi and persuade him to confess his treachery…"

"Perhaps with your newfound eloquence," said Mollie.

The sergeant looked hard at her but she kept her gaze.

"But that hope was not to be. The Zulu was no fool and had discerned our change of plan. When we approached him, thinking him asleep, he leapt to his feet with a dagger in his hand and struck out at me."

"Oh!" said Mr Proudlove. His hands leapt from the tablecloth, his fingers spread in a gesture of anticipation.

"Corporal Briscoe reacted more quickly than I. He pushed me aside, brought his rifle to the aim and put a bullet through the blackguard's heart."

There was a brief silence.

"It was all over in a moment," said the sergeant. "After that, we decided on a day's march round the base of the escarpment and ascended a hill on the further side, thereby allowing us to come from behind and catch the bandits unaware – with the added advantage of higher ground and our Snider-Enfield rifles. I suppose there is little else to tell. The plan succeeded and we dispatched the gang of them."

"Bravo!" cried Mr Proudlove. He seemed to become suddenly aware of his raised hands and he applauded.

"And we found the body of our loyal Ayanda, cruelly injured in ways I will not describe." The sergeant glanced again at Mollie. "There are some things about which one must ever stay silent."

"And was this action," asked Mollie, "the fatal campaign that ended the life of Lieutenant Castleden?"

"It was. On my recommendation, he was awarded the Distinguished Service Order."

"You are a generous man as well as a brave one," said Mr Proudlove.

"I give each man his due," said the sergeant.

THEY RETIRED TO THE DRAWING ROOM, sitting on the pink chairs. Lisa lit the gas lamps. Mr Proudlove asked her to bring a jug of cordial for Mollie, together with a wine glass which he was permitting her to use on account of the grown-up company; also the bottle of Glenlivet and two tumblers for himself and the sergeant. "I bought it for my curate's birthday but that is not for several weeks yet," he said, "And I regard this as a suitably special occasion. We do not have such entertaining company every night." And, for the second time that day, he brought out the cigars.

"I suppose," he said, "the African sun must be truly horrendous for a white man. Is it true that no white man can survive without a pith helmet?"

"I believe," said the sergeant, "it may be true of some *officers*."

Mollie, who was running her fingers along the top of the wine glass in order to make a high-pitched sound, said: "But you have very brown skin, sergeant."

The sergeant smiled. "My mother was Italian."

"Is that how you came to be called Lorenzo?"

"It is."

"Do you therefore *speak* Italian?" It had suddenly occurred to her that in her father's company he had descended little into the use of those Scotch words she had heard from him at their first meeting.

"I *do* speak Italian." He raised his glass and began:

"Nel mezzo del cammin di nostra vita

38

mi ritrovai per una selva oscura
che la dirritta via etra smarrita.
Ahi quanto a dir qual era e cosa dura
esta selva selvaggia e aspra e forte
che nel pensier rinova la paura. "

He sipped his whisky. "Dante," he said, "the opening of the First Canto."

Mollie leaped to her feet, spilling cordial. "Poetry! You read poetry! And we have it! We have it in the English!" She ran across to the bookshelves, ran her fingers along the spines. "Yes! Yes! Look here!" She flipped the pages, ignored the woodcarvings and the list of contents, found the start of the First Canto and began:

"Midway upon the journey of our life
I found myself within a forest dark
for the straightforward pathway had been lost.
Ah me! How hard a thing it is to say
what was this forest, savage, rough and stern,
which in the very thought renews the fear. "

"Mr Longfellow," said Mr Proudlove.

"A fine translation," said the sergeant.

A sudden thought occurred to Mollie. "Do you," she asked him, "ever read Mr Browning?"

Chapter 5

THERE WAS A MORNING MIST on the tops of the hills. It was going to be another hot, bright day, thought Sergeant Joseph. He had left the water closet, which had taken him a while to master, closed the door, walked round to the front of the house, put on his bowler hat against the sun, and was buttoning up his trouser front, when he met Mollie.

She was dressed in a pinafore of bottle green and a cleaner but otherwise identical version of yesterday's dress. She said: "Will you be going over to Mr Truss's house to retrieve Snowbird?"

He admitted he was.

"Then I shall walk with you." She swung her satchel across her shoulder and lengthened her step to keep pace with him. "I have eaten breakfast and I am going to school, but sometimes I let that Truss boy escort me."

They marched across the field at the back of the vicarage, as Mr Proudlove had directed him, down a dusty narrow lane and into more open fields beyond.

"I had hoped to see you at breakfast," said Mollie, "it was boiled eggs with Mrs Tordoff's fresh white bread. White is more healthy, my father says, because it is purer."

"I was not hungry."

"But it is good to meet people at the morning table and exchange one's hopes for the day. I trust you have spoken in detail to father."

"I believe I have."

"And what has he devised?"

"That I should begin with Constable Allardyce who, I believe, is responsible for enforcing the Queen's law in this neck of the woods."

"*Neck of the woods*. Well, that is a colourful phrase and one that I shall remember, sergeant." She laughed. "Yes, an audience with Constable Allardyce is a good way to start.

It is true he lives in Granborough, which is ten miles distant. And he is *only* a constable, when all's said and done. But we are normally so peaceful here in Padstone that the Granborough Town Constabulary make only one man available to us."

"Even when a soldier is murdered."

"I suppose," she bit her lip, "they were thinking the soldier was not a local man and the assailants were not truly local..."

"And the people here would as soon forget about it."

"To be honest," her voice now took on a somewhat pained tone, "I have met Constable Allardyce on occasion, as has my friend Christopher. I do not regard him as having much wit – Constable Allardyce, I mean – but I believe him to be a decent and upright man who will do his best on all occasions."

"That is your father's judgement."

"Yes. He and I think very much alike, I find. Well, it is a pity you have to be staying with us when Mr Shollitoe is away visiting relatives. He too is a useful person and has a good baritone."

When he looked hard at her, she added: "I do not mean that his singing would benefit you in your current endeavour. Obviously that would be far from the case. Rather I was trying to give an impression of the range of his talents. He is a good man and close to us. He has often sung *I Dreamt That I Dwelt in Marble Halls* of a winter evening to the pianoforte accompaniment of Mrs Tordoff; and has shared a glass of wine afterwards with my father while Mrs Tordoff has taken her usual tea. I have a mind, in his absence, to celebrate his accomplishments. Do you know that song, Sergeant Joseph?"

"I believe I have heard it."

"And you would very much enjoy his version of *The British Grenadiers*, you being a military man, for Mr

41

Shollitoe is most patriotic. And, in counterpoint, I believe he would have enjoyed your story of last night about Lieutenant Castleden. But I do not wish to paint him as in any way a crude man; he is equally at home with more soft and gentle songs like *The Lass of Richmond Hill.*"

"Does he also recite poetry, Miss Proudlove?"

"Yes, he does. He is particularly expressive with *The Wreck of the Hesperus*. I mention that because Mr Longfellow is now very much in my mind."

"I see you are a generous young lady, Miss Proudlove, and I see that Mr Shollitoe is a man of divers qualities who is worthy of that generosity. And, yes, I do regret I have not yet encountered him."

Mollie hesitated a moment, then tossed her head. "I trust you do not mock me, Sergeant Joseph. But no, I realise you would be incapable of such unchivalrous behaviour."

They came to a five-bar gate with a stile alongside, and Mollie held out a hand for him to help her over. "Of course," she said, "I can manage perfectly well when I am on my own, but it is always a pleasure to benefit from having a gentleman assist."

And now they had come to the field where Snowbird was kept. As soon as he saw the sergeant, he raised his head, snorted, turned and came trotting over, nuzzling against his master.

The sergeant said: "Come, Miss Proudlove, for I know you long to stroke him and feel his wet nose against your palm." He again took her hand, this time guiding it.

Mollie patted the horse and stroked it between the eyes, the way she sometimes stroked the local dogs. "I told Mr Truss he was a beautiful horse and so he is. How did you come to find him, Sergeant? Is he really yours?"

"No, no. I am only a footsoldier in the Queen's Light Infantry, as you well know. Snowbird was loaned me by a friend, a cavalryman who also valued Briscoe and wished to see him avenged."

"But the cavalryman does not *own* the horse."

"No, the regiment owns the horse, but they thought it worth the investment. Along with a sum of money that will go for my expenses. And the Queen owns the regiment. So one might say the Queen has shown her interest in bringing these felons to book. As well she might. And I am her servant in the matter."

"Your Corporal Briscoe was a great man to have had so many staunch and admirable friends."

"Yes, Miss. But I fear his baritone was mediocre."

Mollie looked at him quizzically.

"Och, it is the privilege of friends to mock each other," he said, "In the army, we call it *joshing*. It should not be taken to mean any harm."

They walked across to Mr Truss's white stone cottage and Mollie knocked hard at the window. There was the immediate sound of running feet, the latch on the front door was raised and Christopher's plump face came round the door. That face fell immediately on seeing the sergeant.

"Christopher, you have not met Sergeant Joseph."

"Though I believe we have only narrowly missed each other, Mr Truss."

"Good morning to you, sergeant." The door was opened further and a narrow face with a goatee was exhibited.

"The *senior* Mr Truss," said the sergeant, "Well, sir, I trust my horse has minded its manners and been no trouble to you and your family."

"No indeed," said Christopher's father, "It has been my honour to tend him. But do come in, the both of you."

They followed the elder and younger Trusses into a small, badly lit room where an old table and two wicker chairs fulfilled the role of furniture. Christopher mentioned something about his satchel and ran off into a further room. Mollie ran after him.

Mr Truss said: "I have been told of tha mission here. I can only hope it goes well."

"I am pleased to have your support. Perhaps you were present at the Harvest Festival in September..."

"When your corporal friend was killed. Yes, so I was. As was all the village and beyond, Lord Holtby and his younger daughter..."

"And perhaps you saw, even spoke with, Corporal Briscoe..."

"No, I cannot say I did. Hold a moment and I will find tha saddle and the stuff that was with it. The horse has been fed and watered already this morning." Mr Truss followed after the children and returned shortly with the saddle and stirrups, the leather saddlebag and bedroll.

"Let me help," the sergeant took the saddle into his big hands. "And perhaps you saw those with whom Briscoe conversed?"

"I can remember nowt about that."

"But you would remember to whom *Lord Holtby* conversed?"

"Why, yes. He..." Mr Truss hesitated.

The sergeant said: "I mean no disrespect. It is sometimes true that nourishing one particular memory may provoke another, one which is connected by time and place. I take it that neither Lord Holtby nor his younger daughter would have much reason to exchange words with a corporal. No more than with a sexton."

"Well, they *do* own to the ways of aristocrats. Now, sergeant, I will come out with thee and help with the horse."

The two of them walked out into the morning and the sergeant hailed Snowbird, patting him and stroking him when he sauntered up. The sergeant swung the saddle and stirrups onto Snowbird's back. Mr Truss handed him the saddlebag and bedroll and the sergeant began to strap them in place. The sergeant said: "He was a handsome young lad, my Briscoe, was he not?"

"I believe he was."

"So you do remember seeing him?"

"Nobbut a glance in the distance."

"His uniform would have stood out against the garb of civilians."

"I believe that was the case."

"And both his good looks and his uniform would have provided attraction to those members of the gentle sex who attended?"

Mr Truss laughed. "Indeed, I think they would."

"So you see. You remember more than you thought."

The sergeant had now fixed the saddle bag and bedroll. He patted the horse again. "What I would like to know, Mr Truss, is who these members of the fair sex might have been and where I might discuss the matter with them?"

Mr Truss looked troubled. "Where the names of young ladies are concerned, sir, there is a necessity for discretion."

"But we are speaking, Mr Truss, of a wholly respectable assembly, are we not? We are speaking of a quiet, religious Sunday with a service at the church of St Agnes, where the Lord is thanked for the mercy of his generous provision. And where the vicar and his household lead the prayers."

"Except for Mrs Tordoff, of course," said Mr Truss.

"And afterwards, you repair to an open meadow, with two or three large tents or canopies housing the culinary delights of home-made preserves and cakes of a wholesome nature. The tent with the ale and spirits, I suppose, is set a little aside from the others, so the ladies will be more easily able to avoid the company of those gentlemen who have consumed a wee dram too much, and also to ensure that those

45

who deviate from the paths of righteousness are more easily observed and identified by their neighbours."

"Mrs Tordoff and her friends would certainly be present *then*," said Mr Truss, smiling.

"Oh, perhaps there will be a coconut shy and a Punch and Judy performance for the bairns and Mrs Tordoff will shout: *That's the way to do it!* with the best of them!"

"Ay," said Mr Truss, "she would that."

"I see no reason in such circumstances to doubt the virtue of Mrs Tordoff and those other ladies who attended, nor do I imagine such ladies will have any fear of my doing so."

The sergeant put his foot in the stirrup and swung easily up into the saddle. He looked down on Mr Truss.

Mr Truss said: "Sergeant, tha friend is dead and nowt more can help him except the mercy of the Lord."

"But those who killed him must fear *more* than the mercy of the Lord, Mr Truss – they must fear my righteous anger and the majesty of the law."

Mr Truss turned to walk back to the cottage, almost reached the doorway, then turned again and came back. "I put it to thee, Sergeant…"

The sergeant and Snowbird had not moved. The sergeant had been watching Mr Truss most carefully on his walk to the cottage and watched just as carefully on his return. "Yes, Mr Truss?"

"I put it to thee that a wholly respectable lady might be moved to accept an invitation. For a mere walk, perhaps. For a stroll along the river. In the open. In the broad daylight of an English afternoon. And it would be no wrong thing, nor even an indiscretion in the normal course."

"And I would agree with you."

"Then something might happen, unexpected, out of the blue so it might be said, something bad, Sergeant Joseph, something evil…"

"Murder, Mr Truss."

"Not simply murder, Sergeant Joseph. More than murder. And it might be that this new event, though never the fault of the lady involved, put such a stamp on things it would mar her life forever. If her name were known and voiced abroad."

"I do not voice abroad the names of ladies of virtue."

Mr Truss put a hand to his forehead and considered. He began: "A married woman who was widowed two years ago. A woman from Dovecote. Emily…"

And then the children came running out through the doorway, shouting, chattering, laughing. "You won't! You won't! You won't catch me!" yelled Mollie, and made hard for the field's boundary wall with Christopher in pursuit, hindered by the strap of his satchel being tangled in his arm and the satchel falling momentarily in front of his feet, so he was forced to bend and pick it up again before he could continue.

"Mrs Emily…?" began the sergeant.

"I have said enough." Mr Truss walked briskly back to the cottage and closed the door behind him.

Out in the field, Sergeant Joseph turned his face and his horse towards the terraces of cottages on higher ground. He had been right about the sun, right to wear his hat.

Chapter 6

HE RODE PAST the cottages, onto the unpaved road beyond, and down to ford the stream that flowed from the Ribble.

It stank of sewage – a sign of these modern times, he thought, when water closets kept your bothy clean but distributed the muck more widely. He had decided to ride Snowbird for his visit to the constable, though he had been given from Mr Proudlove the offer of the vicarage dogcart – a two-wheel horse-drawn thing with back-to-back seats on permanent loan from Lord Holtby – and the promise of a further night's lodging if he should wish it.

The road to Granborough now began to move to higher ground. The sergeant rode slowly so as to conserve Snowbird's strength. Every so often, they encountered a small flock of driven sheep or half a dozen cows. They would be passed by a pony cart carrying hay, with one or two youths aboard.

As the road broadened, it became macadammed – the uneven earthy surface segued into a flat one of small stones, almost dainty, cemented together; and even when it reached 30 feet in width, the camber from the edges to the centre was slight. He had been told that the delicate size of each stone was habitually tested by the labourer checking if he could fit it in his mouth.

The traffic increased in both number and kind. First there were more farmcarts, but bigger and with more variety of cargo: potatoes, greenstuffs, even calves, all headed for market. Some also carried their share of farmers' lads, more eager perhaps for the day's carousing than for the market itself, some of them shouting in friendly fashion, admiring Snowbird, others mocking his battered bowler or shabby coat.

Then there were single horsemen who raced past him in a billow of dust, like jockey boys, as though the road might disappear if they lingered. And groups of riders, some of them giddy from drink and the heat of the sun, who veered and halted and cursed their mounts before slithering to the ground and running off behind the roadside bushes.

Occasionally came a trap or landau or stagecoach, carrying even ladies and children and God-knows-who. But more common than he would have guessed, stopping every so often at their prearranged halts, annoying the speedier users of the road, the omnibuses with their teams of three horses, their back-to-back knifeboard seating and their open tops which provided half-price accommodation for strong men prepared to hang on.

For this was the mark of the modern world. Movement. Change. Everyone dashing higgledy-piggledy to wherever. And this, he knew, was the mere beginning. For he had some time ago seen and understood the power of the railroads in Liverpool and London, Bombay and Durban.

Already he regarded these Granborough locals and their nags with the superiority a man of experience always feels for the greenhorn. For the moment, he had adopted their mode of transport – but only because he wished to resemble them, to fit into their crowd.

After a couple of hours, he came to the wrought iron gates at the head of what he knew to be the drives leading up to large houses, the offshoot roads that carried placards **PRIVATE: NO TRESPASS**. He counted clusters of cottages on the roadside that spoke of servants and hired hands. And he could see, beyond these, avenues of limes with their heart-shaped leaves and plane trees with their maple look, tall but somewhat cropped on the sides so they had a neatness foreign to nature.

A while later, still following the road, he came upon the shops. First, a hardware store with its sign in the shape of a teapot, a collection of baskets, bags, tin tubs, lamps, pots and kettles hanging above its window, which itself displayed a plethora of cups, saucers, plates and china statuettes in the shape of shepherdesses and cowherds. Next door, a draper with its own statuary – the distinct shapes of women, though only constructed of wire and modestly covered by dresses and shawls and counterpointed by swathes of silk, cotton, linen, all with a cardboard tag indicating price-per-yard.

And then – now this was something to tell the boys when he got back! Here in this veritable backwater was an actual *photographer*, a man who advertised likenesses from life and a colouring-by-hand service for family portraits and pictures of the newly born!

"Snowbird," he whispered, "when we are done with this, I may well purchase a memento of us, two friends pictured triumphant in adversity, and have it coloured and make it a postcard to send to our friends in foreign parts."

AS HE GOT FURTHER INTO THE TOWN, so he came across the tenements and the back-to-back houses. At one stage he took from his coat pocket the small notebook in which he had pencilled Mr Proudfoot's instructions. He checked these against the compass he carried on a lanyard round his neck, and turned Snowbird down a hill and on to a cobbled walkway.

Here were more houses, mostly back-to-backs, all of a uniform red brick, difficult to tell one from another. And the streets, which had been full of shoppers and sightseers earlier, seemed well nigh deserted. "Perhaps they have all gone to market," he remarked to Snowbird, "let us hope *our* man is in his proper place."

The lack of people at least meant that he was less distracted. In any case, his eyes were sharp enough to glimpse the blue sign with the word **CONSTABULARY** above the wooden fence that surrounded one of the houses, set apart from the rest. He pulled Snowbird across the road, dismounted and tied the horse to one of the fence posts. He removed the saddlebag and opened the small wooden gate, took two long paces over the flags, removed his hat and banged the iron knocker against the unpainted wooden door.

A voice from inside. Loud. "Who is it?"

"A law-abiding citizen come to you on business, Mr Allardyce."

There was silence. Then the sound of boots on paving slabs. Then a man appeared round the side of the house. He was small and wiry, with thinning hair and a pencil moustache. He was dressed in brown boots, blue trousers with braces hanging over his sides, and a dirty vest with long sleeves. He carried a polished brown wooden truncheon with a leather strap.

"And just what is thy business?" he asked. And he raised the truncheon slightly.

"The securing of a murderer," said the sergeant. He reached in his pocket. "I have a letter of introduction from the Rev Eli Proudlove of Padstone."

"So tha says," said the other.

"It is here to be read."

"Thee ad best come inside."

Sergeant Joseph followed the constable round to the back of the house, where they crossed a small yard and entered. The constable closed the door and bolted it. This was his kitchen and his kitchen windows had steel mesh on the inside. One of the windows was broken.

"Best to be careful," said the constable, "Ay, *I* am Constable Allardyce and this is my ome and also my place of office, tha might say. But this is not a place where a peeler is much loved, so I must watch out for myssen. Sometimes they think they can taunt me. But they always pay in the end. I make sure of that."

"There seem to be few enough people here to cause you trouble."

"Hah! Does tha mean the empty streets? Think nothing of that. It is early for the criminal classes to rise from their sinful beds. Be ere in the first breath of evening and tha will see their awakening. And only in full darkness will thee encounter their strongest presence."

"I am Sergeant Joseph." Again the sergeant offered him the letter.

"Thee as come from Mr Proudlove?"

"I do. And here is the proof." Yet again he offered the letter.

Allardyce smiled and rubbed his chin. He was, the sergeant guessed, tougher than his appearance. He said: "I do not need to see the letter, mon. I am a judge of character and I believe thee."

He placed the truncheon on a small deal table, pulled up his braces, picked up his blue tunic from the floor, put it on and buttoned it. "Sit," he said, indicating one of three pine chairs. There was a bottle of gin on the table and a single glass. "Get thyssen a glass from the cupboard."

The sergeant did so. Allardyce poured him a generous measure and himself an even more generous one. "Tell me thy story," said Allardyce.

"There was a soldier. He visited the Harvest Festival at St Agnes in Padstone last September. And he was murdered."

"Ay, ay. Briscoe. I remember. A navvy did it. By all accounts."

"By every account except a warrant for his arrest."

"It is difficult with navvies."

"Is this not England, the land of law?"

"It is England, the land of many things. Of railroads and shant towns and men with pistols." Allardyce took a swig of his gin. "Look, tha must understand. There was a lack of witnesses."

"I believe there was a woman present."

"Tha believes correctly. But she was never much of a witness. She was, alas, issterical. She ad undergone an assault. A serious assault."

"You mean she was violated?"

"A blunt word. But ay, tis so."

"A blunt enough word for a blunt enough action. And there is a written statement to that effect?"

"There is not. The woman could not be persuaded to make such a statement. Nor *any* statement."

"Was she threatened with the full force of the law for her refusal?"

"She was not."

"Why not?"

"It would've done no good." Allardyce paused. "Ow did tha travel to this place?"

"I have a horse outside." This time the sergeant paused. "Is my horse not safe, even tethered in front of a constable's house?"

"He will be as safe as I make im," Allardyce picked up his truncheon and his glass. "Come," he said, "bring the bottle."

They marched through to the front room, which commanded a view of the street where Snowbird was tied. The horse was still there and apparently unharmed.

"We can watch him from ere," said Allardyce, "My own orse is normally kept in the yard. Just now he has some sickness and is being doctored. He is at best an old weak orse but it is all the Constabulary permits me. "

The sergeant looked round the room. There was a sideboard and on it two photographs – neither tinted – of an older couple in Sunday best who might have been Allardyce's parents. There were two armchairs, the stuffing hanging out of the upholstery. There was a glass vase with cut flowers on the window ledge and a dirty teacup on the floor. The sergeant knew there was something missing and suddenly he knew

53

what it was. There were no papers, neither in the front room nor the kitchen.

He thought for a moment. Then: "I would interview this woman. She is, I believe, from Dovecote. I have already been given her name." He pulled the small notebook out of his pocket. He read: "Mrs Emily..." he paused. "Now isn't that the *damn'dest* thing! I cannot read my own writing. Is that a *W* or is that an *M*?" He passed the notebook to Constable Allardyce.

Allardyce did not look at the book. "Seabrook. It is Seabrook."

"So it is," said the sergeant. "Now I see it. S-E-A-B-R-O-O-K."

"I believe so."

"You have done me a great service, Mr Allardyce."

"I ope no-one may come to grief from this, Sergeant Joseph. The woman was distraught. I was no match for er. And the other women. From the chapel. They drove me away."

Sergeant Joseph said: "From the *chapel*?"

"Oh yes," said Allardyce, "There's many Methodists and even some Baptist folk go to the Padstone Arvest Festival. For Mr Proudlove is a popular man within and without is church." For a moment Allardyce looked ashamed. "It was a terrible thing to appen," he said and the sergeant feared he would burst into tears. But another swig of gin set him right. "There was talk the soldier came upon the attack and was killed for it. But my sense is that e was there already, that there ad been some intimacy between Mrs Seabrook and Corporal Briscoe."

"Are you certain of that?"

"I cannot swear to what I did not see for myssen. It is only my opinion. And yet it would be a terrible thing to press this lady for a testimony of it."

"Perhaps I will not have to do that. I mean, Mr Allardyce, I will not *personally* have to do it. Perhaps no *man* will have to do it. Perhaps there is another way. But tell me," he poured another libation into Allardyce's glass, "about the navvies."

Chapter 7

"NAVVIES," SAID CONSTABLE ALLARDYCE, "Brawlers, crawlers, thieves, brigands, drunks, vagabonds, fornicators and buggery merchants. I ates em but I respects em.

"They've been about ere some eight months now, buildin this section of the line. Oh, it will be a great thing, say the big railroad bosses, a seventh wonder of the world, when it's finished. But for now it's a picture of Ell, Sergeant Joseph. Ell with mud and blood and shit and stink in place of fire."

The constable glanced suddenly at the bottle. The sergeant saw it was nigh on empty. He stood up, walked back into the kitchen without a word, and returned with his saddle bag. "I have some whisky if that is acceptable," he said.

"Acceptable!" Allardyce drained his glass and held it out. The sergeant took the unlabelled bottle from his bag, uncorked it and poured a good three fingers into Allardyce's glass. Allardyce swigged it and coughed and spat on the floor.

"Now that," he said, "is manna from eaven."

The sergeant put the bottle on the floor in front of the constable, covering the spit stain on the floorboards. The constable said: "Where did I get to?"

"Hell," said the sergeant.

"Yes," said the constable, "Now listen. Does tha you know ow a navvy works?"

The sergeant knew a fair bit, but he shook his head.

"Well, I will tell thee! First you ave a cutting they call a gullet, just wide enough for a single track for the wagons that take the muck out. You ave a downward slope to aul the muck away and there's only one brakesman ridin' each train. That's enough shakin' and joltin' to take tha bones apart, so the brakesman isn't so much oldin' the brake as *dancin'* on it! So e *as* to be a brave man or a fool or both!

56

"Once the gullet is ready for the clever work, you ave the face to contend with. And all the buggers ave is picks and shovels and axes. Now this face – you can ack at it, slice by slice, top to bottom, which is pretty slow if you want to earn t'best money. Or you can cut it away at the foot and let the ole thing come tumble down. That's what they call a lift."

"I'll remember," said the sergeant.

"You can ave a face that's 12 feet tall. You start by oling the bottom – cutting oles there but leaving pillars of earth olding it up. Then you cut a groove down the side of the face. Then you start knocking the legs away – chopping down the pillars that old it up. Now that's a pretty grievous thing to do, all that muck sliding down in an urry. You ave to be spry at gettin outa the way. You *ear* me?"

"I do."

"All that muck gets tipped from and-barrows and orse-carts into ditches and rivers and canals and whatever's there to take it. If there's nowhere to dump it, then they end up buildin a bank of the stuff as tall as they ave to. So whatever they're doin, these navvies, they're always up an down, climbin or slidin, lettin go the muck and keepin out of its way when it *does* go. If there's an orse cart, you'll ave a tipsman in charge and a nipper maybe ten years old guidin the orse. When they slip the ook and the muck goes down... well, like I said, they ave to be fast about it. Lots of them get killed. Maybe undreds. Those railroad firms ave plenty of book-keepers lookin after their interests, ledgerin their moneys in and moneys out, but nobody ledgers on things like that. I'm tellin thee."

He reached over to the bottle on the floor, filled his glass again. He offered the bottle to the sergeant who shook his head and pointed to the level of gin still in his own glass.

"Well," said the constable, "thee be the judge." And then: "That's why they lives like they do. To them, it's nowt, is life. Get through the bloody day an that's good enough for them. More than enough. That's why they put up with Shant Town."

"Tell me about it," said the sergeant.

"A shant can be med of anything – bricks, stones, tiles, pieces of old wood, mud, tarpaulin. Some of these shants are made from sods. And some of the sods are cut wet, so the shants get steam comin off the roof an the walls when they gets hot with cookin and tryin to keep warm. Water gets in the beds and in the clothes. You can wake up in the mornin an pick mushrooms for tha breakfast. In a big sod shant, you'll get maybe 20 people. You will ave to ave one door for in and out, but tha's lucky if tha's got a window.

"Tha cooks thee own meals, taters and swedes – *tommy* is what the navvies call their victuals. And tha gets rabbit and chicken if tha be an andy thief. But if it's the grog tha wants, there's a tapster who's got the keys to the barrels and charges thee top whack for what's in there."

"And when tha's *et* and *drunk*, tha shits in the road. Night soil. And thy shit and piss runs down like the muck tha's shovelled from the gullet. And that's a navvy's life, is that. Everything running downhill and stinking."

"And what of their women?" asked the sergeant, though he assumed the women who followed the navvy were sisters of those who followed the soldier.

"Some women, some *kinds* of woman, will come out ere, it's true, but not so many as'll go round. So there's nights I guess when they make do with sodomy among their own kind. May God forgive em!" He looked hard at the sergeant.

"You paint a sad picture," said the sergeant because he felt the pause demanded comment, "It's surely a pity that more can't be done for these men, who, as everyone tells us, are doing so much for our land and empire."

"I know what can be done," said the constable. He put down his glass and reached over for his truncheon. "Crackin eads is what can be done. An I'm the lad as does it."

58

THE CONSTABLE LAID HIS TRUNCHEON on the floor. "I've another," he said, "not much like this'n. I'll show it thee." He went back to the kitchen and there was the sound of cupboard doors opening and the sound of scrabbling among piled artefacts. Then he returned. The new truncheon he carried was white wood, not brown; matt, not polished; with a blue silk ribbon, not a leather strap; and the device of a lion was stamped on it in blue ink. "What does tha think?" asked Allardyce.

"I think Freemasons," said the sergeant.

"And are thee on the square?"

"I am *not* a member of your Fellowship."

Allardyce looked crestfallen. "It's passing strange," he said, "for I can usually tell. And I ad thee down for a Brother." He sat down and went back to his drink. "Now," he said, "I will tell thee about Fellowship. I will tell thee about Brotherhood. Because a man needs allies in this life, good friends to share the weight of the world.

"It was north of ere, Hawick, border country, as Scotch as it's English, and they were buildin a railroad there, five years ago, before I was a proper constable. But yet I was called upon, now and then, to serve Queen and country, just as much as *thee* might have been, I do believe.

"It was my first brush with the navvies. I was called in by an agman, a gent who bids to finish a section of the line, then ires is own gangers to recruit and run the labour. An agman doesn't do things to be charitable nor even respectable. An agman is ard, takes the cheapest and the most dangerous, relies on the strength of is arm to keep them in order. But sometimes there as to be sugar as well as salt. Sometimes the gangers get restless if the pay is poor and the work excessive. There are times when the agman overreaches."

"*A man's reach must exceed his grasp, else what's a heaven for?*" the sergeant put in. Allardyce stopped and looked at him strangely. "Browning," said the sergeant, "I was reminded of Mr Browning only yesterday."

Allardyce resumed. "The agman sent out word that e needed enforcers. E was a Brother and is call could not be refused. I answered. As did a number of our Brothers and also many others, for we all of us considered the pay for enforcement was good.

"There was 30 of us. We was settled in good lodgings on the Monday, with food twice a day at table. And we carried sticks and one of us ad a pistol for extreme cases. On the Tuesday, work was rained off. A navvy called Gregory was startin fights around the town, picking out any lad oo seemed better off than issen, which meant just about everybody. But this Gregory was on is own, so it didn't rightly affect us. It could be taken care of in the normal course of things.

"Then e took it on issen to brawl with a lad called Currock who worked in The White Art, a public ouse in the town. Currock was cut up a little and bruised. And when e come in to the public bar, the landlord said: *That's it then.* And e shut for the day.

"Course, it was the worst thing. For the navvies started groupin outside, thirsty for beer then thirsty for blood. One of them threw a stone through the window, smashin some glasses on the bar. The landlord ad bolted the doors, now e put up the shutters downstairs. Im and this Currock went up to a bedroom and looked out and saw there was maybe a dozen or so of em, with more joinin all the time. But they was all up at the front. So the landlord said to this Currock: *You get out the back, over to the lodging ouse and bring out the enforcers.* And this Currock was a good lad and that's what e done.

"So we made no bones about it. We took up our sticks and the lad with the pistol put it in is pocket and we swaggered over to the White Art. There was about 40 of em by this time and when they saw us comin there was some navvies, the clever ones, who said: *Alright, lads, I think we're done*. And they sloped off. But there's always a few, no, more than a few, as I'm sure tha knows, that won't be talked to, won't be made to think. And they stayed. About 20 of em. Course they did.

"Now the leader of our bunch was a Scotchman called Goodacre, or at least e pretended to be Scotch. And the navvies was mostly Scotch with a sprinklin' of English, and this Goodacre also knew there was a small section of the navvies that was Irish and Papist. And e asked the navvies what they was doing fightin *honest* men when there was Fenians in the town they should jump on. And, by God, e was a silver-tongued one, this Goodacre, and after ten minutes e ad em eatin out of his fingers like pigeons. And a load of them decided to go seek out the Fenian scum and pump *them*. And they did. And that kind of thing was nowt to do with us, it not being strictly a railroad matter. So it looked all over.

"And then we eard it. *Bang!* Like it nearly took yer ead off with the sound of it. And this party that ad the pistol in is pocket, e'd only took it out for what reason nobody knew, and fired it, or it went off, or summat like that. And this big navvy, who was int' front row of the mob, e fell over and just lay there. And you damn well knew e was dead. Couldn't be no other way. Oh, we settled over im and tried to raise im up and pretend it wasn't too bad, but there was blood all over is ead, like strawberry jam on a sponge cake.

"And then them navvies come at us, sticks and bricks and stones and a knife or two, and we went back at *them*. And it took mebbe arf an hour before we quelled em, but we did it. And we made out to the peelers it was the navvies ad shot the fella and im just strolling in the street, all innocent like, not part of the gang at all. And is wife was appy to keep er own counsel, for the railroad stepped in with a widow's pension. And the White Art brought in the glazers and opened up on the Wednesday and trade came good again.

"And I acquitted myself. And I was noticed. And I was recommended for regular Constable work and so you see me ere and now. So there *is* some justice in the world, but you ave to fight for it.

"But I know them navvies, always did. Me father was a navvy and I was a nipper on the Manchester Canal 30 year ago. But I've got over it and made summat of myssen. So I respects em but I ates em cos they've not got so much sense as me, not so much sense as any proper man should ave, to leave and get a better life. And that's why God above ates em too!"

Chapter 8

THE SERGEANT UNTIED SNOWBIRD AND MOUNTED. He rode at a brisk trot for about 150 yards when the horse began to snort and stumble.

The sergeant got down and took in his hand the front left leg which Snowbird raised. He looked at the hoof, saw with anger the sharp stone pressed into the inside of the shoe. "Well," he said, "well, well. And who has done this to ye?" He prised it loose and threw it away. "I should be more attentive," he said, "When I go to windows to guard you, I should not be distracted." He rubbed Snowbird's nose. "We will walk you awhile."

He swung the saddlebag down and draped it over his left shoulder. Then he walked slowly, looking straight ahead, but using his ears and the far corners of his eyes to remain aware of any disturbance on the periphery. It was only two minutes before the disturbance began.

"Ey, you with the saddle bag! Thee with the at!"

The sergeant halted, looked round. A group of five young men were strolling towards him from the side street on his right, on the far side of Snowbird. They wore dirty waistcoats and shirts, ragged trousers and hobnail boots. He checked to his left to see if their plan might be to surround him. But no. The five, he guessed, had no reinforcements and precious little strategy. They were on their own territory, they outnumbered him, and they had the natural confidence of unruly youth.

"Ey you, stranger!"

"Ey you! The bobby's friend!"

"Ey you! What're you doin in *our* street?"

Four of them stood in front of him, grinning; the fifth was further to the right, still on the other side of Snowbird. If the fifth started to move to the back of him, he would have to act quickly.

"What am I doing on your street? Well, I am walking." The sergeant grinned. The young men renewed their own grins.

"What's in that saddle bag?" asked one of the four in front of him. This one was smaller than the others and more aggressive. The other three had fanned out behind him, as though acknowledging him as Leader.

"Nothing of consequence."

"We'll be judge of that!" shouted one of those standing behind the Leader.

"It's us own street, Maister," said the Leader, "And we levy us own tax on strangers, us own road tolls, tha might call em. Don't we, lads?" He reached down into his shirt and withdrew a long knife on a string round his neck. He ducked his head to free it.

"You hurt my horse," said the sergeant.

The Leader sniggered. "Nicked is foot a little. E'll get over it."

"What's in that saddlebag?" shouted the one who had shouted before.

"I have my razor. I have my Bible...

"Keep your bastard Bible! But we'll mebbe take thy razor and shave thee!" shouted the one at the other side of Snowbird. He giggled. He was now further back than previous, was moving behind the sergeant.

The sergeant unbuckled the bag and put his hand inside. "...and I have my pistol."

The one on the other side of Snowbird stopped moving. The Leader stopped grinning. One of the others behind him shouted: "Don't listen to im, Jed! Don't take no bloody eyewash from the likes of im. E ain't got no gun!"

"A Colt 44, a most impressive gun, believe me. Made for the US navy."

"US navy be buggered," said Jed. He raised his knife hand.

"Tha'll not shoot us!" It was another of those behind Jed. One who hadn't spoken up to now and presumably felt he needed to do so. "If tha shoots us, tha's gonna swing for it!"

"Only if I kill you. And perhaps not even then."

Jed made a lunge with the knife. But the sergeant already had his fist round the handle and the large blue revolver was cocked. It took him the blink of an eye to bring it out and fire it.

Kerakkkkkkkkkkkkkkkkkkkkkkkkkkkkk!!!

The report filled the street. Black smoke rose over the sergeant's head. His arm and shoulder shuddered with the recoil. Snowbird whinnied, reared a little.

Jed collapsed, screaming, clutching his left boot.

The sergeant swung round, located the one on the other side of Snowbird, pointed the gun at his chest and cocked the hammer again, resting the pistol gently on Snowbird's saddle. The cavalry horse was quiet again and remained still.

"Now, laddie," said the sergeant, "move up towards your friends." The other did so slowly. The sergeant's pistol followed him every inch.

Jed was still crying – but the sound now was less a scream of terror, more a retching moan of pain. It would grow in volume once more, the sergeant guessed, when the initial shock had evaporated and the nerves came alive again.

One of Jed's bully boys was kneeling over him, trying to unlace the boot. "Tha nearly bastard killed im!" he shouted.

"Nicked his foot a little. He'll get over it. Now..." The sergeant waved the gun in their faces. "All of ye get down on your knees."

They looked at each other. They looked at the squirming, weeping Jed. They looked at the sergeant. They got down on their knees.

"That's good." The sergeant threw the bag over Snowbird's neck and mounted the horse, still with the Colt in his hand. "Now I am going to ride out of here, taking my own good time, and ye bonnie lads will be pleased to stay *very* still. But I have grand hearing and if any one of you loons so much as pishes himself, I will hear it and I will come back and shoot him. Ye hear me?" They were silent so he repeated the question. This time they offered their "*ay*s" or "*ye*ses" in ragged fashion.

He looked round at the houses, noted the twitching curtains in those windows where there were any curtains at all. "I imagine there'll be a lot of people out on the street once I'm gone. Tell them to get your friend to a doctor."

He stuck the Colt in his trouser top and kicked his heels against Snowbird's flanks. The horse, thankfully, was walking normally again. The sergeant allowed himself a good hundred yards before he stepped up the pace.

For all his outward calmness the sergeant was nervously alive to every sound, every sign of pursuit. But there was none. He rode in fairly leisurely fashion for the first five or six miles, then stopped at an inn called The King of Bohemia where he returned the gun to his saddlebag. He carried the bag inside and ordered bread and cheese and a pint of porter and got into a lively conversation with the landlord about the merits of ale and stout. He wondered if the incident would be reported direct to Constable Allardyce. He doubted it. But he did not doubt the constable would hear about it soon enough and make his own inquiries. A man who could not read must develop compensatory skills and the constable had done so.

THE SERGEANT RETURNED to the vicarage at something after five. Mrs Tordoff opened the door. She looked drawn. "Mr Proudlove is not at home," she said, "but I have orders to admit you." He thanked her. "Lisa is also away. Mollie is up in her room," she said, "I will call her."

"No," he said, "it is *you* I wish to speak to."

66

She looked at him with suspicion. "Well, I believe I have left the kettle boiling."

"I shall come down with you." He took off his hat.

She had *not* left the kettle boiling but she offered to make him a cup of tea while he waited in the kitchen and he thanked her again and sat down. He put his hat on the table. "You do not go to Mr Proudlove's church, do you, Mrs Tordoff?"

This time she did not look at him at all. "No, I do not."

"Mr Truss mentioned it but I did not think to take him up on the matter. Because you are a Methodist, are you not? You are chapel folk, not church."

"I believe as I believe." She warmed the pot, poured away the water, spooned in the tea.

"Which is why you do not drink strong liquor. After Mr Shollitoe sings in his fine baritone and you accompany him on the upright, he and the vicar drink their wine and you drink your tea. Miss Proudlove told me that."

She poured boiling water onto the tea leaves and put on the lid. "Give it a minute or two, Sergeant Joseph. Give it time to brew."

"And it is because of Mr Proudlove's benevolence – and I think also because of you – that a large number of chapel people come to the Harvest Festival. *For Mr Proudlove is a popular man within and without his church.* That is what Constable Allardyce says."

"Ay, Mr Proudlove is a true Christian, even though he clings to the strange fancy of his church for graven images. He believes in making less of the differences in people and more of what they have in common."

"And Mrs Emily Seabrook is also a Methodist and a friend of yours."

After a while she said: "I will pour the tea." She did so.

67

"I had meant to speak to Mrs Seabrook. But perhaps she may be spared that ordeal."

"I wish to God you *would* spare her. It would be no less than His mercy if she *were* to be spared any more."

"For it may be that you have already spoken with her at some length."

Mrs Tordoff sipped her tea. The sergeant pressed her. "Mrs Tordoff, I must know what happened when Corporal Briscoe died. And I must have some notion of who killed him, a description perhaps..."

"A description? A description of those who did it? Hounds from Hell!" Mrs Tordoff grabbed the pot in both hands and threw it into the hearth where it smashed and the tea poured out and hissed and bubbled on the hot tiles.

"Yes. Hell is where they belong. Help me send them back there." The sergeant took a wet cloth, picked up the particles of crockery and wrapped them in yesterday's newspaper which was lying on a chair. He came back to the table and laid the package down.

Mrs Tordoff said: "Ten years in this house and that teapot is the first thing I have broken."

"You were sorely taxed. I regret I have played my part in that. Now. Please. To spare Mrs Seabrook, you must tell me what you know."

"Then tha must ask me direct. There may be things I have no words for."

"Corporal Briscoe and Mrs Seabrook were known to each other."

"She wrote to him. She wrote for a soldier. She had been six years since her husband passed on. She wrote for a soldier and he replied."

"As you say, she was a widow. Corporal Briscoe was unmarried. There is no shame in such a correspondence. So. He came here to visit, to meet her."

"Their very first meeting. The corporal was to stay with her brother, who runs The Blackamoor at Dovecote."

"*He* is not a Methodist then? The Brother?"

"Neither was *she* until she wed. But she has kept it up in deference to her late husband."

"A good woman then."

"I think so. She takes in mending and alteration for she is deft with a needle and her brother is generous as much as he can be. But it makes for a meagre life."

"Corporal Briscoe arranged to meet her at the Harvest Festival. They contrived to walk away along the river."

"Along the beck. A walk in broad daylight..."

"In England. I know. And the gang attacked them and killed the corporal. And molested Mrs Seabrook. I will have to ask..."

"Sergeant, there is nothing a man can do to a woman they did not do to Emily. I trust thee ask no more of me on that side of things."

"I am more interested in the men who did it. They *were* navvies then? From Shant Town at Hallock Hill?"

"They were. *Some* of them were."

"And how did she know this?"

"From their talk. From their clothes. From the fact they were strangers. There are few in these parts that are not known to everyone, both church and chapel. Only the navvies are strangers."

"But I am told there are near enough 700 men in Shant Town. And in any case, the miscreants may have moved on. If so, I will need to follow. I will need descriptions..."

"There were four of them. She remembered them well. How could she not? And afterwards they stole her purse. Wait." Mrs Tordoff got up, walked across to the pantry, opened the door, took a white canvas bag from the hook behind it. "She told me these things while the rush of it was still with her, before she had to push it all away, before she had to *make* herself forget. I wrote some of it down. I don't know why."

She came back to the table, sat down again, laid the bag next to the pieces of teapot. "Yes, I *do* know why. Because I knew that one day someone would come here, someone would ask me. Someone like thee. And then I would need to remember."

She took a small sheaf of papers out of the bag and leafed through them. The sergeant saw they were written in blue ink, in a small and regular hand. "Description, description, wait..." She cleared her throat. "One of the men – tall, thin, long brown hair, red rash round the mouth, bald spot on top..." Perhaps she saw the sergeant made a face at the hopelessness of it. "I also have names," she said.

It took a moment for the information to sink in. He said unbelievingly: "You have *names*?"

He saw her smile for the first time since his return. "They are all of them *given* names. Not given names as thee and I would know them, given by mother and father to some precious offspring. Oh no, these are the names the men have been given by their neighbours, their workmates, sometimes their enemies, but these names are more true than the names their parents gave them. Because these are the names they must live by.

"When I took the descriptions to the constable, he gave me their names alright. He knew them all. But he said it were useless. He used a word..." She took a moment to remember. "*Hearsay*. That was it. He said if she wouldn't testify for herself in court, the descriptions were useless."

She looked back at the sheet in her hand. "But he knew the man with the bald spot. Called him Derby George. So I wrote it down. And then..." She studied another sheet and her face lit up. "A young 'un, a baby-faced boy with a missing front tooth. He's not a navvy, just somebody hangs

70

out with them. The constable gave me a name, and I put it down: Shaun Halloran. He's Irish. *Handsome* Halloran, people call him. And then..."

She thumbed through another three sheets before she came to the one she wanted. "A big bearded man. Tall, heavy build. Scar across his right eye where a knife had almost blinded him. The constable got that name straightway. Moleskin Jimmy. And the fourth... well, that description wasn't so strong because he used her when she was already fainted away. But the constable said: *wherever Moleskin Jimmy goes, Cockney Charlie Gallister goes with him.* So I reckon that's the gang of them."

"You knew my business when I came. Why did you not tell me these things before?"

"I had to be sure thee was the right one, Sergeant. No court will convict unless Emily is there to testify. And she won't do that. But I've listened and I've watched and I've made up my mind. Thee is the one. When tha does catch these men, and I believe tha will, I know there'll be no courts nor judges nor juries. And that's the way it must be."

Chapter 9

THERE WAS A LOUD JANGLE OF BELLS in the kitchen – the set above the cooking range that connected to the front door.

Mrs Tordoff got to her feet. "Mr Proudlove is back. Well, the excitement of the day is not over yet, I think." She made her way up the steps and the sergeant followed. "You have not asked but I will tell thee. Mr Proudlove has been to High Grange. With Lisa and Mr Mortimer. And Mr Shollitoe. And now we shall discover the result of this."

When they got to the front door, Mollie was there before them. She hugged her father and he responded warmly. But when he finally broke away, his face was dour.

"Mrs Tordoff, I think hot tea for all of us including yourself. It is most fitting that you join us." Then he became aware of the sergeant. "Welcome to you, sir. I trust the day has gone better with you than it has with me. The matters I have to report do not directly concern you; and indeed are the cause of our great embarrassment. But you are our guest and I have no objection to your presence."

The sergeant glanced at Mollie but she looked away. Mrs Tordoff turned back down the steps while the others went into the drawing room.

When they were seated, Mr Proudlove said: "Never before have I enjoyed the luxury of a journey in Lord Holtby's landau. In any other situation, on any other day, I would have commented upon the fine suspension which provided such comfort on the ride; I would have complimented the driver on his handling of two very fine coal-black horses; and I would have celebrated their handsome blue-and-silver livery. And I have not yet mentioned the upholstered seats… "

After that, they sat in silence until Mr Proudlove said: "Mollie, I sometimes chide you for your childish ways and I

72

send you to your room whenever the talk veers towards those subjects which might be considered the proper address of the grown-ups. But this time you may stay. This time you may count yourself one of those grown-ups. Though I believe you will not thank me for what you are about to hear."

She looked up for the first time. "I will be as grown-up as you wish, father; or anyways, as grown-up as I can manage."

They remained in silence again until Mrs Tordoff came in with the salver of tea things. She laid them out on the teak table and began to pour.

Mr Proudlove said: "Is this a new teapot, Mrs Tordoff?"

"It is one I had stored away, sir. There was an accident earlier and our usual vessel was broken."

"The accident was *my* fault," said the sergeant.

"Well," said Mr Proudlove, "no mind. We have more misfortune than a broken teapot."

He cleared his throat. "I have a serious announcement to make, though one at least of you may have anticipated me. Mr Shollitoe and Miss Mortimer will not be returning here. They will be travelling to his family home in Cumberland where they will wed within the fortnight. It was to prepare the way for this outcome that Mr Shollitoe had been visiting his brother-in-law these last few days, though I was not aware of such a purpose. Today he returned to Padstone. And before he came here, he visited Lord Holtby. To make a clean breast of things."

It was noticeable to the sergeant that no-one had picked up a teacup.

Mr Proudlove continued: "I have no doubt some of you will have surmised that something untoward has happened with Lisa – Miss Mortimer – and Mr Shollitoe. But I must speak it in plain language so there can be no doubt. Lisa is with child."

73

"Oh, father, poor father," said Mollie.

"Well," said her father, "poor Mr Proudlove indeed. Now I will be castigated for permitting such behaviour under my very nose. But rightly so. There is justice in that. Poor Arthur Mortimer is even poorer than I. For he must suffer ignominy whose only crime was to have a daughter. He has resigned his post as verger."

"Father, you must not let him!"

"Yes, I must. For someone's head must roll. And if it is not to be mine, it must be Arthur's. He is resigned to it." Mr Proudlove laughed. "*Resigned to it!* I did not mean to make a pun, to jest at Arthur's expense. I am perhaps not so much in command of my language today as I am wont to be."

"I will not," said Mrs Tordoff, "have you chide yourself, sir. We were none of us aware of the true state of circumstances until today. They have been so cleverly secretive…"

"*I* knew nothing, father, who have shared a room with her. You must believe that."

"I am sure you did not."

"How could they do such a thing? How could they damage us in this way?" Mollie clenched her fists.

"And," said Mrs Tordoff, "there can be no hope of his continuing in his present profession."

"No," said Mr Proudlove, "this is one of Arthur's prime concerns, that a man who had a fine career in the church now has nothing in the way of a living."

He gazed into the middle distance for a few seconds then slapped his trouser leg with what appeared a sudden false jauntiness. "But here I am, lost in my own troubles. We have a guest, and our guest has a horse that must be quartered. We must see our Mr Truss about it straightway. Mollie, will you do so? And Mrs Tordoff, will you, in the absence of our housemaid, see to providing the wherewithal for our guest room?"

For the first time, Mollie turned to the sergeant. "Shall the two of us take Snowbird across the field?" she asked.

THEY WALKED THE HORSE slowly in the twilight. Mollie repeated her question of half an hour previous: "How could they do such a thing?"

The sergeant said: "I cannae look into their hearts."

"But you can look into your own. *You* are a man."

"Ah. I take it you blame Mr Shollitoe, the weightier of the two. Is it because he is ten weeks older?"

She darted a glance at him. He let her see he was grinning. She said: "Are you amused? Is this the level of your involvement with our family that you are amused by our misfortunes?"

"I believe your father will survive this misfortune. And I believe *you* will survive your embarrassment, Miss Proudlove. You are naturally disquieted because this affair has been happening unbeknownst to you despite your intimacy with Miss Mortimer."

"And *Mr* Mortimer? Will he survive also?"

"He too. He will find comfort in the role of grandfather."

"But it is so unfair that he should be forced out of his post on account of someone else's misdemeanour. Why did father not stand by him?"

"He had no choice. A sacrifice was demanded. It is, after all, the way of religion – the sacrifice that leads to redemption. It is also the way of the military that a man must sometimes be lost for the good of the company. I suspect it is the way in every walk of life."

"I wish he had stood up for Mr Mortimer."

"Then it might be your *father* who is without his post. And his daughter who is without her home and education. No, your father has behaved honourably. He has made the best of

75

things. As I believe he did when your mother died. As he always does when Lord Holtby summons him. I know of no better principle to make your way in the world."

"And will Mr Shollitoe and the future *Mrs* Shollitoe do the same?"

"They have made a good start. I do not condemn them in your own wholehearted manner. If we are all of us sinners, is it not a kind of blasphemy to pretend we are not? Is it not a heresy to expect your Mr Shollitoe and Miss Mortimer to behave as the angels? I do not condone what they have done. But I say it has been punished enough by their exile into Cumberland. Mr Shollitoe has done the right thing by his mistress. He has done the right thing by his unborn child."

"And should I forgive them?"

"You have been in no way wronged. Perhaps you should wait until they are wed, then write to them, offer congratulations on their matrimony and best wishes for the expected child."

"Should we then remain friends, Lisa and I?"

"It is always a bad mistake to discard friendship."

Mollie stopped and faced him. "You have never discarded your friendship for Corporal Briscoe."

"Nor will I – as long as there is a debt to be paid."

"I have never told you this. But I saw the corporal at the Harvest Festival. I remember him well. It was from a distance so there was no opportunity to converse. In any case, what would I have found to say? I am still a child – as you have now shown me clearly. It was a wet and misty afternoon, but for a time the sun shone and it seemed to shine down on him alone. He looked very handsome in his tunic. There. I believe I have said another childish thing which is of no help to you."

They moved on to the boundary wall of Mr Truss's field. The sergeant said: "I wish my own father had had the courage to face *his* misdemeanours."

Mollie turned to him again, her hand leaping to her mouth.

"Oh, my sergeant!" she said, "My poor sergeant!"

He put out a finger and touched her lips. "Alas, Miss Proudlove, I am a little too old for your tears."

Chapter 10: Interlude

ALL OF A SUDDEN 11-year-old Mollie Proudlove was struck by the unexpected sight.

She had been standing near her father, her hymn book still clutched in her left hand, her right hand holding up the skirts of her ankle-length dress to avoid the mud of the field, already plastered on her boots, when she raised her eyes to a splash of redness which the sun's September rays momentarily caught at the periphery of her sight. She looked, she absorbed, she focused on the stranger.

He was perhaps 20 yards away and there was a handsome woman on his arm – possibly a chapel friend of Mrs Tordoff's – carrying a parasol. But *he* was the handsomer. The splash of red was his army tunic, adorned with gold braid. But the man who wore the tunic lent it a new and different beauty.

He was in his early twenties, with hazel coloured hair that fell in a quiff across his forehead. She began, almost involuntarily, to walk towards him, listing as she did so the details of his beauty in her head. For she was a great lover of lists, as was her father. And she was a great lover of beauty, having visited with Mr Proudlove the art galleries of both Manchester and Leeds, and seen and admired the sunsets of Mr Turner, the brilliant skies of Mr Constable.

She noted first his tallness, for he was half a head taller than the lady; second, his boyish, unlined face, the wide-set eyes whose colour she could not yet distinguish, though she had already decided they were a piercing blue.

When she was five yards distant, she caught the flash of his even, white teeth and marvelled at the confident friendliness of his smile.

At three yards she saw that his face was not entirely unlined after all: but his skin was pale and pure and those

78

lines she now distinguished were laugh-lines, arguing an amiable and outgoing disposition.

Suddenly he looked across at her and his eyes took her in. She stopped, turned slightly, made as if she were searching the meadow for a particular friend, then made off, back towards her father. For what would she say to him? What would the vicar's daughter say to the beautiful soldier?

The Harvest Festival was, as always, a wholly respectable assembly. The quiet Sunday service, overseen and orchestrated by her father, had seen the Lord duly thanked for the mercy of his generous provision. The Proudlove household, herself and Lisa Mortimer – for Mrs Tordoff was chapel folk – had led the prayers as usual. Now the merry-making, such as it was, had begun.

They had repaired to this meadow, with two tents housing the wholesome country delights of fruit preserves and cakes, and one, set slightly apart to protect children like herself, the less wholesome concoctions of the brewer.

The tents were there to protect them all from the rain. And it had rained without cease all the previous day, hence the mud. But today – surely another sign from a merciful God – the heavens had stayed dry and signs were promising that the day would end in the sort of placid joy that her father, as a good Christian, regularly aimed for. Even so, she admitted to herself, there was little joy for someone of *her* age beyond the occasional slice of rich fruit cake or treacle tart.

Which was why the arrival of the soldier set her thoughts racing. When she had once again repaired to her father's side – he was speaking something about the reform of the Anglican Calendar with that Fat Fool Lord Holtby – she allowed herself to watch the woman on whom the soldier gazed with such obvious admiration.

The woman was slender and vivacious – her own glimpsed teeth not quite the equal of the soldier's, Mollie thought, but nonetheless all present and well tended. How old would she be? Perhaps slightly older than her companion, a little more worn by the vicissitudes of life, perhaps by five years or more, which made her seem very old indeed.

Mollie attempted to paint a mental picture of herself at such an age. How could she ever contrive to enjoy such glances as the soldier proffered? How would she ever learn such whiles as would compel such clear adoration? It was beyond her.

Suddenly she noticed Mr Truss, the sexton, making his way to the beer tent and she thought about her schoolfriend Christopher. Occasionally they would play together and she would allow him to steal a kiss or to run his fingers through her untidy fair hair. But Christopher was a fool – poor at his schoolbooks, slow in speech, awkward in gait. He annoyed her with his limitations. Even so, she began to look round for him, a temporary panacea for the boredom that was creeping up on her. But he was nowhere to be seen.

They had their own trysting tree, of course. At least, Mollie thought of it as such, though it was doubtful whether Christopher knew the word *tryst*. Once she had used it when re-telling him the story of Tristan and Isolde, and he had confused it with the word *twist*. Or perhaps he was teasing her. But she did not think so.

She wondered now if he had gone to the tree, a tall rowan on the path to Dovecote. Last year she had found him there with a bottle of black beer, which she knew to be an inebriating drink. They had taken alternate sips and she had felt nothing untoward, but *he* had become quite boisterous until he heard his father's voice calling him. Then he had washed his face in the beck, swilled the cold water round his mouth, and sped off without even farewell.

She decided to look for him at the tree. It was easy enough to slip away from her father and the Fat Fool, who had brought his annoying daughter Hermione – a nearly-woman whose habit was to beat the air with an embroidered silk fan even in high winds. *Yes!* Mollie had decided. She *would* make for the tree.

She edged away behind her father, feigned a sally towards the cakes tent, but veered suddenly towards the lane. Five minutes later, she was at her destination. Surely enough he was there. But he did not look pleased to see her. He had a small cigar like the ones her father kept in the box in the drawing room. For a moment, she suspected it *was* one of her father's, secreted away by Mr Truss. But she suppressed such a thought as unworthy.

She studied the fuggy air that surrounded him. "Well," she said, "shall I call out and raise the fire alarm with the Harvest revellers? They have many pales of water round the field for just such an emergency."

He coughed and took the cigar out of his mouth. "You must not tell," he said, "though my father allows me to use them on occasion at home." She wondered if this were a lie, but there was no way to test it. She motioned to him to hand it to her.

"It is not for *girls!*" he said in a tone of indignation.

"Then," she said, "I *will* call out!"

"Very well," he said and handed it to her. She put it to her lips. It was unpleasantly hot and bitter. She blew out some smoke.

"Now give it back," he said.

"Perhaps I will not," she said and took another breath of smoke. Now it made *her* cough.

"I told you. It is not for girls!" And then he broke off. For there were voices and the sound of footsteps in the bracken. He stubbed the cigar against the bark of the tree and they both ran for cover behind the tree in the surrounding shrubbery.

The handsome soldier and the almost-as-handsome woman came into view. They paused, looked round, stood beneath a plane tree on the opposite side of the path, and the woman lowered the parasol to cover their faces.

"What are they doing?" Christopher whispered.

Their action was equally hid from Mollie's eyes, but she knew exactly what they were doing. "They are kissing," she said.

After a while, the soldier reached down to his buff-coloured military trousers and began to unbutton them. He reached inside. The lady placed her hand over whatever was there and began to pull at it, first slowly, then increasingly fast.

"What are they doing?" This time it was Mollie's turn to ask.

But Christopher did not answer. When she turned to him she saw that he had unbuttoned the front of his short cotton britches. She had many times caught a glimpse of his boy parts when he urinated behind bushes and she had never been either particularly curious or alarmed. But the expression in his face alarmed her now. And suddenly she knew what expression the soldier's face must have behind the parasol.

"We must leave," she said.

"No, no!" he whispered fiercely

"Else I will tell about the cigar." And she started off, as quietly but quickly as she could, in the direction of the Festival field. After a few seconds he caught up with her.

"Promise you will not tell," he said.

"What will you give me?" she asked. And she suddenly wondered what the handsome soldier had given the almost-as-handsome woman.

Part Two: Moleskin Jimmy

Chapter 11

THE MAN IN THE MOLESKIN WAISTCOAT stood by the side of the beck, his hands in the pockets of his blue chalkstripe trousers, his dirty bottle green frock coat caught up behind his wrists, his battered stovepipe hat tipped a little way over his forehead.

He was a tall, broad man with a full brown beard. A scar ran across his right eye where a knife had almost blinded him in a fight with a tavern landlord a score of years ago. His ruddy face was expressionless except for the pursing of his lips. He whistled. Then he shouted. Then he took his hands out of his pockets and he clapped them.

"Biter! Biter!" he called. His voice was hoarse as always. And again: "Biter!" Another clap.

The 18-month-old black-and-tan terrier on the other side of the path raised his head and barked. Once. The man beside Moleskin Jimmy said: "Call that a dog? I doesn't call that a dog. I calls that a mangey creature that'll eat yew out of ouse and ome."

"Thou speaketh foolishly," said Moleskin, "Straight from the time he come to me, I knew he would be my great beast, my leviathan, though many mocked me. I tell you: that dog was without form and void. Now I've trained him, I've been like a father in my dominion over him. I've made him the animal he is. I never leave things as nature leaves them, Charlie. I conquer them, I capture them, like an army, like Joshua at Jericho. That's what I'm like. You know me, Charlie."

"I does," said Cockney Charlie. The earlier comment, as Moleskin knew, was for the sake of conversation only. To pass the time on a hot July afternoon. In reality, Charlie never disagreed with Moleskin because Moleskin didn't enjoy disagreement. He bristled at such nonsense.

Right now, he saw Charlie nod his head in satisfaction. If there was one thing Charlie thought he knew, it was Moleskin, his brother, his comrade. It was reassuring for Charlie to think there was something he *did* know, something in the world that was constant as the bad weather in winter. He thought he knew Moleskin and Moleskin let him think it. Why not?

Charlie was as broad as Moleskin but without the height. He wore a tattered cape over an old grey cardigan and a pair of cotton britches held up with leather braces. His face was pock-marked and his teeth were black and rotted.

"Look like a pale of shit, you do," Moleskin would say to him, and Charlie would laugh, pleased as punch to be so addressed. "You look like a pale of shit that's been took out of the gullet and nobody's had the belly to wash it away." How that made Charlie laugh!

Now Charlie was watching Biter as fierce and affectionate as Moleskin did. Charlie had never owned a dog, Moleskin knew, nor anything else that had lived. So he enjoyed the fact of Moleskin's dog, the feeling of closeness that something of Moleskin's gave him.

Good. He was loyal, was Charlie, that's all you could say of him and all you'd need to say. Unlike some *other* people that might soon wish they had acted differently. But Moleskin would get round to *them* in a little bit of a while.

"Come on!" shouted Moleskin, "Come on over here, you pug of Satan!" And straightway Biter bounded through the tall grass, ran up to Moleskin and pushed his wet muzzle against Moleskin's leg. Moleskin laughed and grabbed him by the throat. "Look," he said to Charlie, "look what I done to make him a good dog. Look, won't you?"

Charlie looked, prepared to be amazed. "He used to enjoy himself," said Moleskin, "tearing to pieces any accursed thing he could touch. But I taught him differently. I taught him obedience. Like the schoolmasters could never teach *me!*"

It was a point of pride with Moleskin that he'd had schooling, that he could read *The Times* or The Bible, or *Self-Help* by Samuel Smiles, that he could write a letter to threaten an enemy or sign his name whenever he remembered which name he was using.

"First day I got this dog," said Moleskin, "he bit me most severe. But I was rather pleased than otherwise. First thing I did to calm him, to make him a fit Christian dog, was – I took him to Jack Tracer the blacksmith."

Charlie nodded. He knew Jack Tracer the blacksmith.

"And I said to Jack Tracer – I want his tail docked and his ears cropped. Make him look like something, like a dog that's *owned*. And that's what he did. Oh, you *did* scream, didn't you, Biter?" Moleskin rubbed the dog's throat so it choked a little. "Oh yes, you screamed! But I rubbed some lard in his ears and that quieted him! After a while."

"Lard's good," agreed Charlie.

"And then I trained him up to catch rats and mice. First mouse he caught, he swallowed it whole. I thought – that's a good dog! Keep him on the right diet and the less I give him, the more he'll catch for himself. And I was proved right! Now I wouldn't be surprised if he wasn't the best mouser in Christendom!"

"Best," agreed Charlie.

"But those *rats* was more difficult. He had a long road to travel, didn't you, Biter? First rat I got for him, we kept it in a box. And first time I let it out, it *bit* Biter. Biter bit! Stupid dog."

He hit the terrier across the nose and it whined and jumped and made Charlie wince despite himself. "But this dog did not kill the rat. No, no. To my great disappointment. So I put the rat back in the box. Oh, I fed it with morsels and I gave it water. Because, you see, it was useful for me to do that."

"Seems to me you as a natural kindness," said Charlie and nodded.

Moleskin looked hard at Charlie to make sure there was no insolence in the remark, no undertow, but after a moment of thought he considered it sincerely meant. "And then I waited till the rat was quite fresh and fit again and I let the dog have another try. This time he killed it. But by no means speedily. I thought to rebuke him for it, but then I reconsidered. He had done his job in the end. That much demands reward, I thought, so I made sure he had water that night."

"You as a way with im," said Charlie.

"And then I made him grow up. Didn't I, boy?" Moleskin ruffled the fur on Biter's head. "Went back to Jack Tracer and had his milk teeth loosened to help him grow up faster. And I said to Jack Tracer – I'll bring you all the rats you might want at tuppence a rat. And we shook on it. And then I trained him up, this dog of mine. I got another rat and I held the dog's foot against the rat's mouth till the rat bit his foot. And that was the thing that made the difference! Oh yes!"

"Oh yes!" echoed Charlie.

"After that, a beautiful scene came to pass, a proverb and a byword among the nations. He shook that rat splendidly and had it killed in about one minute."

Moleskin let go of Biter and gazed about the scenery. "They should be here theirselves in about one minute, I reckon. They would be well started out by now." And he took the big knife from his coat pocket. It was the hilt of a sabre, with the blade whittled down to nine inches in length.

"I reckons you're right," said Charlie and fingered the wooden club that dangled by a strap from his right wrist. "I knows what to do," he said, then added: "Tell me more about the rattin'"

"Oh," said Moleskin, "This little dog has slain his thousands and his tens of thousands. I made half a crown the first day. Though after that, of course, there was fewer rats and the money was not so good."

"Right," said Charlie, "I can see that."

"But training a dog is a lifetime's work, I tell you. So I didn't waste any of the time God gave me. Once he'd got well used to ratting, I wished to make him my boon companion when mine enemy might find me, so he could smite them hip and thigh when they appeared. But he did not take straightway to attacking men, except that, when provoked, he bit *me* again! Even more severe. On the forefinger."

He held up his hand. "But I did not thrash him for that, for it showed the kind of nature I needed in a dog. No. I only gave him a touch of the whip when he after refused coming to heel."

"You knows a lot about dogs," said Charlie.

"Oh, I have a way. Like the way I made a mariner out of him. I made him up a little raft, pieces of wood out of a broken barrel that was left in the shant. Tied it with string. Went out to Hindshead Dam, put him on his little raft and floated him downstream. So the only way he could stop from going under when he hit the rapids was swim for it. And he did. But then half a week later he forgot what he had learned. And you can't have a dog forgetting. We went down to the dam and I threw my cane in the water and told him to get it. But he would not. So I threw him in. That made him remember!" Moleskin fell quiet. "Listen! Do you hear something?"

"Voices," said Charlie.

"Quiet!" said Moleskin, half to Charlie, half to the dog. Both responded immediately, Biter dropping to a sitting position, Charlie standing bent at the knees.

The voices were louder now, the other side of the birch trees, round the bend in the path. A man's voice said: "We'll be there in time for dinner if I'm not mistaken. And a glass or two." And then they turned the corner and stopped in their tracks.

"Moleskin," said the man who had spoken previously. He was a heavy, middle-aged man in a black coat, silk scarf and shiny top hat. His companion, a younger bare-headed man in a calf-skin jacket, remained silent.

"You have a thing of mine," said Moleskin.

"I can't think to what you are referring," said Top Hat.

"You owe me eight pounds, no less, Mr Bakey, for certain services that I performed for you in recent times. Services to do with a man that had crossed you."

"No man crosses *me*," said Mr Bakey, "so I'm sure I don't know what you are meaning."

"This man that crossed you, he'll not cross you again. Not after what I performed. But the lucre solemnly promised me has not come my way. And a labourer is worthy of his hire."

"I heard of some sort of incident, Moleskin. I heard of something untoward that occurred to Mr Blenkinsop that had been my clerk and had been passing on wagers to a rival bookmaker while taking my pay. When I found out about his disloyalty I naturally dispensed with his services. As would any man in my position. I then heard that he had met with an accident involving a fall into the Ribble which left him drownded. But such are the vicissitudes of life, Moleskin. I know of no connection between thee and me, and no connection between thee and Mr Blenkinsop."

"Falling into rivers is not a regular occurrence for a sensible man, Mr Bakey. Neither is it sensible for any man to hire the services of Moleskin and then renege on said agreement."

Bare Head said: "Perhaps you should tell this man we are armed."

"I would not expect different," said Moleskin.

At that point, Mr Bakey reached into his coat pocket and Moleskin cut across his right hand with a single blow from the whittled-down sabre. A Derringer fell to the ground alongside three of Mr Bakey's fingers and a pool of blood. Mr Bakey screamed and clutched his mutilated hand. Bare Head made to reach into his jacket also, but stopped as the blade was thrust close to his eyes. Behind Moleskin, Biter had begun to bark. He ran back and forth, circling Moleskin, his tail wagging.

"Maybe," said Moleskin to Bare Head, "I would be taking out only *one* of your eyes. So for all your life you might see the damage your foolishness had done."

"Foolishness," said Charlie and laughed.

Biter sniffed at the fingers and picked one up in his teeth.

"Bind up his hand," said Moleskin to Bare Head, "Use his scarf." Bare Head did so. By now, Mr Bakey's screams had shrunk to feeble moans. He swayed, and Bare Head had to grasp him round the shoulders to keep him from falling.

"Eight pounds," said Moleskin, "That is what is owed. Rifle his pockets till you find that much."

"What about me?" asked Charlie. He waved his club at Bare Head.

"And fifty shillings for my assistant," said Moleskin, "for that is a legitimate expense undertaken in this collection."

Bare Head let Mr Bakey slump to the ground, then opened Mr Bakey's coat to reveal the money belt round his waist. Bare Head rummaged in the leather compartments and counted out the notes and coins.

Bare Head handed over the money. He said: "Take it all if that's what you want!"

"No," said Moleskin, "we are *gennelmen* and we do not rob in any wanton fashion. But Charlie here'll take that midget's pistol of Mr Bakey's and he'll take the one *you* carry also. But I warn you – be very caring how you take it out of its pocket so do you do not alarm Charlie or me."

Bare Head did as he was told.

"And you," said Moleskin to Barc Hcad, "saw nothing! You were round the corner when this outrage occurred."

"Yes," said Bare Head. He cradled the head of the unconscious Mr Bakey in his arms.

"You are escaped," said Moleskin, "by the skin of your teeth."

And Charlie and Moleskin sloped off with Biter close behind.

Chapter 12

THE MISSION WAS A SQUARE WOODEN BUILDING at the end of a row of shops. It stood on the north side of Dovecote which was still small enough to be a village to on the outskirts of Granborough. But now, the sergeant knew, it threatened to become a suburb, what with the recent addition of a regular omnibus service between Granborough, Dovecote and Lord Holtby's estate.

The Mission had small windows, some broken, and a front door with a loose handle. Its outside was unpainted and looked drab in the twilight. Sergeant Joseph rode on the opposite side of the road until he came to an apple tree, tied Snowbird to its trunk, pulled down a green apple and munched it. When he had thrown away the core, he took a large paper from his saddlebag, walked up to the door, knocked once for politeness sake and pushed his way in.

The inside was unpainted like the out. The two people in the room were a man in waistcoat and shirtsleeves at a large wooden desk whose top was covered with papers; and a woman some way behind him at a smaller desk, methodically altering and marking text with a steel-nibbed pen. Both looked up when the sergeant entered. The man smiled uncertainly. He had grey receding hair brushed back from his forehead. The woman put her head down and resumed her close work before the sergeant could get much of a look at her.

The sergeant walked across to the man. "Mr Galbraith?" he said.

"I am," said the man. He rose and shook the sergeant's proffered hand. "What may I do for you?"

"I have a copy of your excellent paper," said the sergeant and unfolded it.

"I am glad you think so highly of it."

"Oh, indeed I do. It seems to me not only excellent in its content and presentation but of a high moral character and social usefulness."

"We like to think so," said Mr Galbraith. He smiled. "Though it's only our *Letter*. The *Yorkshire Quarterly Navigators' Letter*. We hardly dare call it a newspaper."

"It is far more canny than many which *do*," said the sergeant, "Not only is there a liveliness that commands the reader's attention but a respect for detail and some real knowledge, Mr Galbraith, some real understanding of the people of Shant Town."

"Oh," said Mr Galbraith. His face fell. "We do not call it Shant Town, for such would be disrespectful to those who built it and must live in it. No, no, the navigators call it Hallock Station – for on a day to come, they say, there will be a railroad station there at the heart of a lasting community."

"It is good to hear of such faith and optimism." The sergeant once again scanned the pages which he had studied only an hour before. He had sat in the public bar of the Coach & Horses a mile down the road, and now he felt he knew the stories by heart.

Mrs McGregor begs her daughter Mrs C Kenny to write her at once... Will Morrie Cooper come or send for his little girl, 10, before she becomes destitute... Stocky Daniels please send the month's board you owe Mrs Granby... Beware of Dandy Harold he is a thief and dirty in his habits... All young women and girls beware Coal-Eyed Granger is a married man... Mr W. Stanford warned his mates against Slim Thornton, with a scar on his nose, who stole ten shillings in a purse and hid the purse under a dog kennel before he sloped off... Mrs Huxtable of Greenside complained that, having just lost her husband and brother both, in a falled-in gutter trench disaster, she would like to put it in the Letter that some men from the canal dig promised to act as bearers and not one turned up, causing her great expense and further sorrow...

The sergeant turned back to Mr Galbraith. "And yet," he said, "you do not inhabit the heart of Hallock Station but rather prefer the environs and outskirts, a few miles distant."

Mr Galbraith looked suitably apologetic. "There are many of us who would wish to be in the very hearts of the people, sharing their burdens, bearing their sorrows. We would do so gladly as Dr Livingstone did among the negroid peoples of Africa."

"I believe the negroes of Africa were often more welcoming to Dr Livingstone than some of these navigators," the sergeant rolled the word round his tongue, "would be to a man of your station and calling."

"No, no," said Mr Galbraith, "that is not at all the general situation. The great majority of these men respect the Church and are strict in their moral outlook. They welcome the word of the Lord. We would never be afraid to live amongst them. But..."

He looked round at the woman with the steel-nibbed pen, and his voice dropped, "the truth is that we cannot, in good conscience, put at risk the many of our sisters who carry out the routine aspects of our work. For their sake, we must hold back from the centre of things, for they are vulnerable."

"Indeed," said the sergeant.

"Also," said Mr Galbraith, "we depend on preachers from outside the district, outside the run of the established Church, and it is difficult to attract great numbers when there is such a problem with their transport. The roads to Hallock Station are difficult at best, impossible when there is rainfall." Mr Galbraith did not mention the omnibus.

"Indeed," said the sergeant again. He took another look at the woman with the pen. Though he could still see very little of her – the burnish of her chestnut hair piled and plaited high on her head, the cut of her high-necked fawn dress which reached down as far as her ankle boots – yet there was something about her movements, something about the slant of her head as she studied the papers, that was familiar. When he realised his gaze might become obtrusive, he turned his head and scanned the whole room, taking in the granddaughter clock on the west wall, the hand-written notices for religious services, the hanging oil lamps.

"Mrs Barraclough and I are sole occupants at this time," said Mr Galbraith, as though called upon to apologise for their isolation, "but when the preachers are here and the congregation arrives, why, then it is packed and lively."

Then: "What precisely can I do for you?"

The sergeant sighed. "Why, sir, my name is Mr Joseph. I represent the legal firm of Haworth Moorhead & Jones of Harrogate. Many of the men who inhabit these dark places nevertheless have kin in more respectable neighbourhoods, as I have no doubt you are aware. Many of these kin are elderly and have comfortable amounts of money preserved over the years. Then many of these people die. Now we are instructed, for a percentage of the legacies, to find the rightful heirs. I am therefore of a mind to place notices in your *Letter,* as I know others do, so that the persons affected may be made aware of their inheritances."

"I am sure we can be of help. There is a small fee involved in such notices when they are intended for a commercial purpose."

"Of course," said the sergeant. He gave Mr Galbraith the paragraphs he had written out in his notebook in the Coach & Horses. Mr Galbraith returned to his desk, motioning for the sergeant to sit opposite him.

"Ah," said Mr Galbraith, "Halloran... Gallister... But are there no surnames for the other two?"

"These navigators and their strange-sounding names!" The sergeant clapped his hands and laughed. "But they are so long gone into this world of navigating that to use their proper names would help little to alert their companions to their presence and might even be an embarrassment for the principals involved."

Mr Galbraith nodded as though he followed the argument. He counted the words and suggested a number of shillings which the sergeant straightway handed over.

"Mr Joseph, the timing of your visit has been most fortunate. Tomorrow is what we call our press day and Ada – Mrs Barraclough – will be taking the last of our copy to our printer in the next half hour."

"I am grateful," said the sergeant. Both men stood and they shook hands. The sergeant made his way out without any further glance towards the woman with the chestnut hair.

THE SERGEANT TOOK ANOTHER APPLE from the tree, bit off several pieces and fed them to Snowbird. He studied the front of the Mission until he saw Mr Galbraith, now dressed in jacket and hat, come out and make his way along the main road. The sergeant patted Snowbird then strode across the street to the building.

There was a second door at the back, above a short flights of steps. The sergeant positioned himself half-way along the side of the Mission so he had partial view of both front and back exits. He put his hands in his pockets and resumed watching.

Presently the door at the back opened and the woman came out, locked it and walked down the steps. She carried a large canvas bag which she clutched to her side. The sergeant followed the woman. He gently increased his pace until he was level with her.

He said: "Mr Galbraith calls you Ada then? When he does not call you Mrs Barraclough?"

She did not turn to look at him. "And what if he does?"

"But I will always call you Adele."

Still she did not turn; still she kept on walking at the same steady pace. "Adele is too Frenchified for him. So he turns it into English, turns it into what he knows. Is there any point to your comments, Sergeant?"

"No," he said, "*Mister*. Here I am *Mister* Joseph, I represent Haworth Moorhead & Jones of Harrogate."

Now she turned. "I know the people *you* represent, Sergeant." She had, just as he remembered, wide-set eyes, pale and gentle skin, fine high cheekbones and a slight pout to her lips even now, even after all that had happened. "I have known them so many years, Sergeant. I have known their epaulettes, their armbands, their tall hats with feathers, their high boots with spurs, their bugles and trumpets, their sabres and pistols, their instruments of music, their instruments of death, their instruments of life."

"I heard about Ben," he said.

"Of course you heard about Ben. But you did not come to see."

"What could I do? He was gone, only the earth left to take him. I was a world away."

"But you came home for your corporal." She turned away, continued to walk.

He continued to keep pace with her. "Because for him I can still do something. Something needful."

She stopped. The bag slipped from her grasp. Suddenly the world seemed too much for her. "So you didn't come to see Ben. So there was no need, you thought. So you didn't come to see *me*."

"Would that have been right, Adele? What would we have said? What would other people have said?"

She had recovered herself. She picked up the bag. She continued her course.

"How far is the printer, Adele?"

"One or two streets more."

"I will carry your bag."

97

"Like a schoolboy? Like the schoolboy you still are?"

"That is not fair on me. That is not proper."

She handed him the bag. She said: "This is no matter of chance, no wild card in the deck. You knew I was here."

"I remembered Ben's love of the Chapel. A woman said to me the other day that some Methodist's widow had kept his faith even though it had not been her own before marriage. I asked myself what *you* would do, where you would go. I came to see if I was right."

"And it fitted with your purpose."

"It did."

"Those names... There *are* no legacies, no inheritance. We both know that. You are setting a trap. Do you think the lion so stupid he will not see how the goat is tethered?"

"These men are no lions. And I am trusting their greed will overcome their good sense. In any case, I have no better way to proceed."

They had reached a small brick building with a glass-fronted door and the sign *Hemmings Printers*. He gave her back the bag. "I will not come in with you. I will not make occasion for talk."

She took it, opened the door and went in. He gazed back down the street to where Snowbird waited. When she came back, carrying the empty bag, he said: "I will need some place for my horse."

She said: "We have a yard. And it is well known I take in lodgers. There is already a laundress from County Mayo in the downstairs back."

"Then we are chaperoned."

"She has a schoolmaster come back on occasion."

"Then she will have no wish to make gossip among the neighbours. Is it far? "

"A mile."

"You can ride Snowbird. I will walk."

"I cannot ride a horse in this skirt. Not if I am to remain respectable."

"Then we will both walk."

Chapter 13

THE PLACE SHE LIVED IN was a red-brick terrace house, built inside a crescent, overlooking a small, neat garden with a single birch tree.

It was narrow and single-fronted with a passage at one side. The parlour opened off the passage and the stairs led up to the bedrooms. The second floor, he soon saw, contained two attics, one at the front and one at the back. There was a slate roof. It was the kind of house he had lived in with his mother. Like Adele Barraclough, his mother had taken in lodgers to pay for it. In a way then, it was like coming home.

"I want no show of intimacy in front of others," she said.

"I intended none," he assured her.

As she had told him, there was a small paved yard at the back and this was where the privy was sited. He unsaddled Snowbird, tied him to a drainpipe, groomed him and fed him with hay from a field at the back. He carried his luggage back into the house.

"You love that horse," she said.

"He has been my friend and companion on this sad journey."

"Do you love him as much as you loved the corporal?"

"I love him according to his station."

"Do you love him as much as you once loved me?"

"I love no creature as much as I love women. And I have never stopped loving *you*."

When they went inside, she introduced him to Miss Haggard, the laundress from Ireland. Miss Haggard, contrary to her name, was a plump, big-breasted woman, perhaps in her late twenties, whose oily skin glistened with sweat. Adele said: "The sergeant has prevailed on us for lodging for a few days."

100

"I am most pleased to meet you, sergeant," said Miss Haggard and glanced back at him as she went to her room.

"She is always elated when I bring a man into the house," said Adele, "Perhaps it makes her own position appear more proper. Come upstairs and I will show you the room."

He followed her. "And are there many men you bring back?"

"None for whom I would openly risk my reputation." They reached the room and she opened the door and remained on the landing as he walked inside.

He noted particularly the large sash window, offering easy escape in the advent of danger; and the small writing desk, dressing table and water jug. "It is a small bed."

"All my lodgers are bachelors and spinsters so it is more than adequate. Does the room not meet your standards?"

"It is better than army quarters."

She raised an eyebrow. "What is *not* better than army quarters? Come. You will need refreshment." He followed her down.

When he had hung up his hat and coat in the passage, he followed her into the parlour, and again studied the tall windows, similar to those in his own room. The methods and routines of escape were always of interest to a soldier.

She took off her shawl, exchanged her boots for slippers, donned an apron, went into the tiny kitchen at the back and fried bacon and potatoes for their tea.

"I am my own mistress here," she said, "I have my own kitchen and water tap. I even have my own bedroom and parlour – though, as you see, there is but a drape between the two." She indicated the red velvet curtain which matched the upholstery of the sofa and armchair.

"I share the privy but my lodgers all have chamber pots so there is no great run on it except early morning and late at night. My lodgers are all working people of one kind or another who spend their daytime away from here. The men are mainly office workers and, as I have told you, all of them bachelors."

"So do they not hope for a more accommodating bed?"

"They may hope all they want."

"And shall I dare to hope?"

"You may also hope all you want. You do well not to dare, but we all of us may hope."

They sat at a sturdy lace-covered table. She made a pot of tea and produced two earthenware mugs. He took the whisky from his saddle bag.

"I see you have not turned temperance," she said.

"I hope also you have not." He poured a measure into their tea.

She said: "This is not as elegant as the sergeants' mess."

"You josh with me. I do not believe we sergeants ever put much store by elegance."

They drank. She said: "Ben's uncle was proprietor of the hardware store two doors down from the Mission. This was *his* house. But he was an old man and widowed and had no children and needed help with the business. When Ben quit the army, we came here. For four years Ben made the store his own, ordering the stock and manning the counter, learning the trade. I saw to the books. What revenue came and went over that time, I listed and put in good order. But I did not know... Neither of us knew...

"There were debts of a long-standing personal nature. Mortgages taken out against the house and against the store. When Old Nathan died, we did not have the capital to continue. The banks foreclosed on the store, but we managed at least to retain the house. So Ben sold his labour to Lord Holtby, to the colliery. When the disaster happened...

102

"A flash flood. You know all about it. Six men killed, and Ben one of them. Water seeped into the gallery from an underground spring and then the coalface collapsed. For a while it looked as if I would receive nothing in compensation. Then Mr Galbraith brought in the Combinations man, Johnny Roseberry…"

"Combinations man?"

"That's what they called him. The man from the miners' union. It is well attended in this place. The navvies came into the area, and the regular miners were fearful the navvies will undercut them and take their jobs. So they paid into a union and made sure to attend the meetings. Lord Holtby is a man to be feared round here, but Johnny Roseberry was not afraid of him. He discovered an old chart which showed the existence of the spring. It was a fact of which the company was well aware. As a result of the company's guilty knowledge, the widows and orphans received their just payment.

"Also because of that, I am able to make my way in the world. And because of Mr Galbraith and the Mission. The work is regular but not hard – if you can read and write, add up the figures. It is little different from the hardware store, yet I do not have the heavy merchandise to haul about."

She paused. "Mr Galbraith knows of this machine called a *typographer* which I am told is somewhat like an accordion but produces printed words instead of musical sounds. However, I have never seen one in operation and I am content to use my own hand in copying. It would be a scandal if the beauty of handwriting were to die because of some foolish invention."

"*Cembalo scrivano*," said the sergeant, "A harpsichord that writes. It was invented in Italy. You should not mock it. I saw a model in the army HQ in Delhi. True, they had only one and no-one seemed able to use it. But that

103

will change. It is, I think, to handwriting what the locomotive is to horsemanship."

She made a grimace that sprayed tea from her lips. Then she resumed her story. "Mr Galbraith has given me work and Johnny Roseberry has given me property."

"And did they receive their just reward, *Ada*?"

She laughed at his use of the name. "Trevor – Mr Galbraith – is my friend, no more. But if it were different, his wife is long dead and my conscience would be clear. As for Johnny Roseberry, he has received his reward from others."

She took another sip of the tea-and-whisky. "His intelligence and courage were well remarked at the time. As a result, Lord Holtby approached him and found him better employment with greater remuneration. He is now a colliery manager in Nottingham."

It was the sergeant's turn to laugh. "The way of the world," he said, "but we did not make the world."

"Then it is God we must blame," she said.

WHEN THEY FINISHED THE TEA, he poured a second measure of whisky. She sipped at it. "This legacy. These navigators. It is nonsense, is it not? You are hoping the murderers are foolish enough to come forward and you will apprehend them."

"Or that their friends will peach on them. I have suggested there might be a reward for information from friends."

"Meaning those who are not friends at all. Well, the *Letter* is out day after tomorrow. We will have to see."

He reached over and touched first her wrist, then her neck, then her hair. A little later she said: "The light is fading. If you and I are to have further business, we must execute it quickly. We are unchaperoned, but that is sometimes unavoidable in the relationship between landlady and lodger."

"The light of day gives an air of the respectable."

"But by the time it has dimmed to night, you must be in your room. You must make heavy footfalls on the stairs and cough loudly on the landing and close your door with a respectable slam."

She got up and walked across to the alcove and pulled the velvet curtain aside.

He said: "You kept the double bed."

"I could say I did in memory of Ben, but that would not be the whole truth." With her back to him, she began to undo the hooks of her dress.

He got to his feet. "I will help you."

"Do you think I am a little girl?" She had already completed the run from neck to waist. She peeled off the bodice and dropped the skirt to the floor. She wore a white lace-trimmed petticoat which she pulled quickly over her head. She turned to face him. Her breasts were full and white and shapely.

"No," he said, "you are never that." He walked across, took hold of her wrists and kissed her full on the mouth.

"An army kiss," she said, "There is always something fine about an army kiss. After whisky"

MOLESKIN JIMMY HAD FINISHED his sixth pint of red-brown ale in the big sod shant that was his current home. There were 15 others in the shant, not counting Bignose Betty, the shant mother and tapster, who had final say over bed and beer. It was lit with oil lamps and candles but there were two windows so you could see time of day without stepping outside. Right now there was still some daylight but it was waning fast.

Cockney Charlie had stolen a chicken from a farm about a mile away and they had boiled it for their tommy with tatties and swedes that came from the same establishment.

105

At one point, they had nearly been rumbled by the farmer or one of his hands. The man had turned the side of a tree and come across them of a sudden and it could have been nasty. Nasty for *him*. But he had the good sense to turn off and walk away without challenging them. He was a sensible farmer, not like some.

"I cooks good, Moleskin. Doesn't I cook good for you?" said Charlie.

"You are priced above rubies," said Moleskin. He wondered about a seventh pint in his pewter mug, taken three years ago in a burglary where the householder had not been as smart as the farmer and had paid dearly for it. Moleskin prized the pewter mug for its beauty and its cash value but also because it had cost a man's life and that put a sort of shine on it.

Money was no problem for either of them. They could drink themselves stupid and miss out on tomorrow's work and still be set up for the week – in Moleskin's case, maybe a month – following their dealings with Mr Bakey the bookmaker. So Moleskin didn't have to reckon money into the night's strategy.

But pissing was different. He didn't like to exert himself unduly while he was boozing. He would need to leave the shant to take a piss in a while and maybe a shit too. So he weighed the pros and cons. Do it now and get in maybe three more before he had to go again? Or hang on past his seventh, maybe past his eighth? Trouble was he might get wobbly on his legs, just a bit, and then the others would notice when he went out again and they might take it on themselves to say he couldn't take his liquor. Which he would *not* take in good part, no.

Or they might even take it on themselves to rob his bags or his bed while he was outside. That meant him taking all his lucre with him each time or cashing up every time he got back. Either way he felt awkward.

He looked round at the other inmates. Mebbe he worried too much. They were a sorry crowd, not up to much at all this time of day, not with a ten-hour shift behind them. They were all coughs and spitting and hanging the head and mumbling and swearing against the bosses, against the police, against the Irish papists who had come across the water to take their jobs, against God Himself sometimes. Except Moleskin did not tolerate swearing against God. As some of them had already learned. But that didn't mean they would still *remember* their lessons.

He glanced across at Biter, lying still but awake at the side of his chair, relaxed and grateful after some chicken meat. It was no good trying to leave Biter as guard. For one thing, he wouldn't stay anywhere long without Moleskin. Had to follow his master out for a piss to know when *he* could piss too.

And Charlie was little better. In fact, Biter was worth more than Charlie when it came to a fight or a match of any kind. "Be sober, be vigilant," Moleskin said in a whisper and Biter raised his head to listen. "Because the devil walketh about, seeking whom he may devour." Biter sighed and laid his head down again.

Charlie said: "What's that, Moleskin? What's that you says?"

Moleskin laughed. He decided he *would* have another drink right now. He got up and went across to Betty, who was smoking something foul in her clay pipe. She looked as much of a man as she did of a woman, with her thick arms, lined face and gapped teeth. It was only her woman's clothes that went some way to revealing her true sex and these had worn shapeless and years ago lost their colour.

Today she also wore a bandage on her head after one of the navvies had clipped her good and proper for refusing him credit. Not that it did the navvy any good. The others had ganged up on him and thrown him out after searching his purse for coins and finding two shillings. As was right. The shant queen often got belted by some lodger or other but that was bad for the whole lot of them. It meant the landlord would be round come morning with a couple of men and some heavy sticks.

Moleskin took his pint and handed the cash to Betty. She said: "Come into some, ave we, Moleskin? Come into some lucre?"

And he said: "Consider the lilies of the field. They toil not, neither do they spin." Oh, he would get up *very* late tomorrow, might even buy some bacon off Betty for his breakfast.

THE SERGEANT STAMPED with all his considerable weight on each stair. He alternately pushed and pulled at the bannister rail so it swayed and creaked. On the landing he coughed loudly as ordered. When he opened the door of his room, he did so slowly and firmly so the hinges whined. He kicked the wall for good measure, walked into the room and slammed the door.

"Respectable," he said, "Hah!"

Chapter 14

TWO DAYS LATER BIG BRENNAN'S GANG was rock-breaking early morning. There was a crew of five navvies working a single drill and Derby George was the drillholder. He sat splay-footed, holding the steel rod between his knees while the four hammer lads struck – *Kerlang! Kerlang! Kerlang! Kerlang!* – each in turn. After half an hour, Derby George raised a hand as a signal.

"I need my rest," he said, "I need my rest from all this!" And it was right and proper that he should. Even though he didn't have the hammer power of the others – it was all in the shoulders and he knew he wasn't much of a man for shoulders – it was right and proper that he should take his turn with the gang. He wanted to keep his knees a few more years. He would have need of them, he had no doubt.

"Very well," said Big Brennan and he too raised his hand as a signal. He was the ganger, the man who led the crew, it was *his* signal that counted. But Bob Scobie, a powerful man with a red face and large nose, was taking his strike and maybe didn't hear him or see the movement, being concentrated on the task in hand. And it may be that Derby George was pre-emptive in his movement anyway because, as he twisted his body and moved his right leg, Bob Scobie's hammer came down with a crash on his shin.

George gave a yell that resounded down the gullet, down to the stretch of rail already laid where the surveyor was running over blueprints with his foremen, down to the sluicepit and beyond that, across the hills and – some said later – over as far as Nettles Farm where old Nettles and his daughter were finishing off the milking and looked up in shock.

Brennan said later the devils could likely hear it in Hell and know they wasn't so bad off where they was. But Brennan was known for his sly sense of humour.

It took them half an hour to tie a splint on the shouting, crying, fidgeting George and get him up to the road. Then Scobie and Little Manning helped him back to his shant, the two of them holding him up under his armpits and taking his weight as he hopped and skipped very slow homewards.

It was a single-storey, all-wood shant with a bit of veranda made of old beer crates. When they got there, Yellow Kate, the shant queen, guffawed at his situation. She scratched her white hair under her cap and said: "Any old excuse to get out of work, pet."

What George said was loud and predictable, but Kate had heard worse. Truth was, she didn't like him much – he knew that – but he was a regular who paid on the nose and never laid a hand on her, so she tolerated him. The other nine inmates were at the gullet this time of day and the quiet of the place was surprisingly peaceful to George. So by the time his mates had sat him down and paid for a glass of strong ale, he felt well enough to tell his story.

"That bastard there," he said, pointing at Scobie, "that bastard there nearly done for me. He's broke my leg, that's what he's done, and I'm laid off something terrible with the pain."

"I didn't use my full force," said Scobie by way of mitigation, "because I could see you was moving. Just as the ammer was falling, I glimpsed it and held back a little." Perhaps he had gained confidence from Kate's joviality. "And it ain't broke. I've seen broke and *that* ain't broke!"

"If that ain't broke," George shouted, "what is it then?"

"Bad bruised," said Little Manning, "but it'll heal up in mebbe a day or two an' appen we'll take you back right as rain."

George noticed there was a copy of the *Letter* lying on a stool by the grate. But he thought nothing of it. Kate always got the *Letter* on publication day, brought over first

110

thing by her nephew who ran a bawdy house in Granborough. But now, as soon as her eye fell on it, she seemed to remember something important. "Well, well, never mind, pet. I shouldn't wonder if you didn't look back on this day as a sunny one in a bleak life, George. Youse in the paper."

"What?" George was startled, as were the others.

"What you been doing now?" asked Little Manning and winked at Kate.

"Can't be nothing good, knowing you," said Scobie.

"I ain't done nothing," said George. He said to Kate: "What's it all about then?"

"Oh," said Kate, "it's legal writing of some sort about hearing summat to your *advantage* if you go to the Mission in Dovecote."

"Hymn-singing. That's what it'll be! Them Mission folk think hymn-singing is *extremely* to your advantage!" That was Little Manning.

"Not the way *they* sings the 'ims," said Scobie, "More fool them!"

"Now, now," said Kate, "I'll have no bad words said about the Mission and the good people there." George knew she favoured the Mission to a lop-sided degree.

The prayer meetings and hymn singing brought people in from Granborough, and many of the men, on their return, sought out her nephew's establishment. She put it down to the mixing of the sexes, she had told him, with the Mission women often wearing fresh linen and sometimes silk that rustled with their movements and was likely to arouse a young man's mind or other parts.

"Give me the paper then," said George and waved aggressively at the stool.

"I see you've forgot your leg of a sudden," said Little Manning.

"Hasn't he just?" said Scobie who was clearly feeling less guilty by the minute.

111

"It'll do you no good, pet," said Kate, "you knows you can't read an inn sign without it has a picture of a tap."

"I can read enough to get by," said George, "though I believe I've left my spectacles in the gullet."

They laughed and it angered him but there was little he could do. "You read it for all of us," said Scobie to Kate.

She picked up the *Letter,* opened it, and read in a slow, deep, stumbling voice: "To whom – it may concern – Derby George – who is believed to be a navigator – on the Settle to Carlisle railroad – should contact the Mission – in Dovecote – to hear something – to his advantage – following the death – of his relative in Derby."

"Why would I have relatives in Derby?" George muttered.

"Cos that's where you come from," said Little Manning.

"No, it ain't." George now regretted speaking up.

"Then why'd they call you Derby George?"

George took a moment to reply. He knew there would be more unavoidable laughter. "Because I won money on the Derby, didn't I? The one at Epsom."

But first came the astonishment which would make the laughter all the worse. "How long ago was that?" from Scobie.

"Ten year or more."

"And ow much?" This from Manning.

"Two shillings."

"Then how come you ever fell on hard times?" said Kate who was known to have a sense of humour only a mite less sly than Big Brennan's.

ADELE BARRACLOUGH was sitting in the Mission reading the *Letter,* still checking for errors and omissions. She knew that if anything went wrong, they would get the usual queue of customers. Some people came in to deny the veracity of an

112

article, others to support some published indignation and repeat the words they had this morning read as though they were delivering new truths; some argued with the spelling of names, others with the positioning of commas. That was why Trevor made a point of coming in late on publication day. It was already past noon and there had been no sighting of him.

Not that this bothered her. It was true that, in any case, the Mission attracted strange people on a regular basis: they came in to give information, having seen appeals in the paper – or *thought* they'd seen appeals on some matter that, on reflection, turned out to be a thing entirely different. Others came to raise queries of their own, asking for help on how to word things. And some came simply for the chance to talk, prompted by what they'd read or been told was in the paper; to reminisce about characters they'd known; to ask questions to which they already knew the answers.

She didn't mind them. She didn't mind at all. Trevor often complimented her on her ability to handle "members of our great public" as he referred to them. Part of it, he thought, was her bringing of "the feminine touch", the gentle confidence to which both men and women obviously responded. But he was also aware, she knew, of his own shortcomings in regard to the public; of his being looked on somewhat as an outsider, a man whose class and background divorced him from both the readership and congregation.

It was a cross he must bear for the sake of his conscience. Nonetheless, he was reassured by having his Ada support him in her own unprepossessing way. Sometimes he would reach over and squeeze her hand to express his gratitude, then withdraw nervously – whether because he feared her uneasiness at the gesture or because of its possible observation by "our great public," she was unsure.

In particular, she had never feared to be in the Mission on her own. Never once during three years there had she met any situation which had unnerved her, though the

113

sometime intrusion of unintelligible young men "the worse for wear" was occasionally discomfiting.

At twenty-five past one by the granddaughter clock, the door opened and a man with a crutch appeared. He was tall, thin, with long brown hair, bald at the top, and had spots round his mouth. He was dressed the usual way navvies dressed, the only *un*usual thing being that this afternoon his right leg was bound in a splint.

She looked twice at the crutch and saw it was an upside-down flat broom of the kind the Shakers sold, but with most of the bristles worn away. That made her smile. She rose to her feet as he came across to her.

"I've come," he said, "about me name int' paper."

"Oh yes," she said, "Mr…"

"Derby George."

And a cold chill ran through her. "Can you remind me…?" she began but she needed no reminding. She could have put her eye direct to that page, direct to that item, direct against the name *Derby George*. She realised she had started to perspire. She took out a handkerchief and dabbed her brow. "It is a warm day," she said.

"I've known warmer," said Derby George, "When you work as I work…"

"Yes," she said, "I understand."

"It's to do with my advantage," he said, "to do with my relative that's died and the advantage he might be givin me. I take the meaning there's money."

She flipped over the pages because, she decided, she did not wish to find the item too quickly, to give the impression that it might have somehow played on her mind before his arrival. When she did find it, running her finger down the column of type, she found she was trembling.

"Yes," she said, "that Mr Joseph. From Harrogate. He is the one who will be able to advise you."

114

"Mr Joseph? Harrogate? Advise me?" George snorted. "If it's money coming to me, then I won't be needing much in the way of advice."

"No," she said.

"I know all there is about spending money! I do that! It's just the getting it has escaped me int' past!" He laughed, then: "Where do I find this Mr Joseph? I don't fancy walkin to Harrogate in my state of injury."

She started to reach for a pen before she realised she should *not* be writing her own address on the sheet of paper in front of her. "Well," she said, "isn't that strange? I had thought Mr Joseph to have left a local address but he appears not to have done so."

For the first time, a flash of something like suspicion appeared in the eyes of Derby George. "Then tell me how I can find this Mr Joseph if e's left no local address!"

Should she ask for *his* address? Would that make him *more* suspicious? Should she tell him to return to the Mission some time later? That had its risks but would surely be the best course of action, though she disliked the thought of having to see him a second time. She made up her mind to this.

She said: "Mr Joseph has promised to be here at 10 o'clock tomorrow morning to review the results of his advertisement."

"Good," said George, "because I *do* want to see him soonest. And I am injured, as I remarked, and therefore cannot now do my regular work. I have needed the help of two fine friends to get me this far today, and they are even now waiting across the street for my business to be completed."

He looked at her with an expression of some pleading. "If a man can come from as far away as Harrogate to tend to such a business, there must be a tidy sum involved. And it does seem a mercy from God that this bad thing which happened to me only this morning should mebbe be outweighed by a grand financial prospect."

"Yes," she said.

"Because I *do* believe in God as much as *you* do in this Mission with all your singing."

"Yes."

"And I like to be a-singing meself now and again. If the songs is good and the company right."

"Yes."

"And if I am to come into money, then I might settle down and..." He licked his lips. "What be *your* name?"

At that point the door opened and Trevor came in, doffed his hat and called out: "Good morning!" then: "Oh, but I see it is afternoon." And he laughed. "No, no, carry on," he added as if aware of interrupting, "I see you are entertaining a client."

Derby George looked back and forth between her and Trevor. He smiled. "I think my business is done. For now." He said to her: "Ten o'clock tomorra morning." And he winked. And turned. And hobbled out past Trevor.

And Adele felt her nails sink into her palms. And she thought: *Today I have talked with a murderer.* And then she sat down.

Chapter 15

"GEORGE," SAID YELLOW KATE, "I'm tending to you like a wet nurse, I am!" She was helping him put on his navy blue frock coat. She had already refused any similar service with his twill trousers or boots.

It was not from squeamishness with the nether regions of the male body, she explained; rather, it was that she had once had a lodger whom she urged one day to remove his black stockings or face the prospect of fungus in his feet and was told by him that he never *wore* stockings. It was a story she enjoyed re-telling.

"I would do it myssen," said George, "But I am in such a poor way with my injury. When I am rich," he added, "I shall have servants to see to such routines."

He was getting as much attention as she was now giving him, she said, only because it was the fullness of the morning and the others had already gone out to earn her rent. "And I trust," she said, "I shall soon have you back in fine fettle and making payments, pet. I do not offer charity."

Nevertheless, it was clear she shared some of his excitement at the prospect of a windfall. That was why she was glad to see him use the navy blue, his alternative and Sunday garb. It was important to make a good impression where money was concerned. As with yesterday, she allowed him full use of the broom. And, as with yesterday, Scobie was on hand to help him hobble the distance to the Mission, though Little Manning was absent, having pleaded the necessity of earning regular money.

"Well," said George, "he is no kind of friend, and shall have no share of my good fortune. But Scobie here, even though he did me the bad turn of injuring me, yet I will recognise his good works in helping me out."

"I thank you," said Scobie, though he had already expressed disbelief that there might be a pot of gold at the end

117

of this rainbow. He was, he said, offering his services purely on account of conscience.

"If you *do* come into money," asked Kate, "what will you do?"

"I shall invest and live off the interest."

"You need a business," said Kate, "and if you want to invest, why, this very establishment is in need of more partners. You are already settled here and part ownership would see you stay in the place you know without upset. You would have no need to go off working every day, for profit from the premises would be yours. And the ale would be free because you would already own it, George."

He stopped and considered it. It was only a throaty laugh from Scobie that dissuaded him. Kate looked daggers at Scobie. "Don't go damaging me broom," she said to George.

ADELE AND THE SERGEANT sat in the Mission studying the clock. It was already ten past the hour.

"Mebbe he smells a rat," said the sergeant. He kept his voice down a stripe so Mr Galbraith across the room would not hear.

"I am sure he does not," said Adele, "He has no reason to."

She had said the same the previous evening when she had informed him of George's first visit. But the sergeant had been suddenly fearful of the plan failing.

"I did not expect any of them to come so soon," he had said, "I reckoned on a few days for the notice to make itself known. I had not taken into account the obvious popularity of your publication."

And he had gone on to express an irrational doubt that they would be successful. "As you yourself commented, I have hunted lions this way, with a tethered goat rather than a notice in a newspaper. And the best of them, the best of these creatures, are canny enough to sense when something is wrong. For no obvious reason, with no slip on the hunter's part, the lion may suddenly think better of it and bolt."

"This one," Adele had said, "is far removed from a lion or any sort of grand creature."

Now, as they watched the clock, she remembered the flash of suspicion that had crossed George's face and felt again the sense of horror with which the episode had infected her. Perhaps, after all, he would not come a second time. And a sense of relief at the thought stole over her despite herself.

And then the door opened and George was there.

"Even down to the broom," said the sergeant and grinned. He leapt to his feet and waved at the new arrival. "Mr George! Welcome!" He clapped his hands.

An answering grin crossed George's face. He hobbled across to the sergeant, ignoring Mr Galbraith.

"And you will be Mr Joseph," said George.

"And I am that," said the sergeant.

HANDSOME HALLORAN KNOCKED on the door of Kate's shant. Though he did his share of anything that came along when he needed to, Handsome was mainly a player, a cardsman. And he had been in a profitable game of poker in Granborough last night when someone had mentioned Derby George's sudden share of both bad luck and good.

"Why," said Handsome, "Derby's a friend of mine. I was set on visiting him anyway. And if he's laid up, he will sure enjoy a game of cards. And if he's laid up with *lucre,* then *I* will sure enjoy it too."

Later he had gone down to Flash Thompson's whorehouse back of the haberdasher's store and enjoyed a girl called Libby. She was short, dark-haired and plump and her nipples were the colour of chocolate. But she had upped her price afterwards, denying she had ever settled for five shillings.

119

He had thought to call on Thompson to umpire, because he heard Old Flash was an honest man. And then he remembered hearing also that Flash was Yellow Kate's nephew. And that had reminded him about Derby George. So he settled seven shillings on the woman, thinking himself a generous fellow, and thought to make up a lot more than the difference once he got in touch with George.

So here he was. And Kate, he thought, was obviously pleased to see him. Well, he was a fine looking young man, was he not, with his wavy blond hair, his bright blue eyes, his boyish face, shaved clean every day? And he had dressed up today in his finest cardsman's pinstripe three-piece and bowler hat with hatband. What woman should not be pleased to see him? Though Kate was too old and ugly to present any real interest.

"I know who *you'll* be wanting to see," she told him, "I know what brings you out here while the sun still shines, pet. But your good pal George has gone to seek his fortune in Dovecote, where the streets are lined with gold."

"So I have heard." Handsome took off his hat. "May I come in, ma'am? I would be pleased to have an opportunity to discuss the matter, so I would." When Handsome spoke, his words were eloquent enough but he slurred the pronouncing of them. This was a consequence of him staying tight-lipped to cover the gap in his front teeth.

They went inside and Kate sat him down. "Now," he said, "what's it all about? Mysterious. That's what I think. George come into some money, but from whom?"

Kate bent her head towards him. It was seldom – he knew – that she heard the word *whom* from the men she dealt with. Years ago, a woman who fancied him and had some sort of education, had explained when to use it and he had realised its potential in smoothing his way in society.

Kate said: "It's relatives, that's what the paper says. I'll read it to you." She picked it up from the table and began to unfold it.

"Ah," said Handsome. He stood up, reached over and took it from her grasp, gently touching her elbow with his other hand as he did so. "Let me spare your eyes, ma'am. I was five years at my schooling and I have forgot nothing. Just point it out to me if you will."

She did so. He read it, skimpily at first, just to comprehend the gist. His eyes took in the words: *Derby George, contact the Mission, to his advantage, death, relative in Derby.*

Then his eyes slipped down the page. There were other such notices. *The Mission, to his advantage, death, relative.* The words repeated. And further down, the same. And even further down...

And then he picked out some of the names among the lucky ones, the ones whose advantage was mooted. He read: *Cockney Charlie Gallister, Moleskin Jimmy... Handsome Halloran.* His own name was there! Something Kate, with all her reading, had missed!

He reached in his waistcoat pocket and took out the coins. "I wonder if I may trouble you, ma'am, for a dram of refreshment?"

"Porter, Handsome? Or would you be wanting ale?"

"I'll be wanting whisky, ma'am. And you can make it a double measure."

BOB SCOBIE WAS GETTING TIRED of waiting on Derby George. He had stood across from the Mission for a good half hour and had eventually taken to pacing back and forth. There was a handsome tall grey hitched to an apple tree and he reached out and touched its flank.

"How you doin, boy?" he whispered, "How's the life that doesn't ask you to drive yourself with pick and shovel to

121

force a living every day? What d'you think about that God above who decreed you could get by on grass and like it? I wish *I* could get by on grass and like it, that I do!" He stroked the horse's mane before turning and starting back.

At least the sun was still shining. "If it comes on to rain, I'll go in and sort him out myssen, see if I won't!" He was annoyed; and the guilt of the previous day was now utterly dissipated. Damn fool George, letting his leg get in the way! Hadn't he got eyes and ears and a brain? Didn't he know better after all this time on the gullet?

And then the door of the Mission opened and George himself came out, still hobbling, but all smiles. So. Pot of gold after all. Well, well. And the man with him... Funny looking cove, clothes didn't seem to go together at all. Not like a lawyer's clothes anyway. Still, if he's the man with the money...

George waved from across the road. When Scobie went across, George said: "Now then, I've took up enough of your time, Bob, me old pal. You'll be losing pay over our little arrangement, so I absolve you from all blame for our accident of yesterday and I free you to return to your labour here and now. As Mr Joseph is my witness."

"Many thanks," said Scobie, unsure of what he really felt. "There's lucre then?"

"Indeed," said Mr Joseph.

"Indeed," said George, "more than I could ave hoped. From an uncle I never knew I ad."

"We should all have that kind of uncle," said Scobie. Then: "But don't you still want takin ome?"

"All of Mr George's needs will be looked after," said Mr Joseph, "by the firm. And by myself." He executed a little bow, a touch of mock formality that Scobie immediately disliked.

"By the firm," repeated George, "So run along, Bob. And you can tell the others about my good fortune if you will, for I do believe *fortune* is no less than what I have fallen into today."

"I'M AFTER HURRYING OVER," said Handsome, "but I didn't think to find you in."

"We came into money," said Moleskin, "the both of us. So we are playing the prodigal for a while."

"Come into money," said Charlie and giggled.

They were sitting up by the door of Betty's big sod shant. Moleskin's Biter, an ugly dog for whom Handsome had no affection, was laid out on the stone floor fast asleep. Moleskin and Charlie were both drinking strong ale and Betty took Moleskin's order for Handsome's whisky and brought it over.

My second of the morning, thought Handsome. *To be sure, all my friends are coming into money these days. It's clearly made Moleskin generous and I wonder if Charlie would like a game of poker.*

Handsome knew Moleskin never played cards, but Charlie was fond of the pasteboards. And Handsome wouldn't even need a stacked deck to take it all away from him. Still, that was for later. Right now they had something more pressing to discuss.

Handsome had made them sit by the door because it was the opposite end of the room from where Betty kept her casks. He didn't want her listening.

"I don't want to know the source of your sudden wealth," said Handsome, "but I take it there's no connection with this newspaper." When they looked at him bemused, he took the *Letter* out of his pocket and handed it to Moleskin. *No point handing it to Charlie.* He pointed out the notices to Moleskin and Moleskin read them. And Moleskin put down his glass.

"Somebody's got our names," said Moleskin. And then: "I don't reckon *you've* been over to the Mission?"

123

"That's one place I'm staying away from."

"How'd they get our names? What's the connection, Handsome?"

"The only connection between the four of us," said Handsome, "the only connection that would interest anybody…"

Charlie started up from his stool. Even *he* could see what Handsome was getting at.

"So," said Handsome, "it's a bad one, very worrying, no two ways about it." He took a sip of his whisky.

Biter, in his sleep, began to whimper. He could be having a nightmare, thought Handsome. Dogs often did.

Chapter 16

GEORGE LIKED THE RIDE IN THE PONY CART. "Hired special for your good self," said Mr Joseph as he tied his grey to the back of it and climbed into the driver's seat. Better than walking or the clippety-clank of the omnibus.

George liked the terrace house that Mr Joseph brought him to, built inside a crescent, overlooking a small, neat garden with a single birch tree. He would get a house like that himself. Probably.

When they had tied up the pony in the street and deposited the grey in the back yard, Mr Joseph took George inside. The parlour opened off the passage and the stairs led up to the bedrooms, though there was nobody else about at this time of day. They went into the front room. George admired the blue striped wallpaper and the pictures of stags, soldiers and shepherdesses on the walls. He had always planned that one day he would be a patron of art, though his taste ran mostly to nymphs and satyrs, as Moleskin called them, while he himself referred to them in more down-to-earth terms as bare-arsed women and goatmen.

"Have a seat," said Mr Joseph, dropping his bowler on to the table "Will you have tea or coffee? Or something a little more raw?"

George liked the sound of the word *raw*. He thought that something *raw* would be perfect for wetting his whistle. "I'll have some of *that*," he said.

Mr Joseph went into the kitchen and brought him back a whisky glass full to the brim.

George leaned his broom against the table and sat heavily in the nearest armchair. He took the glass, put it to his lips and gulped it down.

"Aaaaaaaaggghhhh!!" He dropped the glass and jumped to his feet. But Mr Joseph hit him square in the mouth and he fell back. "Aaaaaaaaaaghhh!" he screamed again, "What the fuckin hell...?" Again he struggled to his feet.

"Mind your language," said Mr Joseph, "there are ladies present." He indicated with a wave of his hand the shepherdesses on the walls. Then he hit George again. George reeled back again and the chair swung on its castors and hit the wall. Mr Joseph grabbed the arms of the chair and swung it round so George was facing him.

He said: "I didn't have any Scotch or Irish left, so I thought the turpentine would do. Strip some paint off you, George! Strip some paint off your insides!"

"What...!" began George. His voice was hoarse and indistinct. It was hard to speak at all because his throat burned so badly. He clutched his throat. But Mr Joseph clutched it also. And tightened his fingers on George's Adam's apple. "Dear God!" George shouted, but it was a *quiet* sort of shout.

"Calling on God, are we? A mite too late for that, some would say." Mr Joseph took his hand off George's throat and stood up to his full height. "You can have some water with your drink. It'll be good for you." He picked up George's glass, poured the remains of the turpentine on to the carpet, turned to a jug of colourless fluid on the table, poured a dose of it into the glass and handed it back to George. "Here," he said, "this time it's only water."

George hesitated. He had started to moan and tears filled his eyes.

"Take it," said Mr Joseph, "I wouldn't lie to you, George. Not now. Not from this point on. I'm going to kill you, make no doubt about that, but I won't lie to you any more."

George trembled. But he took the glass and sipped it. His voice began to come back. "What you doin?"

"Killing you, George. That's right. That's what you heard. You drink too much, George, and sometimes you lose your voice. But it doesn't make you deaf, does it? That's good. Because when I kill you, I want you to know the reason."

"I never done…" George didn't finish his sentence. He *didn't know* what it was he should be denying. He knew nothing about this mad Mr Joseph, knew no reason why the Scotchman with the moustache should want to harm him. It was so unfair! He began to sniffle. "Please…" he said.

Mr Joseph leaned over him again, their faces almost touching. "Is that what the woman said? Mrs Seabrook? *Please, please don't!* Is that what she said, George?"

"Woman? *Woman?*" This man was going to kill him over a woman! George could hardly believe it. What sensible man would kill another man over a woman? As if women weren't plentiful enough? If you had a few coppers.

"Did you shoot the soldier first? Is that what happened? So the woman was in terror then. She knew what you were capable of! You and Handsome and Charlie and Moleskin!"

And then he knew. And then he remembered. It was something that hadn't even crossed his mind for six months or more. The woman hadn't even been that pretty, though pretty was not a thing he normally required. The horror of it now struck him full-on. *Being killed for a woman that wasn't even pretty!* And the soldier…! But *he* was innocent of killing the soldier, he'd never done *that*! No jury could…!

"It was Moleskin!" he shouted, his voice coming back strong this time, thank God! "It wasn't me shot the soldier! Where would I get a shooter? It was Moleskin!"

"And loyal!" said Mr Joseph, "Loyal to your comrades in arms!"

"Now look," said George. He took another swig of the water. "I can lead you *to* em. The lads that done this. It wasn't me. I swear. I was just there. It's those other lads you want, that Moleskin with his gun. And the rest."

"Tell me," said Mr Joseph.

127

George rubbed his throat and put his fingers down his collar. "Don't kill me!" he said, "I don't deserve to die."

"There's plenty don't deserve to die, but it doesn't make any difference in the long run," said Mr Joseph. He took a notebook and pencil from his coat. "So. Moleskin. Where will I find him?"

"In a sod shant on Waterloo Street. Betty Hannah's sod shant. Big-Nose Betty. And Charlie too. They're good pals, Moleskin and Charlie!"

"Stick together, do they? Sentimental types. That's good to know." He wrote something down. "And Handsome?"

"He gets around more. He's a cardman. Games around the shants. Games in Granborough. Sporting lads all know him. He's always around."

"Gambler," said Mr Joseph as he wrote. "But I reckon you've *all* gambled this time, George. More than any of you can afford."

"Tell me," said George suddenly, "Is there really any money? From this relative in Derby?"

Mr Joseph straightened up and laughed out loud. It was the moment George needed. He pulled up his trouser leg and snatched the knife from where it lay hidden in his right stocking, and plunged it into the other man's thigh.

Mr Joseph shouted and fell. Then George was upon him.

MOLLIE TOOK THE RIFLE from Joel Truss. "This is the Girandoni air gun," he said, "You see the stock. That's the reservoir. That's where the air comes from. That's what fires the ball. It takes more than a thousand strokes of my and pump to fill that. But there, I have done the work already. Now comes the pleasure. When you young people have a day off school, I think you *deserve* some pleasure."

128

He went on: "The magazine is that thing on the side of the barrel. That's where you keep the shot. It holds 46 calibre round shot. It can shoot 20 balls in a minute." He paused. "*Magazine* and *calibre*. They'll be new words to you, I don't doubt."

She nodded. She did not wish to appear stupid in front of Mr Truss and Christopher. "I like new words," she said. She fingered the wooden stock and tried to raise the gun to her shoulder, but it was too heavy and cumbersome.

"As you see, it is almost as big as you are and weighs ten pounds or thereabout. So we must find you a place where you can rest the barrel on a ridge or on a log as you aim. And..." He paused, presumably for dramatic effect, "you must always be careful. You can kill a man with that."

"I don't want to kill a *man*," she said, "Only rabbits." She thought about it. "Perhaps a partridge if it were in season."

"Perhaps," he said. He smiled. Christopher, behind her, laughed. Mr Truss said: "You're not dressed for it. You will need to dress like a boy for ease of movement. Also for modesty's sake. But we can see to that. My boy has some britches he can let you have. Christopher, go show the young lady."

Christopher took her to the smaller of the two bedrooms at the back of the cottage. He picked up a pair of corduroy britches from a pile of clothes on the floor and handed them to her. She took them and put them to her face. "They smell," she said.

"No worse than most of the time," he said.

"Well," she said, "I'll need a shirt." He went back to the pile and brought her a black-and-white check cotton shirt. She took it. "Well?" she said.

"Well?" he said.

"Well, if I am to undress, I would not wish for *you* in the room."

129

"We are friends," he said.

"Friends or not," she said.

He went out. She closed the door, stripped off her dress and put on the clothes very quickly. She was afraid he would make an excuse to come back. When she looked at herself in the mirror on the dresser, she noted the bagginess of it all. "I look like a clown," she thought. She had once been to a circus with her father in Granborough. She sighed.

The three of them went outside. They walked across a field, through a copse, over a narrow stream. The sun was very bright and she wished she had worn a hat like the other two. They came to an ash tree and sat down in the grass.

"This gun," said Mr Truss, displaying it again, "was once used by the Austrian army. The advantages of the air rifle are its lack of noise and lack of smoke. It does not give you away like a firearm would. But be wary. It is a delicate instrument..."

"Like a violin," she said. She had started lately to tease Mr Truss now and then. She thought of it as *joshing*, a word the sergeant had taught her.

"Like a violin," said Mr Truss, "though I have never played one of those. I will have the gun at all times except when I give either of you permission to shoot. Then I will supervise and govern all actions that you may take. I am your captain. Remember that."

Mollie was suddenly a little shocked by his manner, by the way he had not bothered to address her as Miss Proudfoot or even as Mollie. He clearly wished it brought home that he was in charge, that his word was paramount. Still, when she thought about it, she did not really object. It was, in its way, reassuring.

Since the scandal of Mr Shollitoe, she had taken a dim view of the male sex, particularly those who might aspire to musical entertainments in a drawing room and employ condescending politenesses. She knew Mr Truss was not one of these and never would be. He was more like, well, like the sergeant, whom she would probably never see again.

"Come," said Mr Truss, "we will seek a suitable hide where we can rest the barrel and await the game."

They walked through another copse, then through a gate and over a stone wall. It was at this point that she realised the necessity of the boy's clothing, especially – as Mr Truss had commented – for her modesty's sake.

Eventually they came to a broken section of wall which stood by itself in the shelter of trees and in front of a grassy hillock. They sat on the hillock and Mr Truss rested the gun on the wall and trained it at various angles.

"This will do as well as any," he said, "Christopher, you shall be first as you are the boy." Christopher knelt against the wall, raised the stock to his shoulder and scanned the fields in front.

Mollie peered over his shoulder, but Mr Truss motioned for her to get down. She realised he wanted them to be as nearly invisible as possible. And she remembered his words about the advantages of the air gun with its lack of noise and lack of smoke which "does not give you away."

And she realised – with a thrill that was delicious – that they were poaching on Lord Holtby's land.

Chapter 17

ADELE TOLD TREVOR she had the starting of a cold. He was sympathetic and let her leave early. True, she was in two minds about it. She did not know exactly what the sergeant had in mind for Derby George; whatever it was, she did not wish to be too close when it happened. On the other hand, she had accepted – as she had always accepted with husband Ben – that she would follow through with all the consequences of whatever he did or whatever happened to him.

Soldiers' wives, she thought. *Soldiers' whores*, for that matter.

She walked home. She saw the cart was tethered outside, and the grey – who whinnied at her approach – was in the yard. She turned her key in the lock and opened the front door. That was when she heard the shouting and the crashing. She had heard enough brawls in her time to recognise it instantly. She ran into the front room.

The sergeant was getting the worst of it. Both men struggled on the floor; George was sitting on top of the sergeant with a knife in his hand, the sergeant forcing his arm back to avoid the blade. This surprised Adele because she knew the sergeant to be an able-bodied man of strength and ruthlessness and George a weak man with an injury.

But terror, she knew, often brought sudden strength. Then she saw the blood on the sergeant's left trouser leg. And she saw the broom – George's crutch – against the table.

Enough of being surprised. She ran across to the table, picked up the broom and passed it quickly over the top of George's head, fastening on his throat. Then she pulled it back with a jerk and heard his throttled scream.

He did the only thing he could do – he dropped the knife and grabbed the broom handle in both hands and pulled at it desperately. Straightway, the sergeant punched him twice in the stomach and George went limp. And the sergeant hit

132

him again, twice in the face, and George collapsed unconscious. Adele began to ease the pressure of the handle.

"No!" shouted the sergeant, "No! No!" He lunged forward, grabbed the broom handle where she clasped it, his hands tight over hers, pushing while she pulled.

Adele froze for a moment, then she realised the necessity. The sergeant was wounded. The fight had come to *her*. He was right, and she was wrong to let up. Now she pulled as hard on the broom handle as he was pushing: harder and harder, till she heard the squelchy sound of flesh bursting and finally the *snap* that said it was over. She let go as the sergeant let go and George crumpled and fell, lying like a heap of laundry.

The sergeant fell back and lay panting. Adele ran to the kitchen and opened the cupboard where, like all soldiers' women, she kept bandages and clean cotton cloths and Dr Tichenor's Patent Medicine for cleaning wounds.

She brought them in on a tray with a pair of scissors and began to cut away at his trousers.

He was groaning. "Damn it," he whispered hoarsely, "these are the only good trousers I own."

"There," she said as she pulled them off, "and I thought your moaning was from modesty."

He nearly cried out when she poured the fluid into the wound. But he lay still as she bandaged it. "I do not believe," she said, "that it has cut through any organ of importance."

He managed a laugh. "God's mercy that it was not higher! But that does not make it less painful." She helped him into the chair.

"I am angry," he said, "angry with myself for being careless. I thought I had the rat trapped. But, like all rats, he was most cunning and fiercest when frightened. I had briefly forgotten the nature of rats. He had the knife concealed. Well, it is a trick I shall remember. I shall have my own dirk ready from now on, pushed into the top of my stocking in the tradition of all good Scotchmen." He held out his right hand and she took it. "You," he said, "you were…"

"Magnificent?" She too felt the need to laugh. "Useful? A murderer?"

"Do not think of it as murder…"

"Why should I not? The judge and jury will think of it as murder."

"Then we must make sure they do not hear of it."

There was a sudden noise from the hall. "It is Miss Haggard. She has returned."

"Go out there, woman. And see she does not come in *here.*"

Adele did as she was told. She traded the normal afternoon pleasantries with the woman from Mayo, and watched from the hall, and listened to the turn of the key, to make sure Miss Haggard was in her room before she went back to the sergeant.

"This is how it is," said the sergeant. "We must wait till dark. We must find some way to parcel Mr George…"

"A laundry bag," she put in, "I have plenty. For my guests." She was surprised by the continuing quickness of her mind. She was surprised at the things of which she now seemed capable.

"And I must take him on the cart…"

"*We* must take him."

"No. You must be here, you must be doing the usual day-to-day things that you would otherwise do. That your guests would expect. I must take him somewhere to dispose of him. The river."

"Yes." She nodded, knowing he was right. "But first we must strip him, remove any indentification, cut up the clothes…" She thought: *What have I become?*

"And *I* must have new trousers…"

"I have an old pair of Ben's. I am sure of it. I do not know if they will fit…"

"Otherwise I must borrow from Mr George."

Suddenly they both laughed. Then, just as suddenly, stopped.

"I will adjust Ben's trousers without delay and tomorrow I will buy you a second pair." She remembered she had a tape measure in a kitchen drawer. "I will have to discover your measurements."

"I will enjoy that. But the people in the tailor's shop will ask themselves what sort of woman buys a man's trousers."

"Fortunate then that I still wear my wedding ring."

"Fortunate that I have found myself a respectable woman."

This time she did not laugh. This time she leaned forward and kissed him.

CHRISTOPHER WAS TAKING HIS TURN and taking his time. Mollie beat a snappy rhythm with her fingers on her strange trousers. Hardly worth a measly rabbit, she thought. But then she sighed. In her heart she knew *he* was right and *she* was wrong. Patience was not a thing she found easy to come by. She knew this because she had for some time been making a list of her virtues and vices with a view to building up the first list and diminishing the second.

So far the Seven Official Virtues read: *Charity* – yes, by and large, if you did not take into account her attitude to Lord Holtby; *Faith* – absolutely, in God, in her father, in the progress of the human race; *Fortitude* – well, she had valiantly overcome her contempt for the bumbling Christopher in order to continue a friendship in which she knew she played such an improving role; *Justice* – she was not sure of this since she could see it conflicting with the already mentioned Charity; *Temperance* – which, she had been told, somehow included Chastity, a virtue she could not properly define; *Hope* – well, she was always hoping for things, though she was wise enough to know that the great river of Hope probably included Patience as a major tributary and here she knew she was wanting; and *Prudence* – the least said of that the better, since she was even now poaching on Lord Holtby's land.

And the Vices, the Seven Deadly Sins which everybody knew by heart even when they did not know the Virtues? She did not believe she was *Slothful*, because she worked hard at school and helped in the kitchen; nor given over to *Gluttony* because she ate a lot less than her father; nor lost to *Anger* because she had remained friends with Christopher (see under Virtues).

Was she *Covetous*? When she asked herself this, she had to admit she coveted certain things such as the *Poems of Lord Byron*, which her father had not seen fit to purchase, even though he had given accommodation to Mr Browning. *Envy*? Well, she did not envy Lord Holtby his wealth since he had such a dreadful wife. That left *Pride*, which she straightway conceded – she was proud of her cleverness, but then her father encouraged her in this. And that left only *Lust*, of which she did not understand the meaning any more than she understood Chastity.

She was pulled from her reverie by the sudden jerk of Christopher's body which marked the recoil of the gun. He threw up his arms and was about to shout, but his father put a hand over his mouth. That must mean Christopher had hit his target. Well, she should accept this with equanimity, she supposed, since to do otherwise would be to give way to Envy. At least Christopher was good at *some* things.

Mr Truss waited a minute or two then scampered out to pick up the rabbit. "A fine one," he said and ruffled the boy's hair in affection. Christopher suddenly took on a glow of achievement and looked back at Mollie. She pretended to study an elm tree nearby.

"Your turn," said Mr Truss. He looked at Mollie and she returned the glance. Christopher grinned and moved to one side. Mollie took up her position behind the gun. The stock felt sharp against her shoulder and the gun was heavy and ungainly, even with its barrel resting on the wall.

Well, she thought, I am proud of my cleverness. Let us see if I can be clever at this.

She scanned the field for a likely victim. Mr Truss had spent some time rehearsing with both children the procedure for preparing to shoot, but it had been another excursion into *magazines* and *calibres* and she had not listened well. Should she wait until a rabbit or bird planted itself directly in front of her sights? Or would she be able to manoeuvre the gun, heavy though it was, to home in on the target? She would have to trust her instincts.

The seconds moved on and became minutes. Mollie became acutely aware of the roughness of the fabric of the boy's clothing. And the sun was heavy now and she had begun to perspire. Perhaps she should wipe her brow. But she had left her handkerchief in the pocket of her dress. Would there be such a thing in the pocket of Christopher's trousers? And if so, what would be its state of cleanliness?

She felt suddenly vulnerable. *I am a girl*, she thought. This was not a usual or frequent thought for her. What it meant was a question which she did not often ask: *If I am a girl, should I really be doing a thing like this?*

The minutes became something else: not quite hours, but extended and elastic. She began to lose her sense of time but not her sense of discomfort. She could hear her heart beat. No, more than hear it – feel it. She longed for the silence around her to be broken – for Mr Truss to cough or Christopher to laugh. She could not see them since they were behind her and she suddenly wondered what they might be doing.

137

Could they have left her on her own? Had she not known Christopher to run off in times of crisis? Yes, that afternoon when the sergeant came riding in...

But Christopher's father would not leave her. No. She became suddenly calm. She said to herself: *I will shoot. Soon. I will have the chance to shoot and I will do so.* And then she saw it. A partridge landing in the middle of the field, just left of her aim. One of the kind called *redlegs*. It was small, of course, scarcely worth the shot if she were honest – the partridge season, after all, was months away.

And she felt for a moment a stab of pity. Poor little thing. She felt like Herod about to massacre the innocents. Then she realised how silly that was and how... *blasphemous.* She manoeuvred the gun as best she could, took aim and pulled the trigger.

There was a jolt that shuddered her from head to foot.

And the sound filled her head and seemed to fill the world.

And the partridge flew off.

"Never mind," said Mr Truss, "you did your best."

"Well," said Mollie, "I will get better." She was disappointed about the things of which she was not yet capable.

ADELE HANDED THE REINS TO THE SERGEANT. She glanced at the linen bag which the sergeant, despite his wounded leg, had carried out gamely five minutes before and deposited in the back of the cart. Its spreading bloodstains were next to invisible in the moonlight. "Well," she said, "you go out with a passenger. Do not bring any back."

"Wish me Godspeed," he said.

She did so.

Chapter 18

MOLESKIN JIMMY STUDIED THE PAPER AGAIN. "We must find the man who wrote this. We must have words." Moleskin and Handsome still sat at the opposite end from the casks so as not to be overheard. But since the significance of the names in the newspaper had struck home to them all, there had been little conversation.

Moleskin took a sip of his drink. "We read in Proverbs: *Wisdom is the thing, therefore get wisdom.* The man who wrote this notice will have the answers we need."

"But wait," said Handsome, "the immediate problem is not this man who writes notices. It's Derby George. Where is he? Has he been shootin his gob? Don't you see, Moleskin? We won't know what to do until we've talked to George. George will tell us how much this meddler knows. And that will tell us what we have to do."

Handsome was playing with the brim of his hat now, running his fingers round and round it. "All I'm saying is there'll be no harm if George keeps his gob shut. The only word against us would be…"

"… the word of a whore of Babylon."

"That's right. What jury would take the word of such a woman?"

"It would have to be a *jury* of whores."

"Exactly." Handsome laughed, but only briefly. "So," he said, "first of all we have to talk to George."

"Talk to George," said Charlie. He stood peering out of the window as though seeking an answer in the distance.

"If we ever *get* to talk to George," said Moleskin, "If he's still on this earth to do any more conversation. If he's not already with his Maker."

Handsome put his hat on the table. "What d'ye mean by that, Moleskin? Why in God's name shouldn't we get to talk to George? You think the man who wrote the notice is set to cut George's throat or hang him from an oak tree or some similar action?"

Moleskin remained silent.

"That is foolish," said Handsome, "to think anyone might harm George. It will be some lawyer, I believe, some agent from a solicitor's office, mebbe seeking some reward, I don't know. Sure, he knows our names but he cannot have much hope of prosecution, otherwise the peelers would be out lookin' for us all in the open instead of Mr Lawyer laying his plots."

Moleskin touched his nose and winked. "Think about it. He knows four names and the only reason he should connect them is the killing of the soldier..."

"*I* dint kill no soldier," said Charlie, turning away from the window, his voice raised in indignation, "I never had no gun."

"Hush," said Moleskin very quietly.

Charlie hushed.

Handsome said: "No dead man ever made a good witness."

"True. So we must ask ourselves," Moleskin leaned back and his chair creaked, "what is Mr Lawyer's game? Apart from us four, there are only two people in the world that could inform on us. One is dead, as you have well remarked, like a veritable a voice in the wilderness! The second is a whore! And *she*, if she gets to court, must make admission of indecency so gross that she will lose her credulity..."

"Credibility," said Handsome. And was pleased Moleskin failed to hear him.

"So what's he up to, this Mr Lawyer, if he cannot get a prosecution?" asked Moleskin.

Silence answered him.

"If 'tis not a prosecution he is seeking...?" began Handsome.

"Then mebbe," said Moleskin, "it is a personal thing? Mebbe the soldier was a friend of his. Mebbe the whore is his own private whore, or he *thought* she was. Mebbe it is not a day in court Mr Lawyer is aiming at. Mebbe it is blood for blood."

Handsome jumped to his feet. "Moleskin, you've too much drink taken! What sort of man...?"

Moleskin was also on his feet now and his hand slapped hard on the table top so the glass was overturned and Handsome's whisky spilled. "We have a dead soldier. And who cares about a dead soldier? Nobody round here! Because people are afraid of soldiers as they are afraid of peelers, and nobody other than a soldier will stir himself to help one! Likewise, nobody other than a navvy will stir himself to help any one of *us* when we need it!"

"Hah!" said Handsome, "even supposing that's true, suppose this fella is a soldier playing at being a lawyer? What harm is one soldier to us? Can he rally a regiment of horse? He may play God Almighty in the Africas or India, but England is a civilised country under rule of law!"

"Civilised," said Charlie.

"Civilised!" laughed Moleskin, "Oh, I pity thee, Handsome, as I pity any man who can gaze upon this place, this shant, this street, the gullet where we work, the town where we dwell, and say this is civilised! As Sodom was civilised before the God of the Hebrews smote it! Oh, I pity a man that can do what you have done to that woman and watch that soldier die and say this is civilised work." He looked round to see if others might have heard, but Betty was nowhere to be seen. He turned back to the two of them.

"I'll tell you what sort of man this is! What sort of man has cunning and nerve and what sort of man would care!" The drink had got to him by now, had filled his great heart like the warrior he knew he was, like Gideon and Saul, and he suddenly cared nought who might hear him. "I'll tell

141

you *his* sort! He's a soldier alright! He's a soldier come back for his vengeance for his mate, his fellow soldier. And he's more than that! He's not just your ordinary footsoldier, your man who takes orders. He's a ganger, that's what he is! He's a leader! He's a man who can't leave vengeance to the Lord!"

Moleskin's face was red now, red with the excitement of it. "You ask what sort of man? That's the only sort of man he *can* be. A man who lives with killing! See if I'm not right! What sort of man is he? He's a man like *me*!"

He sat down again and the others did likewise. "Now here's what we do," he said, "We don't wait on our brother George, for we cannot count on his return. What he has said to Mr Lawyer or Mr Soldier we do not know and so we must act notwithstanding.

"Handsome, you will go down to the Mission first thing tomorrow and you will give false name and you will say you may know one or more of these names in the notice in the paper and you are looking for a reward. Ask about the man who writes notices. But say nothing that will incriminate.

"If you cannot find this man, find out *about* him. What he calls himself, where he comes from, what he looks like, where he lodges if he lodges locally. Anyone who knows him, anyone you think might be useful, be friendly with that person."

"Very well. I will do that. And what will *you* do?"

"I will seek out the one witness who might be our undoing."

"The woman?"

"The woman. The whore. For though she *is* a whore and only a jury of whores would take her word over that of ordinary men, yet I say to you: those townies and country folk, either together or separate, will always find against a navvyman, even on the evidence of a whore. Oh, we live in bad times, lads, when every man's hand is against us. So we must take what chance we can and do what we must."

142

"You mean to kill her," said Handsome.

"I will," said Moleskin, "Oh, I will. If I can find her."

"There was a purse," said Handsome. The others stared at him. "There was a purse," he repeated, "that came my way. There were letters inside. I have brought them to you." He reached in his inside jacket pocket and put the papers on the table.

"You took her purse," said Moleskin. He was amused.

"Though I did not kill the soldier, Moleskin, yes, I took the whore's purse."

"And you know from the letters where she lives."

"I do."

"If youse goin killin, Moleskin, an Andsome's goin to the Mission, what will *I* do?" Charlie's voice rose in a wail.

"Why, Charlie, you will bring up the rear as usual."

Handsome smiled. And Charlie laughed. Poor useless sinner, thought Moleskin, what would he do if he didn't have me? And Moleskin was suddenly filled with a sense of goodwill to Charlie and – if not to all men – then certainly to those who were never likely to stand in his way.

He had had a good day today. He could see new purpose and direction for himself and his flock. He was not simply a warrior but also – again like Gideon and Saul – a giver, a father, a host and protector to his comrades and people.

ACROSS FROM WATERLOO STREET and down an alley running with piss and shit was a shant made up from an old barn which had been there when all around was farmland. The ground inside was a dormitory for navvies who lay listless in the stink of it and ate their tommy and drank their tapster's grog.

But the hayloft was the cabin of Carribee, and his straw was clean. He was the tall, shaven-headed ebony-skinned man who had sailed round the Capes of Horn and

143

Good Hope and the southern tip of India and only lost his mind when he came to England, so now he would speak only in grunts.

Carribee worked for the hagmen – the subcontractors who paid the smallest wages and therefore had most need of a strong and fierce presence to protect them. But it appeared also that he could read in French, though no-one knew what his half dozen French books might be, except for one Bible; and some claimed he only pretended to read anyway, because he was mad.

Carribee was Moleskin's friend, if any man was, because once the black man had been attacked by gypsies on market day in Granborough; and Moleskin, passing by, had slashed a gypsy's face to ribbons and helped Carribee escape.

"Gypsies," Moleskin told him, "are the children of the Egyptians who held the people of Moses in slavery. That is why I hate them."

When it got dark, when Handsome had left for some poker game and Charlie had slunk off to his bed, Moleskin shouted to Biter and they went out to visit Carribee. When they reached the barn, Biter found a small corner of ground and lay down obediently while Moleskin climbed the ladder.

Moleskin and Carribee sat on Carribee's straw and Moleskin said: "You are Cush, the son of Ham and grandson of Noah. Your race was turned black because Ham fornicated while aboard the Ark in violation of God's commandments."

Carribee, naked, sat perfectly still in the orange light of an oil lamp hanging from the roof. He grunted.

Moleskin said: "Though you are outcast from God on account of your forebears, yet I believe you are to be redeemed when the final trumpet sounds. For you have only to believe, like me, and you will be saved." Then he said: "Though you are black like the gates of Hell, Carribee, yet I find thee beautiful."

Afterwards, he addressed the more mundane business of his visit. "The bag," he said, "and the instrument of my salvation on this earth."

Carribee dug deep into his straw bed and produced a tarpaulin bag. He handed it to Moleskin, who unlaced the top of it and briefly checked the contents. "Because you are my friend," said Moleskin, "I trust you with my most valued possession. No man must know what passes between us here."

Carribee grunted. Moleskin turned and went down the ladder. Biter got to his feet and wagged his tail. He had grease round his mouth.

"Have they been feeding you, little dog?" asked Moleskin, "I can see you'll not need supper then."

It took a mere five minutes to get back to Betty's shant and Moleskin kept the bag tucked beneath his arm all the way. It was not until he was under the blankets that he took out and caressed the Williams & Powell Revolver with its wooden chequered grip and packet of six bullets.

Chapter 19

MOLESKIN WOKE EARLY IN HIS CLOTHES covered by a single blanket on the floor of Betty's shant, a foot or two from Charlie who was snoring. Moleskin was cold, but then he was always cold. He knew straightway that this was a special day. He looked forward to it.

"Oh Lord," he whispered, "for what we are about to receive, we thank Thee." Biter heard him, sat up and whined. "Good boy," said Moleskin, reached over and rubbed his head. "Stay," he said. Biter lay back on the floor.

Moleskin went to the pump out back of the shant, poured cold water into a wooden bowl, went back inside, stepped carefully across the sleeping bodies that filled the room, until he stood by a curtainless window. He put the bowl down on the window ledge, went back to his tarpaulin knapsack, which he always used as a pillow to protect his possessions from the wicked world.

"Not used ye in a long time," he said to the razor. "Nor ye," to the piece of shiny metal he used as a mirror. He dashed water in his face, rubbed a piece of lye soap into his skin and shaved off his beard, slowly, meticulously. "Oh yes," he said when it was finished, "You are still the handsome one, Jimmy." He rubbed his face dry on his blanket.

He then made his way to the door of the back room, locked and bolted, where Betty slept. He rapped lightly, careful not to wake the sleeping navvies and knowing that Betty would *always* be awake. He called her name softly.

"Is that Moleskin?" she called back.

"I need to do some business," he said, "that will mean lucre for you."

She unlocked the door. Like him, she had slept in her day clothes – for her, a long cardigan over a printed cotton dress. "Speak that business," she said, behind the chain that

146

still protected her. Then: "Well, you've got a face at last. Now that's a turn-up and no mistake."

"A face at last," he repeated, "But I still need some tailoring, Betty. Something to go *with* the face. A pair of britches that do not look like mine. A coat that is dark enough for nobody to be dazzled and look twice. A hat that will give good cover to my handsome head."

"Since when," she said, "have you started wanting style, Moleskin? Since when have you followed any fashion? Nuthink I've heard from you has prepared me for this."

"Since I woke up this half hour."

"Come in," she said and unhitched the chain.

Inside the room was her iron bedstead with three layers of sheets; a table with a wash bowl, a bottle of gin and a glass; an oil lamp stood on the floor; and an old oak chest in the corner.

"I do not cut the cloth myself," she said, "as you well know, but I sells it at fair prices." She opened the chest and he saw the piles of clothing, neatly folded.

"I can put faces to some of this," said Moleskin, "I can recollect the very bodies that wore them."

"And none of them still in need," she said, "Not *one* of them complaining if I might have helped meself to a garment or two when they passed on to the Good Lord's mercy and I had no further prospect of their rent."

He began to sort through the material. It took perhaps 20 minutes to kit himself out.

"Is it cash?" she asked.

"It is."

"Only I can do you a partial trade with your own vestments if you so wish."

"No. I will have further need of my present clothes after today."

"Ay. And good reason to burn the ones you bought from me, I don't doubt. And to grow that beard again."

147

"But no-one must hear of such a thing, Betty."

"They will hear nuthink from me."

"I know they will not. For thou art a good woman. And a good woman is priced above rubies."

"Good job for you my old clothes is cheaper."

They settled on a price and he returned to his bed with a dark brown coat, a grey worsted trouser and a woollen cap. He changed into the newness of it, rolled up his old garments and put on his regular boots. Then he gave Charlie a kick.

The other man rolled over, clutching his blanket to his chest, his face stitched in a pattern of alarm which did not dissipate when he saw who had kicked him.

"Charlie," said Moleskin, "be awake."

"Awake," said Charlie.

"I am away today. An excursion you might call it. And here's what you will do. You will see to my clothes that I am loaning you and my belongings that I leave here. You will feed Biter and take him for his constitutional. You will keep to yourself any tale about my being at large. You will tell no-one what I am about."

"But I *dunno* what you're about, Moleskin." Clearly, Charlie's memory did not encompass much of the last twelve hours.

"Well then, that's something to warm my heart. *Rejoice; again I say rejoice!*" Moleskin stood up and Biter again raised his head. "Stay with your Uncle Charlie," said Moleskin. Biter snorted and began to growl but lay back again.

"He never likes to be away from me, but he does as I tell him. Now don't go teaching him your bad ways, Charlie. I shall know on my return if he should practise unaccustomed disobedience, and I shall lay it at your door." Moleskin picked up his knapsack and was gone.

MRS TORDOFF HAD PUT ON HER BEST BONNET, the one with the rose-coloured trimming. "It is not often I get treated like a lady," she told Joel Truss, "getting fetched and carried like this."

"It is no problem for me, Freda," said Joel, "I have people to meet anyway in Dovecote, and we may as soon use the dogcart as any other way."

"It is surely a Godsend," she said, "for occasions such as this." The occasion was a visit to her friend Mrs Seabrook.

"I do believe she needs cheering," Mrs Tordoff told Mr Proudlove, "for the recent trouble is still very much in her mind. I am taking her a sponge cake made with butter and cream."

"I understand," the vicar had said, "I realise it is too much a feminine area for a blundering man such as myself to trespass, offering words of comfort. I believe you are the perfect person to bring relief to your friend for I know you to be both strong and compassionate. And I am sure she will adore your cake."

The journey went pleasantly enough, with Joel allowing the horse an easy jogging pace. Finding the two-up-two-down that housed Mrs Seabrook was easy since it lay just below the sign of The Blackamoor; though Mrs Seabrook, a little embarrassed perhaps by her brother's business, liked to describe it as "opposite the draper's". Joel helped Mrs Tordoff down from the seat. "And I shall return at four to collect you," he said, "and we shall have a fine journey back for the sun will still be strong."

"And I am sure there will be a cup of tea left. Perhaps more than one. I will speak to Emily."

He doffed his woollen cap and said goodbye.

MOLESKIN HAD READ the letters from the whore's stolen purse. An address next door to a tavern! What sort of woman… ? Moleskin had even been in The Blackamoor on occasion prior to the killing of Corporal Briscoe. Had he known, he might have had some previous fear of recognition and dispatched the whore at the time. Well, he was confident he would not be recognised *now*. But the result, though delayed, would be the same.

He carried a Bible on his journey and held it always in his right hand and consulted it now and again. It was a book that gave him great comfort, particularly those passages about the Hebrews claiming the Promised Land. But also it was useful for a journey such as this.

When he heard the sound of a farm cart trundling behind him, he would wave the hand that held the Bible, for he knew these were mainly Chapel folk and would usually give a ride to a righteous man. At the third attempt he was lucky. A fat yokel with brown buck teeth pulled him up among the hay and chattered interminably about the rainfall that was already overdue. Moleskin advised him to trust in the Lord and it seemed to comfort him. *I have missed my calling,* thought Moleskin, *for I might have gone among the unrighteous as a preacher and converted many.*

When he arrived at Dovecote, he soon found The Blackamoor – a small, dingy room with tiny windows, a few odd tables and a dozen stools, inhabited by an equally dingy barman of indeterminate age. He ordered a half pint of India pale ale, kept his face turned away, sat down near a window, without further conversation.

He drank and read a chapter of the Good Book, though he could not afterwards remember which one. At some point a dogcart drew up outside and he squinted to get a good look through the narrow glass near his table. There was some to-ing and fro-ing with a woman called Freda and another called Emily, which he knew to be Mrs Seabrook's given name.

A man was also involved but he mounted the dogcart and departed as the women went into the front of the house. Moleskin drained his glass.

It was time, he knew, and he would have to kill *both* women. Still, he had enough bullets. And some to spare.

He got up, put his glass on the counter, nodded to the barman, went out into the street. Slowly he walked round the block, pretending to be interested in the fripperies of shop windows, but feeling himself an agent of a higher power, *sent to spy out the land* as it says in Numbers.

When he came to the back of Mrs Seabrook's house, he pretended to drop his knapsack and used the moment to retrieve his pistol and put it in his coat pocket. Whatever he did would have to be done quickly, no prevarication. He studied the back door, wondering if it were on a bolt as well as a lock. He thought it unlikely since these Chapel folk were much of a muchness, wandering at will into each other's houses and unlikely to be so protective.

Still, Mrs Seabrook was an especial case, having suffered considerable fright and much else all those months ago. So he could not be certain. He would have to chance it.

He stretched to his full height, squared his massive shoulders, put his weight on his back foot, then charged the door. It splintered with a crash. He suddenly found himself in the small back room with purple flowers on a table. He waved the gun at the flowers. Then out into the hall, still waving the gun, glancing left and right, knowing any surprise was already lost.

The women came out of the front room, alarm on their faces but no screams yet. The Seabrook woman was in front, the woman called Freda just behind. Moleskin raised the gun.

JOEL TRUSS WAS HALF A MILE out of the village when he realised there was a problem. A brown paper parcel still

151

nestled on the back seat, unobserved by him till now. Freda's sponge cake! And the women would be having mid-morning refreshment very soon!

He snorted and his horse snorted too, as though picking up his mood. *Ah well, there was nothing for it.* Joel pulled at the horse and turned the dogcart round and trundled back the way he had come.

THE FREDA WOMAN PUSHED MRS SEABROOK over against the wall. Moleskin fired.

Kerrrrakkkkkkkkkkkkkkkkkk!!!!

The bullet hit the Freda woman square in the chest, and she screamed and buckled and blood spurted over her bodice. But she fell against the wall, obscuring his view of Mrs Seabrook.

He fired nonetheless. His bullet hit the glass in the front door and shattered it. A part of him knew he should be afeared by now because he was always a careful man, always prided himself on the fact. But a fierce joy had taken hold of him and the noise only fed the joy.

And then the front door swung wildly open and the glass in it shattered a second time. And in the doorway was a man in a woollen cap carrying a brown paper parcel.

It made no sense to Moleskin. He laughed. And he fired again. And the bullet took the man in the left shoulder and he spun and hit the door jamb. And Moleskin fired again and the man fell back into the street. And Moleskin fired at Mrs Seabrook again, but the bullet hit the Freda woman in the face and her head burst open like a pumpkin at a fairground shooting gallery. And Moleskin laughed again.

But he knew the game was up. He had used five bullets. And now he had to flee, as had often happened in his life, and he would live to fight again. But he would need the remaining bullet if he were to guarantee his escape. He ran through the doorway out into the street, waving the gun,

152

watching them, the mob of people, as they shouted and ducked and ran. *Ducked and ran!*

He also ran, first down the street, past the shops again, then across to the fields at the back of the haberdasher's, then across more fields, running, running, feeling the ecstatic pounding of his heart and the piston motion of his legs, into trees, into woods, across a stream, feeling the spray, drinking in the warm air of summer.

I am escaped with the skin of my teeth, he thought and: *Keep me as the apple of Thine eye, hide me under the shadow of Thy wings!* And he thought: *In the hand of the Lord there is a cup and the wine is red!*

And then he fell, exhausted, lay his head on softest grass and fell straightway into deep sleep, full of so many dreams.

Chapter 20: Interlude

THE BEARDED MAN IN THE MOLESKIN WAISTCOAT stood by the pathway, his hands in the pockets of his chalkstripe trousers, his dirty bottle green frock coat caught up behind his wrists as was his wont, his battered stovepipe hat tipped a little way over his forehead.

"Biter!" he called. The eight-month-old black-and-tan terrier, relieving itself against a rowan, wagged its tail and ran across to him.

"This Blenkinsop, e's not coming," said Cockney Charlie.

"He will come ere long," said Moleskin. But in his heart he thought: *No, you're right, Charlie. Just don't rile me now.*

Charlie was stupid but at least he obeyed orders; and Moleskin liked to have him come along in these matters, if only as audience.

But Moleskin regretted his decision to let Derby George tag on. It was unlikely Blenkinsop would have anybody with him, so killing him should have been a one-man job.

And coming across Handsome Halloran had been a sour twist of fate. "I was at the Harvest Festival, Moleskin," the Irishman had said, "looking to start a game, but the place is half full of Methodists and I couldn't get going." Once their paths had crossed, however, it was easier to take him with them than let him wander round with his loose mouth.

"I was told," said Moleskin, "that Blenkinsop would be here at this very time. On his way to the Festival. I was told by Mr Bakey."

"But he's not come," said Handsome, managing to sound a lot like Charlie. He looked worriedly at the pale September sky. "And it's gonna rain, I can tell it's gonna rain! Bloody English weather!"

154

"Wait," said George, "there's somebody coming."
They all heard it now. Footfalls on twigs. Voices.
"A woman's voice," said Handsome.
"A woman," said Charlie.
"So it'll not be this Blenkinsop," said George.
"A woman is unexpected," Moleskin agreed.
"What can we do with a woman?" asked Charlie, and Handsome and George laughed.

Moleskin whistled for Biter who came running. Then, at a wave of Moleskin's arm, they all retreated under the cover of the trees and watched. Moleskin put his hand over Biter's mouth and whispered the usual mixture of endearments and threats to calm the dog.

A couple were walking along the path, coming closer. They were perhaps ten yards away – a young man with a handsome woman on his arm, carrying a parasol. But he was the handsomer, thought Moleskin, studying them awkwardly from his kneeling position, still holding on to Biter's muzzle.

The man, Moleskin saw, was in his early twenties, with hazel hair that fell in a quiff across his forehead. He wore a bright red army tunic. Moleskin noted his tallness, for he was half a head taller than the lady and would surely be a fighter in a tight spot. True, he had a boyish face with wide-set eyes, but the tunic told its own tale. The woman? Well, Moleskin did not reckon *women*. But the others did.

"She's a corker," said Handsome. He kept his voice to a whisper but gave a high-pitched giggle at the end of his sentence.

"Corker," said Charlie very quietly, for he knew the depth of Moleskin's anger.

"She does my eyes powerful good," said George. He rubbed his eyes to indicate his pleasure.

"Now, now," said Moleskin. He knew it was a weak response. He was uncomfortable in his kneeling position and agitated at the failure of his plan to ambush the man

155

Blenkinsop. It was still possible that his quarry would be along in the next half-hour or so, but now...

Now Moleskin studied the woman, trying to make sense – as he was wont to do occasionally – of what the others might see in such a creature. She had a broad but not uncomely face, fair hair of the kind he liked on some boys, and a youthful figure that probably owed more to corsetry than to the natural distribution of fat. She was, he reckoned, an acceptable example of her kind but by no means a beauty.

The soldier and the woman with the parasol had now come upon a fallen section of tree, axed perhaps to broaden the path, then left there by the woodsman. They stopped. They spoke. They laughed. She nodded and they sat on the fallen tree.

"Well," said Handsome, "and what's this all about?"

"I think we're gonna see some lovey-dovey," said George.

"Lovey-dovey," said Charlie.

"Shut your mouths," whispered Moleskin.

The woman put down her parasol and the soldier leaned forward and kissed her on the mouth. She made no resistance. He put his arms tightly around her and kissed her again.

"Go to it, my boy!" said Handsome.

"I said: *Shut your mouths!*" Moleskin felt Biter strain against him. He could see he was losing control.

The soldier now had his hand on the woman's bodice, his fingers outlining the breast beneath. "Ooohh, this is tasty," said George.

The soldier took his hand away from her breast and unbuttoned his tunic, so it fell open. He then began to unbutton his twill trousers at the front.

"He's gonna take it out," said Handsome, "I'm gonna cheer if he does."

"You will not," said Moleskin. But he too was excited now.

"She's strokin' it!" said George.

"God bless the colleen," said Handsome.

They watched for a time. Then Handsome said: "The whore! The bloody whore! I'm gonna have some of that!"

"Hold!" said Moleskin in a voice louder than he had intended. But it was too late. Handsome and George were running across to the woman. She glanced up, saw them and screamed. The soldier jumped to his feet and lashed out at George, sending him spinning. Moleskin let go of Biter and pulled the Williams & Powell Revolver from his coat pocket. "Damnation," he said and ran after them.

HANDSOME HAD JUST FINISHED WITH THE WOMAN and it was George's turn. She had been screaming at the start but they pulled off her bloomers and pushed them into her mouth to shut her up. She had struggled at the start but they slapped her and pulled her hair.

Moleskin stood a yard or so away, with Biter circling and snarling. The soldier lay at his feet, his head bloodied by the blow from the Williams & Powell. He was conscious and there was a look of resistance in his soldier's face. But his soldier's brain told him such resistance was impossible while he lay on the ground with a gun trained on him. Moleskin knew. Moleskin understood. Moleskin felt pity for the soldier.

He said: "Why do you trouble with this Babylon? Why do you bring shame upon your uniform?"

The soldier said nothing. Moleskin respected him for that. No begging. No crying out. No useless threats. Not like the woman. Why were women like that? Because they had no strength of their own, so they sapped a *man's* strength. That was the reason.

George shouted: "Your go, Charlie."

"Only do it quickly!" whispered Moleskin, "and do it quietly!" He had given up the idea that Blenkinsop would come this way, but others well might. The people at the Festival – friends and relations of the couple – would have missed them by now, but presumably they had not rushed to find them for fear of causing embarrassment.

Those fine respectable Church and Chapel folk! They had been no better than accomplices to the lust of this benighted couple! *Well, their sins have found them out*, he said to himself, *The Lord thy God is a jealous God*!

He said to the soldier: "See how they have found you out!" He wanted to say more. He wanted to explain that there was something better than the softness of a woman. It was a hardness and a strength that he felt – that he *knew* – he shared with the soldier. It was far above what men and women did.

But he knew there was no point in trying to explain. Certainly it was something he would not have considered explaining to Handsome or George or Charlie. *They* were not real men, merely the effigies of men, as the golden calf was an effigy of God. There *was* a real God but he lived in a Book; just as there were real men, but Handsome and Charlie and George were not of that ilk. What they were now doing to the woman proved that.

There was a cry behind him and Moleskin realised Charlie had finished. It had not taken him long. Handsome shouted: "If you want some, Moleskin, better get over here fast! She's passed out under Charlie and there's not much life left in her!" And Moleskin thought: *Dear God, they had used my name out loud*! At least the woman had already fainted…

And Handsome laughed. And George and Charlie laughed.

Were they laughing, thought Moleskin, because of the whore or because they knew about *him*? He was already tense with the whole afternoon – the waiting for Blenkinsop, the awful pantomime of the soldier and the woman, now the

158

sudden danger that had come to him through the stupidity of his acolytes. He raised the gun and was about to turn it on them. Then Biter, sensing something badly wrong, growled at him.

"Ay," said Moleskin, "I should have more sense." He pointed the gun at the soldier instead and pulled the trigger – twice. Both bullets hit the soldier in the throat and he gagged and shook and the blood came out in a fountain, splashing over Moleskin's boots. It was the only satisfaction Moleskin had experienced all day.

The soldier lay still. And there was silence behind Moleskin. But only for a moment

"I didn't mean it!" shouted Charlie, "I didn't mean er passin out!" And then his high, whining voice reached a crescendo: "It's not so much pleasure when she's out like a light!"

PART THREE: SERGEANT JOSEPH

Chapter 21

MR PROUDLOVE EXTENDED HIS HAND. "You are most welcome once again, Sergeant Joseph. I am only sorry that such a sad occasion should have been the sole cause of your return."

The sergeant shook his hand. "It is more than sad," he said, "it is an outrage. And it is right, sir, that you should have alerted me."

"I fear such is the depth of feeling for this infamy hereabout that you would not long have remained ignorant, though you might wear a blindfold and stop your ears with wax. It is a dreadful, shocking business."

He coughed. "For reasons on which I will not elaborate, I am unable to attend the ceremony today. But my daughter Mollie will be there. Also young Christopher, whose father is still too weak to complete the journey."

"I had heard of Mr Truss's injuries. I had hoped to speak with him."

"I'm afraid that will not be possible. He is sleeping currently under the influence of morphine. He needs every moment of that sleep to replenish his strength. I'm sorry…"

"I understand," said the sergeant. "Another day perhaps. Another day soon." But silently he cursed.

They were standing in the vicarage drawing room which was filled with about a dozen people whom the sergeant did not recognise. The sergeant indicated Adele. "This lady is a friend of mine who wishes to attend and offer her condolences to Mrs Tordoff's friends. We hired a pony and trap for our journey." Seeing a slight change of expression flit across Mr Proudlove's face, he added quickly: "Mrs Barraclough is a worker at the Dovecote Mission."

Adele was wearing a full skirt and bodice, her modest Sunday grey, with matching bonnet. She smiled and Mr Proudlove took her hand also. "Charmed, I am sure," he said and to the sergeant: "Could I ask you to take Mollie and Christopher in your trap? I would deem it a great favour."

When he had turned away, Adele said: "He will not go to a Chapel funeral just as the established church will not make its priests available to help with the Mission."

"Adele, he is not a bad man. He does what he can according to his needs and talents."

"And his needs are to keep Lord Holtby happy."

"His needs are to look after his parish and his child as best he can and keep the wolf from the door. He does not seduce housemaids, unlike his former curate, and I wager he does not put his fingers in the church collection. Be charitable, today of all days."

WHEN THEY GOT OUTSIDE, Sergeant Joseph patted the pony and called it soft names while Adele paced nervously to and fro. "Perhaps it is the heat and a surfeit of clothing," he said, "But you are more skitterish than the horse." He himself was dressed in one of Ben's black frock coats and ill-fitting black trousers.

"Do not think to use your whip on *me*," she responded.

And then a small voice the sergeant knew well said: "That is a picturesque turn of phrase, Mrs Barraclough."

And the sergeant said: "And this is Mollie of whom I have told you." Mollie was dressed in a black apron over a white dress.

Adele and Mollie faced each other. "How is it you know my name?" asked Adele.

"My father told me Sergeant Joseph had a handsome lady with him and informed me of your name."

The sergeant thought he saw the hint of a blush touch the handsome lady's cheek. "Well, if you are Mollie, I am Adele," said Adele.

At that point, Christopher came out of the house and walked slowly over to them. He had lost weight since Sergeant Joseph last saw him and there was a darkness about his face. "I trust," said the sergeant, "that things continue well with your father."

"One bullet in the shoulder, another grazed his head," said Mollie, "but Dr Arbuthnot from Granborough says he will be up and about in four weeks with no lasting effect."

"God be praised," said Adele.

"Yes," said Christopher. His eyes turned downwards and his lips set hard.

THE ETERNAL GLORY CHAPEL was on a turning two miles along the road from Padstone to Dovecote. Throughout the journey, there had been little conversation; Mollie had ridden by the sergeant's side while Adele and Christopher rode in the back. Only once did Christopher stir himself to say: "This was a day my father and I would have taken the airgun..." then stopped himself.

The sergeant saw Mollie bite her lip. He hoped there would be no tears just now, for that would upset Adele and he wanted her alert to any gossip there might be among the Chapel women.

It seemed unbelievable that the man who murdered Mrs Tordoff and wounded Joel Truss in the home of Emily Seabrook should be anyone other than the man who shot Corporal Briscoe. And yet... It seemed such a desperate and foolish move. It *was* just possible that the elusive Emily had some other malcontent in her past, in which case he needed to know of it.

The Chapel was set on the far side of a copse with an area containing about 40 graves in front. When they arrived, the sergeant hitched the pony to an elm tree and turned to help Mollie down, but she was already on the ground on her feet;

Christopher quickly followed her and the two children ran off towards the building.

That building was small – looking to accommodate no more than 80 or 90 people – but was grand in style, built of sandstone with a slate roof. The sergeant noticed most of the gravestones were the same sandstone.

The Chapel had five narrow bays with buttresses and a lancet in each bay. The south end, from which Sergeant Joseph and his passengers approached, had an arched doorway with a window above and the corners were square with pinnacles.

Next to the chapel was a single-storey wooden Sunday School with three windows on each of its two long sides and a lean-to porch. Already about 30 people were gathered outside, the adults looking suitably chastened, the children running and playing as they always would.

"Is it not grand?" asked Adele, "And is it not solemn?"

"Do not speak to me of solemn," he said, "I am with the Anti-Christ of Rome and we *always* do things solemn. This jaunt will be my education in sandstone religion."

When they got inside, they found the chapel full to overflowing. There were galleries on two sides, a ribbed vaulted ceiling and an organ to the right of the pulpit. In front of the pulpit on a rough table was the coffin: small, modest – but properly planed and polished, the sergeant noticed.

A woman interrupted the sergeant's reverie by handing out a hymnbook. He and Adele joined up with Mollie and Christopher and made for the back row of pews. Adele and the children found seating together; the sergeant stood behind Adele, scanning the congregation for interesting faces. There was no Emily Seabrook. He was confident he would recognise her from the sepia photograph he had been shown, and had been so taken with, so long ago.

164

The hymn was *O God Our Help in Ages Past*; the voices ran slightly ahead of the organ which was played vigorously in what the sergeant thought of as fairground style – but he liked the effect. Both singers and organist were demonstrating *enthusiasm*, something he occasionally found wanting in his usual church. He was strangely pleased that he had come.

The rest of the service followed the usual pattern: eulogy – in which Mrs Tordoff's sponge cakes were mentioned – sermon and prayer, led by a grey-haired preacher whose face bore the lines and pockmarks of the sandstone around him.

No details of the circumstances of the death were touched on except in the most vague and abstract of terms – "the unforeseen tragedy of a moment" said the preacher – and the sergeant understood instinctively why this was so. The natural horror of violence among people in general often had the result of stigmatising the victim. So best not to dwell on such things; best to summarise with a necessary word – that "unforeseen" – which exonerated Mrs Tordoff from any possible blame for her doom.

Then it was best to emphasise only the well-ordered circumstances of her virtuous life. It was as though the fearful truth of those final moments had been shut outside the Chapel doors by common consent.

But the sergeant was not among people in general. He was a man who lived with violence and its detail held no terror for him.

Then the coffin was carried out by four men, one of whom sported a silk waistcoat of a kind that seemed foreign to the style of the congregation. He looked as much an outsider as the sergeant felt. The congregation filed out to join the procession, beginning with the front pews, leaving the sergeant and his companions till last.

The graveside rites were short and unmemorable, though he noticed Christopher and Mollie appeared transfixed as the casket was lowered. He had not properly thought till that moment of the effect on the children. Both were involved with church ritual through their parents: Christopher indeed was the son of a gravedigger. And both had previously been touched by death – each, he knew, losing a mother while very young. But there is a moment in life, he also knew, when the past and future come together in realisation, and perhaps this was their time. He sighed.

Afterwards the congregation moved into the schoolhouse for lemon cordial and sandwiches. Adele exchanged a glance with the sergeant, then attached herself to a group of women who looked like the gossiping kind. On a hunch, the sergeant moved across to speak with the man in the flowered waistcoat. On the way he almost bumped into a powerful, red-faced man with a large nose who looked strangely familiar; the sergeant apologised and moved on.

The sergeant said to the man in the waistcoat: "Excuse me, sir, but I think I know you. Have I not seen you on occasion in The Blackamoor in Dovecote? Are you not Mr Kilfedder, the proprietor?"

The short, wiry, dark-haired man snorted. "If you have seen me there, sir, then I beg you lower your voice. We are among lemon-drinkers now. But yes, I am the landlord, though I confess I do not recognise you."

"I have been there on only few occasions but I have always thought the ale exceptionally well kept and the company most friendly."

"We do our best for our clientele," said the man and smiled the smile of the professional who has received unexpected praise, "Perhaps you might extend us your custom more frequently."

"I had been thinking the same." The sergeant finished his cordial and placed the glass on a window ledge. "I understand The Blackamoor is next door to where the outage took place. Tell me, have you any notion how the police investigation is proceeding?"

"I wish I did. The officers, as you may imagine, often frequent my inn and nothing loosens a man's tongue faster than a pint of porter, I always say. But I fear I have heard nothing of use."

"I understood there have been no arrests thus far. But does that mean no local man has been identified or denounced?"

"It was not a local man, that much I can tell you." A look of suspicion now clouded the landlord's face. "But it may be you have a personal interest in the case? Or that you feel you have some useful information which will help the constabulary?"

"No, no," said the sergeant, "I am merely a law-abiding citizen eager to see justice done." And he smiled, wiped his mouth on a linen napkin and strolled over to where Mollie and Christopher were sitting on the uncarpeted floor. He squatted next to them.

"When your father is better, young Christopher, I hope to speak with him about this dreadful matter."

Suddenly Mollie's face broke into anguish, she put a hand across her eyes and her body was wracked with sobs. "Mrs Tordoff! Mrs Tordoff!" she cried. "She has been taken away from us! Oh, cruel and evil!"

But the sergeant took no notice. He had suddenly remembered where he had seen the red-faced man with a large nose before today: he was Bob, he was Derby George's friend.

And now he was gone.

Chapter 22

"THERE IS NO GOSSIP TO BE HAD," said Adele as they drove home. "The whole community is shocked. They think it was a burglar broke in to thieve. They think it was a navvy."

"About the second fact, they are right," said the sergeant. "And my money is on Moleskin, the leader of the gang. For I think Moleskin and his friends have decided to take the offensive."

He told her about Bob. "They have sent someone to see the lie of the land. They found us at the chapel, they know I was with you and I do not doubt they will know you from the Mission."

He felt her tense on the seat of the trap beside him. "Then we are in danger."

"We have always been in danger. But we are forewarned and forearmed. Let us not take fright at this late hour."

When they arrived at the house, a familiar voice rang out from the parlour window – which was now open. "Sergeant Joseph, I trust tha's in good ealth."

The sergeant tried not to show his surprise. "Did ye doubt it, Constable?"

They went into the house. Con Allardyce stood up as Adele and the sergeant entered the room. "I ad no *real* doubt," said the constable, "for I knew thee to be a man not easily quelled. There's a lad named Jedediah, known as Jed, who doesn't walk as well as he used."

"I remember Jedediah." The sergeant introduced Adele. "My landlady," he said.

Allardyce touched his forelock. His helmet lay on the table. "The Irish lady allowed me in."

"She is very accommodating," said Adele. She offered to make a pot of tea but the sergeant said: "Of course, I have something stronger."

"Ah," said the constable and smiled.

"Then," said Adele, "I will leave you two gentlemen."

When she had gone, the constable sat down again. The sergeant found the whisky and two glasses and sat opposite him. "You still have no horse, I see."

"Still they treat him for is old age as though it will pass like the scurvy. I ad to come on the omnibus." He snorted.

"Your employers then do not think much on dignity."

"There is one less dignified than I." Allardyce took a long drink. "We found a man in the river," he said, "In a sack in the river, to be exact."

"It is always good to be exact."

"E was naked and the water and the rocks had done their work on im but still I knew the man. Is name was George, known ereabout as Derby George. I believe tha knew im."

"He had come to me believing a relative had left him money."

"And was that so?"

"The information turned out to be wrong."

"Why should e come to thee?"

"He heard I was an agent for some solicitor. That also turned out to be wrong."

"It is a strange business."

"Police work is often a strange business."

"I believe there was a notice in the paper…"

"So I am told."

"Is tha saying thee ad nowt to do with its publication? I must tell thee I ave spoken with Mr Galbraith."

"Mr Galbraith is an honest man but even honest men can be mistaken."

"Thee is denying the connection?"

"I am saying perhaps I should not speak more without the presence of a *real* solicitor."

169

The constable laughed. "Let us speak plain, as we did previous. Derby George was shit. E ad neither kin nor genuine friend that will come forward to demand we arrest the culprit. When a navigator dies, what of it? It will be another navigator that as committed the crime and e will be moved out of the district by the time we find the body. But this Derby George was one of the gang that killed thy friend Briscoe. Tha'll know that already."

"How could I know it?" The sergeant poured the constable a second drink. "You gave me no hint of their names when last we spoke."

"True, I did not." Allardyce picked up the glass.

"Indeed, it might be damaging to your career if anyone should get the notion that you *did* tell me. I mean, in view of this body turning up."

"Career is it?" Allardyce's laughter caused him to spill the drink. "I did not know I ad a *career*. But true, it might affect me badly."

"So I must ask why you are here."

The constable's voice dropped half an octave. "Now a *woman* is also dead. A respectable chapel woman. A woman known to you. I believe you ad words with er after you left me."

The sergeant also dropped his voice. He knew the time had come for gravitas. "I am not aware of any words. And, as you say, the woman is dead…"

"… so cannot be questioned." The constable sighed. "Well, I've tried for a quiet life, tha knows, and it as not been given me. Now I've three murders, two of the victims being decent respectable people. I do not wish to see a fourth. But if there *is* to be a fourth, and a fifth, and a sixth…"

"I see you are a fatalist, Constable Allardyce…"

"… then I would rather see that none of those to come should be decent or respectable."

"And so would I."

170

The constable finished his drink and stood up. "I know what tha's up to, sergeant, and I ave some sympathy. I like a military man. My own late brother was a private soldier in the 19ᵗʰ Foot in barracks at York. So I say to thee, Sergeant: Do not make thyssen too obvious."

The sergeant stood also. "I thank you for the warning." They shook hands.

The constable said: "The Irishman is a card player, well known with the sporting fraternity in Granborough."

"I already know. Does anyone else have his name?"

"I do not believe so."

"Not even Mr Kilfedder?"

"If Tommy knew the names, e would do as you do."

"That was my impression."

When the constable had left, the sergeant went up to his room where Adele was waiting, sitting on the bed. She said: "Well?"

"He is no threat. He may well be an ally."

"But we must be careful."

"We already knew that."

They went downstairs. The sergeant asked for writing paper and an envelope. When she had found them, he took a pencil from his pocket and wrote five paragraphs. The fifth contained three names, none of them his own. He sealed the envelope and wrote on the front: *Tom Kilfedder, The Blackamoor Inn, Dovecote.* He asked Adele: "And do ye have one of those new-fangled penny stamps?"

"More mischief?"

"*Much* more mischief."

"Then we must be more careful. *Much* more careful."

"I will make the arrangements to take you away from here."

"And you?"

"I will remain. I have made them a trap, have I not? Now they may fall into it."

171

"IS THE BIG MAN AWAKE?" asked Halloran, slipping through the door at the front of Betty's shant. She nodded and indicated with her thumb the alcove at the end of the room, cordoned off with dirty blue velvet curtains since Halloran's last visit.

He made his way across, hat in hand, stepping carefully to avoid the pools of ale and occasional piss that puddled the floorboards. There were three or four bodies on the same floor in various states of sleep and undress and he worried for a moment whether this was really a safe place for a heart-to-heart on the dangerous matter in hand. But he knew he had little choice.

Halloran laid his hand on the curtain and pulled it aside. Of a sudden he faced Moleskin Jimmy and the barrel of the Williams & Powell.

"For the Lord's sake, man!" he shouted. Then, more quietly: "Put that thing down, will ye!"

"Thou shalt not take the Lord's name in vain," said Moleskin. He lowered the gun. "For *your* sake, not the Lord's." He was sitting on the bed, fully awake, dressed in his usual outfit of waistcoat and chalkstripe trousers, his legs dangling over the side. His face was covered in stubble.

"I see you're growing it again," said Halloran.

"You see too much."

"And I take it Charlie's exercising that damn dog. You'll not be showing your face outside for a while then."

"You see too much and you talk too much. It's the Irish in you."

"I'm after seeing something which may change your mind. Or rather my *spy* has seen it. And what I have to tell you will change everything for all of us."

Halloran reached beyond the curtain, grabbed hold of a wooden stool and pulled it inside. "I will sit here and tell you of it." Moleskin made no reply. Halloran sat down and

172

continued: "There's a man called Scobie who was a great pal of Derby George. I say *was* because we all know George has gone to better things."

"George has gone to Hell," said Moleskin, "Let us not be mealy-mouthed about it."

"Wherever he is gone, we should be at great pains not to go after him too soon. But there is another we should be sending there. A Mr Joseph."

"Joseph." Moleskin tasted the name. "The only Josephs I know are the husband of Mary and the Hebrew with the many coloured coat."

"Now George's pal Scobie is also *my* pal."

"Since when?"

"Since he lost four pounds to me at poker."

"A friend in debt is a friend indeed."

"And I sent him to the good lady's funeral this morning. This Mrs Tordoff."

"Well. Those who consort with whores are no better than whores."

"And he recognised two of the guests – this Mr Joseph whom he has met on one occasion in the street but remembers well, and the good lady who works at the Mission, a Mrs Barraclough. These two came together and left together. And we know the woman runs a guest house in Dovecote. Scobie last saw Mr Joseph in the company of George. It is dead to rights Joseph is the man who wrote the notice for the paper."

Moleskin slapped his thigh. "Then we are closing in! O, the Lord be praised! We will have him!"

"But also this Joseph is well in with the family of the vicar at Padstone. You know the dead woman worked for the vicar and the wounded man likewise. And our Mr Joseph has stayed there recently."

"They conspire!" Moleskin slapped his thigh again. "See how it is, Halloran. They are not content with the peelers

173

and the narks and the courts of law. They are not content with the jealous God who tells them vengeance is *His*. No, they must conspire against the navigators who live among them but are outcast from their hearths and homes!" Moleskin laughed. "Well, I will show them. I will have my *own* vengeance!"

"But this time," said Halloran, "we will be more circumspect. We will hit the target, not the bystander. We will use our wits as well as our bullets."

"We?" Moleskin gazed steadily into Halloran's eyes. "Will it be you pulls the trigger when next this Mr Joseph comes into sight?"

"I didn't mean…" Halloran ran a nervous fingernail down the crease of his trousers. "You're the one who has the call, Moleskin. You're the one who's our leader. You always will be. But you know that we have to do it right this time, no more bits and bobs, be rid of it once for all."

Moleskin stood up, stretched his arms, pulled aside the curtains, paced out into the room. "Betty!" he shouted, "I'll have whisky. Scotch, not Irish. I've had enough of the Irish for one day. I'll have the bottle. I have thinking to do."

He sat at the table by the door and she brought the bottle and glasses. Moleskin handed one of the glasses back to her. "Mr Halloran has to keep a clear head today, Betty. He has to remember instructions."

"What are you thinking, Moleskin?" Halloran was on his feet now. He patted his suit pockets. He walked across to Moleskin but did not sit down.

"I'm thinking you're a card player, and a famous man in these parts. I'm thinking Mr Joseph need not have wasted his money on that notuce if he had known a few of our gamblers round here."

"Moleskin, it's because I'm well enough known…"

"…that you don't want to take risks. Oh, I can see that. But Mr Joseph already knows *who* you are; it's only finding your whereabouts makes him hesitate. He already

174

knows your name, now let him find your game. I'll send somebody down to the Mission to complain about your crooked dealing, make sure they know where you can be found. Card-playing is a reckless business at the best of times and men have been killed over a bad hand, a crooked deal or a welsh on a bet."

"Sure, Moleskin, this is a terrible risk for me."

"And you, Halloran, are a terrible risk for *me*. Mebbe I should forget for now about Joseph and the whore and rid myself of the most dangerous witness – you!"

Halloran's laugh was forced. "You don't mean that, Moleskin?"

"And why should I not, my handsome young man? And why should I not mean every word I say? Have you ever known me *not* mean what I say? And now... It's not even Christmas but I have a present for you." And he put on the table top Mr Bakey's Derringer.

Halloran felt a wet warmth run down his leg. He held his hat over the stain.

Chapter 23

JOEL TRUSS WAS UNSMILING. "I was a fool," he said.

Mollie looked away. She was not used to Mr Truss confessing his faults in front of herself and Christopher. She glanced at the boy. He was staring intently at his father.

"I am sure," said Mollie, "you did what you thought was right

"I did," said Mr Truss, "but I was a fool nonetheless."

With that he subsided. He was sitting on one of the two wicker chairs in the Truss family's front room and now he gazed vacantly out of the window, his eyes closing, as though he were mesmerised. Mollie thought of a picture her father had taken her to see in Manchester – the *Beata Beatrix* by Dante Gabriel Rosetti.

But there the expression of the eyes had, as her father remarked, a religious significance, eyes blinded by an *inner* light, and was a remembrance of that other Dante's beloved who had died so young. In that picture was what her father had described as an *ethereal aura* which was no part of the elder Truss's current demeanour. She waited on him to say more.

Mr Truss's eyes opened again. He turned back to his audience. "I should have spoken to the sergeant. I should have unburdened myself. But I did not."

"There must," said Mollie, "have been good reason."

"So I thought. I was protecting someone. A lady of good name. Now another lady of good name is dead."

"I am sure," said Mollie, "you cannot blame yourself."

"But I do," said Mr Truss, "and if I could today speak to the sergeant and tell him of my regret, it would lift a burden from my heart."

Mollie looked closely at Mr Truss and once again noted the strong physical changes that had come over him

176

since the death of Mrs Tordoff and his own wounding. His narrow face now looked no less than haggard, his beard was untrimmed and spreading haphazard across his jaw, his body seemed slack and his limbs without energy. His eyes – the eyes, she reminded herself, of a first class poacher – flickered from one object to the next, a sure sign that his mind did likewise.

Yet, she knew, he had escaped the worst potential of his ordeal. Two bullets had struck him in quick succession. One had penetrated his left shoulder and chipped the bone; the other had grazed his neck but missed the artery. It was now almost a month since the shooting. His left arm was still in a sling but the heavy bandaging above it had recently been removed; there was no longer any dressing needed for his neck. Dr Arbuthnot, visiting him several times, had repeatedly exclaimed how fortunate he had been.

Perhaps, thought Mollie, the effects of the morphine might be to blame for Mr Truss's melancholia. He had slept the best of the past two weeks on account of the drug, but it seemed not to be the kind of sleep that brought proper rest. And, as her father often remarked, a man's body is only the vessel of his soul. If the soul were suffering, then the body would show the signs. Of a sudden, Mollie realised there was something she could do to alleviate his suffering.

"I will bring him," she said, "I will bring the sergeant to you."

It was the obvious answer. For a moment she was uplifted up by the brilliance of it. And Mr Truss seemed uplifted too.

"Could you do that?" he asked.

"Of course," said Mollie, proud of her inspiration, "Why, the sergeant asked after you on the day of the funeral and was eager to speak with you. But he was told you were too ailing."

"Would that he had ignored such comments and sought me out," said Mr Truss, "but if you can bring him…"

"We do not know," said Christopher, "where the sergeant lives."

Mollie shot him a withering glance. "But we can discover it! I am told he lives with Mrs Barraclough…" Realising what inference might be laid on what she had said, she added quickly: "Mrs Barracloough is, I believe, the proprietor of a lodging house…"

"But we do not know the address," said Christopher.

This time she did not condescend to look at him. "But we know Mrs Barraclough works at the Mission in Dovecote. We can journey there and inquire."

"But Dovecote is a long journey and father is too ill to drive us there."

The solution came like divine inspiration. "Then we will take an omnibus! There is now a service between Lord Holtby's estate and Dovecote!"

"But then we must travel with the servants of his household. And it is said they are often rowdy." Christopher looked aghast.

"Are we not," said Mr Truss, "all servants of Lord Holtby, in our own houses as in his?" He paused then added: "Begging your pardon, Miss Mollie."

"No," said Mollie, "do not ask my pardon, Mr Truss. What you say is true. He rules our world as Ozymandias once ruled that age in which *he* once lived. But Lord Holtby's monuments, I fear, will not survive a fraction as long."

When she saw how they were looking at her, she added: "I have been reading Mr Shelley." Then: "At least the omnibus is a really useful sort of monument and we should do our best to utilise it while it lasts."

When silence still greeted her, she said: "I see the motion is approved. Christopher, you must accompany me. Although it is quite acceptable for us both to travel with the

178

rowdy servants of Lord Holtby, I do not think it so for a lady on her own."

MOLESKIN LAID OUT THE COINS on the tabletop. "That's what I promised you, Betty. Have ye done the job for me?" He was sat at the table with another whisky in front of him.

"That I have, Moleskin." Betty remained standing. She still had the pipe in her mouth though the smoke had long ceased from it.

"And is it writ down?"

"Now why should it be writ down when I have it in here?" Betty tapped her temple with her fingers. "And why should it be writ down when the writing of it makes a sumthink for police evidence?"

Moleskin laughed a throaty laugh. He respected Betty, old haridan that she was, for being one of life's dependables. A man knew where he was with her.

"And what is it ye say to me?"

Betty leaned over him so he could see the bulging tops of her breasts over the neckline of her blouse. Moleskin frowned and turned away but he cocked an ear.

Betty gave him the directions. From the door of the Mission it took ten minutes or so to walk the distance. Due east and then south west, past The King of Prussia and Hodnett's stables, a terrace house of brick, in a crescent, overlooking a garden with a birch tree, and a yard at the back. "It's a lodging house, so tha can knock and ask about things and have good excuse."

"And who did you have doin the following?"

"A body with sense. A body that wouldn't attract interest. Not to this Mrs Barraclough."

"A woman?"

"Of course a woman. An ugly woman too. For a man would attract suspicion from the woman he followed. And a

179

fine looking woman would be the object of attention from the men in the street."

"You did it yourself." It was a fine joke. He thought even more of her for the way she told it.

"Yes, I did it myssen. Now I want my lucre." She reached across and pulled over the coins.

Moleskin added another. "For your silence in the matter."

She hesitated. "You had that anyway."

"Now I have it more."

"So tha does." She took the final coin.

"YOU WILL GET TOGETHER YOUR THINGS," said the sergeant.

"I have not so many to take," said Adele, "nor do I mean to be absent long."

"These people are to be trusted?"

"They are as close as any and more than most. He was a miner, a friend of Ben's, invalided, given compensation..."

"Johnny Roseberry again."

"Johnny Roseberry again."

"And she...?"

"...is my friend this ten years and we know each other's secrets."

"Even so, do not tell her too much. Even so, do not tell her *mine*."

"I will not."

"No," he conceded, "I know you will not."

There was a silence between them. In the end she said: "I hope you will miss me."

"As you say, it will not be for long."

"Yet still I hope you *will* miss me."

She packed a carpet bag with her clothes, two books, some trinkets. Then she closed it, buckled the straps.

"It is necessary," he said.

"I know. I understand. I am a soldier's widow."

"They followed you today."

"As we expected. A woman. An ugly thing. I noted her for her ugliness."

"They will soon come here. They will find me."

"So you will find *them*. How long do you think?"

"A day. Two days."

"And what will you do?"

"I will settle them as an honest citizen would settle those who burglarise his house."

"*My* house."

"The house of a friend. It makes no difference. The law for once will be on our side."

"And my lodgers?"

"I will protect them as I protect myself. It will give my lawful action added weight."

"And in the meantime? Remind me."

"I will tell them you are gone to visit sick friends. That you have appointed me your temporary agent. They will think you an angel. Which truly you are."

"If I *am* an angel, it is the angel of death." She stumbled against him, fell into his arms.

He clutched her. "Have no conscience for the murderers. And for your lodgers, I will guarantee their safety. As much as a soldier can. Trust me. I believe this thing is nearly over."

"And then... ?"

"And then we shall both be free of our fears. And of our obligations."

"Yes," she said, "so we shall." She stepped back, turned away from him, picked up the bag, refusing his offer of help. "I have merely a short walk to the omnibus stage. I need no escort. The omnibus is a respectable service."

"Respectable. That word again."

"You know you cannot come with me."

181

"I know I cannot leave here until the trap is sprung."

"Then it is goodbye."

"Then it is farewell. Till we see each other once more. Very soon."

"With no more fears. Or obligations." When she got to the door, she turned and said: "God be with you." Then she was gone into the dusk.

"God be with us both," said the sergeant.

"MY FATHER HAS GIVEN US the money for the fare," said Christopher, "that I may be your guardian on the journey."

"Do you think," said Mollie, "that I need a guardian?"

"You said yourself..."

"Yes, I did." Mollie was annoyed with her conduct. She hated the contradictions of behaviour she so often encountered in herself of late.

It had been pleasurable enough to play the grand lady in front of Mr Truss, expecting a beau to escort her on her way; now, in retrospect, she felt foolish. Why should she not make the journey to Dovecote on her own? Why should she not address the grown-ups as equals when she was the daughter of a clergyman? Why should she have wanted such a companion as Christopher for such an important mission?

Yet the truth of it was that if she refused the offer of Christopher's companionship, then she must refuse the money from Christopher's father. And if she did that, she must seek the fare from her own father. And what would he say? He would question her, as was his wont, about the reasons behind her excursion. Even if he allowed her to go, he might want to accompany her. And then, and then...

How would she behave with the sergeant if her father were present? How would the sergeant regard her? Why, as a child! The way her father regarded her!

No, no. Better then to go with Christopher. Better then to put up with his boyishness so that she could meet again the manliness of the sergeant. Oh, better! Better by far! She had recently memorised a newfound verse:

If I were a dead leaf thou mightest bear,
If I were a swift cloud to fly with thee,
A wave to pant beneath thy power and share
The impulse of thy strength… !

It seemed strange now that she had once been taken briefly by Mr Browning. How little did Mr Browning know of life compared with Mr Shelley!

Chapter 24

HALLORAN WALKED SLOWLY through the big double doors of the Marlborough Hotel in Granborough's Main Street. Bob Scobie walked one pace behind.

It was a light, warm, card-playing kind of night, like many other nights Halloran had looked forward to with enthusiasm and enjoyed with great success. But tonight, though he wore his usual chancer's smile and his usual chancer's smart suit, he was nervous, glancing first one way then the other. Scobie had also been told to scrutinise the surroundings.

He had chosen Scobie because Scobie knew the sergeant by sight and Scobie was a big fine lad who would give as good as he got in any sort of trouble. And Scobie, he knew, was carrying one of the Derringers that Moleskin had taken off the bookie; Halloran was carrying the other.

"It's a kiddy's thing," Scobie had said and had been reluctant to own one. But Halloran had bullied him and persuaded him in the end. "This man has a hard thing against me, Bob. And he's a troublemaker, a man who wouldn't think twice over killing me."

"You must have done him bad harm."

"No, no," Halloran declared, rubbing his hands together, "He just can't stand losing at cards. That's how some people are, Bob. They see you turn up four aces to their three tens and they get that red spot in front of the eyes. You know what I mean. The red spot that keeps on growing and gets so big they can't see anything else any more. It gets so big it fills them full of its heat and they explode like cannon shells."

Halloran grinned at his own turn of phrase. Scobie had looked unconvinced but finally he took the gun anyway. Along with the ten pounds Halloran had offered him. "Too much to turn down," said Scobie. But he still looked uncomfortable.

Now Halloran hesitated in the foyer and was wondering again for just a moment whether it might not be better to call the whole thing off, this crazy idea of Moleskin's. "So what if I shoot him?" he had asked his co-conspirator, "Am I expected to swing for it without complaint?"

And Moleskin had replied: "It will stand as self-defence. This Joseph will come armed, mark my words. Pistol or dagger or some such. How do ye think he took care of Derby George? You think he talked him to death? You tell the judge the man had threatened you. You tell him he'd threatened George over a tip on a horse that went wrong. And now George is dead. Then Bob says *he* got threatened too. So you took a gun to protect you. Bob did the same. The peelers must know this Joseph is a wrong'un. Anyway, he's never local; they'll not be bothered over him getting himself killed."

"And if he *does* come armed and ends up killing *me*?"

"Make sure he doesn't. He won't reckon on *you* being armed. And he won't reckon on Bob."

For God's sake, thought Halloran as he stood by the reception desk, *which of us is crazier? Moleskin or me?* He was about to turn on his heel when the tall woman with her long dark hair in a bun came out from behind the desk and greeted him.

It was Roberta Daviot, the proprietor's wife. A winsome woman. "Good evening to you, Mr Halloran. You've already got five or six in the top room waiting on you. Will you want the usual drinks? If so, I'll come up to take the order."

Halloran regularly treated his card pals to a whisky or two at the start of a game or a quart of pale ale. For himself he ensured a regular supply of cold tea in his private decanter. The thought of five or six regulars gave him a sudden rush of

185

emotion, a feeling of being in control. *It's like it always is,* he thought, *I'm the man with all the cards. Bob Scobie is my ace in the hole.* And he suddenly felt better, felt strong.

"The usual. That'll be fine. I'll go on up," he said and he mounted the stairs under the massive chandelier, with Bob's footfall behind him.

When he got to the room, he motioned Bob to go first. A moment later, Bob put his face back round the door and smiled. "No Joseph here," he said, "Nor Mary nor Baby Jesus neither."

Halloran laughed as was expected, but he was enough of a believer not to enjoy jokes about religion. When he went into the room, he was further relieved to see he knew three of the five already.

He was more relaxed now. Joseph wasn't going to show. Why should he? Why risk anything so public? And even if Joseph did turn up, there would be plenty of friendly witnesses to talk to the peelers afterwards.

He greeted the men in front of him, reassuring them that refreshment was on the way. Two of them were already seated round the table they regularly used. There was Copes, a hagman who ran his own team of navvies; and Lone Jacobs who was never known to make a friend.

Halloran pulled out a chair for himself and the three standing players did likewise and sat down. One of them was Abbott, who owned the ironmongers down the road. The other two Halloran did not know. The first was a short, wiry, black-haired man wearing a jacket with a velvet collar and highly coloured waistcoat; the second was a younger man who seemed to be his friend.

There was a knock on the door and Bob, who was standing next to it, opened it a little way, smiled and pulled it open wide. Mrs Daviot entered, carrying a tray. "Some of your Irish liqueur, Mr Halloran," she said and he thanked her.

186

When she had put down his decanter and a whisky glass, she also gave him the pack of cards which she had helped him re-seal the previous night.

"Come on, lads, the drinks are on me," he said and she took the orders and left. He then broke the false seal and took out the cards. This was perhaps his favoured moment of the night, more so even than leaving at the end with the pot in his pockets. He knew all eyes were upon him and he did not disappoint. He shuffled, stacked and whirled the cards in dizzying patterns.

"Would anyone care to inspect?" he asked and held up the newly rearranged pack.

The man in the waistcoat said: "*I'll* take a look, Mr Halloran." Halloran handed him the cards. The man sifted through them, quietly studying with what Halloran recognised as a keen card player's eye. *Well, that was a warning not to get careless.*

Even so, Halloran was confident no fault would be found. "I have to say they look fine to me," said the man in the waistcoat, perhaps a little grudgingly.

As he took back the cards, Halloran said: "Thank you, Mr..."

"Kilfedder," said the man, "And this..." indicating the figure sitting on his right "...is Mr Caborne. He works for me."

"Mr Caborne," said Halloran and nodded. He thought he ought to know Kilfedder's name from somewhere but could not place it. Then Mrs Daviot came back with the rest of the drinks order, handed it round and went out again. Bob stayed on door duty.

Halloran said: "Gentlemen, let the games commence." He put his money on the table and the others did likewise. Halloran dealt the cards.

The first couple of hands he played casually because the pot was only ten or twenty pounds and it had to grow before it was worth his while. He calculated that the stakes by the end of the night would be four times what was being bet at present.

By the third hand, Lone was dealing and the ale was already befuddling him. He had flopped out in the last round and was looking to improve his situation; and from the expression on his face, which he never knew to control, he had a good hand. Halloran folded, wishing to keep Lone in the game. Kilfedder raised and Lone called and put down a straight flush; Kilfedder countered with a royal flush and scooped the pot.

"Mr Kilfedder," said Halloran, "you are clearly a man whose luck is in. And," he added, eager to offer praise, "you certainly know how to read the run of the cards."

"As for my luck," said Kilfedder, "well, Mr Halloran, I cannot say I have been as lucky as some. Not as lucky as you have been these past ten months. As for my reading, ay, I know how to read. Yesterday I had cause to read a letter in which your name was mentioned."

It took Halloran perhaps half a minute to grasp what was being said, which was slow for a card player like himself. Even then, he was unsure whether there was any threat in Kilfedder's words.

"Your name was mentioned," Kilfedder went on, "along with three others: Derby George, Cockney Charlie and Moleskin…"

Halloran jumped up, knocking over the table. Kilfedder, directly opposite, fell back, his chair tipped over and he hit the floor. Halloran realised with horror what had happened – *Joseph had sent someone in his stead! Joseph had sent the woman's brother!* (For now Halloran recognised that name.)

Halloran turned, made a run for the door; but Caborne had somehow avoided the overturned table and was on his feet. He ran towards the door, cutting Halloran off, and lashed out at him with a fist. Halloran took the blow on his right cheek, staggered back, almost fell, but somehow regained his balance. With his right hand, he reached for the Derringer in his inside breast pocket.

As he raised the gun, an arm fell across him, a hand snatched at his wrist. He still managed to press the trigger but the bullet hit the wall and plaster dust shot up in a cloud. Halloran pulled his arm back, aimed the gun at his attacker and fired a second time. Bob Scobie yelled, fell over, crashed down onto his knees.

Halloran grasped the doorknob with his left hand, pulled at the door, ran outside, rushed down the stairs, still waving the gun. Above and behind him were the shouts and scamperings of the stunned card players. Below and in front of him were the upturned faces of the hotel staff and customers, their mouths open wide with terror and disbelief.

Halloran crashed down into the foyer, stumbled, fell, regained his feet, ran out through the double door. He still had the gun in his right hand but it was useless now, the bullets used up. He threw it away. He was crying.

B'Jesus! He had killed his protector! He had killed Bob Scobie! In front of a room full of witnesses!

"YOU'RE A BRAVE MAN," said Kilfedder, "He's a brave man, Caborne. You see what he did?" Kilfedder was kneeling next to the wounded man with Caborne looking down at them.

"He's a brave man alright," said Caborne, "He did well! So did we all!"

"I didn't bring it," said the man on the floor.

"Didn't bring what?" asked Caborne, though he sounded as if he knew it was a foolish question.

"The kiddy's thing. Why would he want to use a thing like that? What was the good of it? All over a card game. The red spot keeps on growing and gets so big they can't see anything else any more. And then it explodes like cannon shells."

"He's delirious," said Caborne, "raving. It's the wound has made him so. Mebbe he's dying."

"Nay," said Kilfedder, "not dying. The bullet's too small for a big man like this. I've heard worse nonsense from half-penny drunks. He'll be fine, don't doubt it. Get him a doctor and his arm in a sling and he'll be fine. It's just shock, that's my opinion. But that brute aimed to finish *me*. He aimed that pistol at my head."

"Not dying?" asked the man on the floor, "Am I not?"

"You're a brave man," said Kilfedder. Someone had told him the man's name was Scobie. He said: "Scobie, you saved my life and I'll see you're alright. How'd you like a job at The Blackamoor?"

But the man they called Scobie had fainted clear away.

Chapter 25

"I'VE BROUGHT YE A VISITOR," said Moleskin. The straw in the loft was still clean, he noted, though he had never doubted it would be. He hoped Halloran would appreciate the benefits of good housekeeping.

Carribee sat on the boards, naked except for a loincloth. He eyed Halloran without any obvious surprise.

"Oh Lord," said Halloran, "have I come down to this?"

"Ye have come *up* to it," said Moleskin, "by way of a ladder. And it may well be that ladder is your salvation as much as Jacob's ladder was for him, giving new hope of safety and success, giving indeed a vision of very Heaven. Yes."

Halloran stood and his hands trembled. His suit was unusually crumpled, his hatless head uncombed, his hapless face unshaved.

"Carribee," said Moleskin, "I have a boon to ask of you. This morning I bring a sinner to your door, this gambler, this brawler, this foolish man, who has risked all and lost all in the chapter and verse of life. He is in need of shelter, in need of your protection. The world is not his friend. But then that world has never been friend to you nor me."

Carribee nodded. Otherwise he made no move.

"You are not one to ask questions, Carribee, not one to belabour the point of necessity with a surfeit of commentary. No. But because I respect ye and because I require your loyalty, I shall tell ye what Mr Halloran has done and why the world has turned on him today."

"I'm after doing what you would have me do," said Halloran. The trembling was now spread to the whole of his body.

"Last night he killed a man," said Moleskin, "killed a man over a hand of cards."

"God damn you, Moleskin, it was not for cards!"
Halloran raised his arms in a gesture that was both anguish
and defeat, his hands seeming to push away the images of
nightmare that had suddenly surrounded him.

Moleskin gazed at him. "Well, we will not dispute the
motive. It is murky enough. Even the victim is not truly
known. We believe it might be a Mr Kilfedder, a purveyor of
liquor and brother to a whore. But Mr Halloran is not himself
certain. The shot, he fears, may have gone somewhat astray."

"I am not used to them," said Halloran, "to firearms. I
have never had much time for them. I have not led a violent
life."

"Until now," said Moleskin, "and it might have been
better for a man in your trade, Halloran, if you *had* made
yourself more expert, if you *had* prepared yourself for this
Day of Judgement. For that Day is upon you now. But you did
not."

Moleskin turned back to Carribee. "Unlike ourselves,
Carribee, who have always known the nature of life and of
God's disposition and spent our time accordingly."

There was a whine from the floor below, followed by
repeated low-key howling. Moleskin said: "That is Biter and
he is upset. He misses me and fears I am caught up with a
great trouble. But I am not. I am filled with joy because I can
now see my way to salvation. However, I require you to keep
Mr Halloran in your care, Carribee, until you hear further.
There may be offices for you to perform."

"Offices to perform?" asked Halloran, "What the divil
do you mean?"

Moleskin ignored him and continued: "His being here
is a secret between us. There is risk, but I promise you the risk
will not be overlong."

Halloran said: "Why here, Moleskin? Why can't I
stay with you and Charlie?"

192

"Already," said Moleskin, "the woman Betty knows too much. And the other navvies are inquisitive. I can risk no more." He grimaced. "I leave you in better hands than you have ever left me." And he moved towards the ladder and began to descend.

Halloran said: "Do not desert me, Moleskin. Else it will be the worse for you. Sure, I know things..." His voice was hoarse and high-pitched.

"You do," said Moleskin, hesitating on the ladder with only his head now visible, "You know enough to hang me, Halloran. Don't think I have forgot that."

Then his head was gone also and Biter was making his usual snuffling sounds of affection below.

IT WAS, OF COURSE, the first time they had travelled this way, and even Christopher showed some excitement, noted Mollie.

They waited with the half dozen servants lined up by the north gate of the High Grange estate. Christopher complained a number of times about the period spent waiting; but Mollie, who had brought along her father's second best watch in the pocket of her dress, had restrained him with a running commentary as the minutes passed. So he was only too aware when the omnibus arrived that they had spent no longer than a quarter of an hour all told.

The servants – including an elderly woman in a mob cap, a self-important looking man who might have been a butler, and three gardeners who talked incessantly of techniques for scarifying lawns – were far from the boisterous characters envisaged by Christopher; and, indeed, sober to the point of solemnity.

It must be, thought Mollie, that they were now so used to this novel form of transport, so inured to its picturesqueness, that such a journey was second nature. But for her it was an anticipated pleasure at least as thrilling as her attempt to kill the partridge with the air gun.

"Whoahhh!" shouted the driver as the omnibus turned the corner of the road and clattered up to them. "Whoahh!" he called again as he pulled up the horses – a chestnut gelding and two dun mares harnessed three abreast.

The vehicle itself was a rectangular box-like structure painted in the navy blue with gold stripe that constituted the omnibus company's livery. There were large leaded windows downstairs and an open deck on top, rounded by a metal railing just above the driver.

"We will ride up there," shouted Mollie, "we will feel the wind in our hair."

"No, we will not," said Christopher, adding quickly: "Riding on top is only for grown-up persons and especially only for men."

Then, even more quickly: "Though I, of course, would support your notion if I had my way for I believe it is much cheaper to ride on top."

The line of passengers-in-waiting moved along to the entrance at the rear of the vehicle and handed their coins to the conductor who stood at the bottom of the stairs. He wore a peaked cap and long coat, also in the company's livery, and carried a leather satchel.

Mollie and Christopher waited for the others to get on first, then groped their way inside. There were two longitudinal benches along which the passengers sat facing each other. She and Christopher sat side by side opposite a young woman with two small children who constantly groped for their mother's breast.

Mollie quickly estimated there were around 30 people downstairs and assumed the same number on top. How big it was! A very Leviathan!

"Oh," said Christopher, "it is more dark than I had thought."

But Mollie was already reminded of Jonah in the belly of the whale and she cried out to him laughingly: *"I have been banished from your sight, yet I will look again towards your holy temple!"*

It was even *better* than the partridge and the airgun!

TWO MEN CAME into the public bar of the Marlborough Hotel. Roberta Daviot was on duty and they ordered a pint of ale and one of porter. When she pulled it, one of them said: "Is this where the papist killed that fella t' other night?"

She shook her head. "I know of no papists," she said.

"But the fella was killed," said the man. He took a sip of his ale. "Shot in the back over a hand of cards." He was a scruffy man, big but not muscular, wearing a labourer's dusty cotton clothes, and not one of her regulars.

She shook her head again. "No-one was killed here," she said.

"Oh, but he was," said the man drinking porter. He was smaller, with a sad try at a moustache, and similarly dressed, and she couldn't remember seeing him before.

"Not here," said Roberta.

"We were telled he was," said the man drinking porter.

"You were telled wrong."

"That's what she *would* say," said the man drinking ale.

"It's not too grand for business," said the man drinking porter, "to have your customer killed by a papist. It's something you'd not let on about. Not to respectable customers."

"It's true we had some trouble over cards," said Roberta, "but no man was killed and I know nothing about papists."

"She knows nothing about papists," said the man drinking ale to the man drinking porter. They both laughed.

195

Roberta looked round the bar room. It was early enough to be close to empty, but there were a couple of fellas in the corner she knew quite well, two young ostlers from down the street who came in most days to sup a while and play dominoes. She picked up a cloth, walked over to their table and wiped up the puddles of beer. "Hello David, hello Seth," she said, "I might need your help in a few minutes. I have a piece of trouble on my hands."

"You can count on us help," said Seth. He put down a double six.

"Bugger," said David. And to Roberta: "Forgive my language."

Roberta walked back to the man drinking ale and the man drinking porter.

The man drinking porter nodded in the direction of the table. "Are those two church or chapel?" he asked.

"And if they're church, is it English or Roman?" asked the man drinking ale.

"I do not know," said Roberta.

"She does not know," said the man drinking porter.

"She should ask them," said the man drinking ale.

"I have my work to do," said Roberta.

"It would not take more than a minute," said the man drinking ale, "and then we would all know for a certainty."

Roberta nodded across to David and Seth and they put down the dominoes and Seth came over. "Two pints of regular, if you please," said Seth.

Roberta pulled the two pints. She said: "On the house, lads."

David joined him. He and Seth stood about a yard from the other two.

"So that's the way it is here," said the man drinking porter.

"Free drinks," said the man drinking ale.

196

"Landlady's privilege," said Roberta. Then: "Drink up."

The man drinking porter said: "Drink up, is it?"

Roberta said: "You hear me. Drink up and leave."

"I think we will stay," said the man drinking porter.

"I think we will stay and have a brace on the house," said the man drinking ale.

"You will drink up and leave," said Roberta.

"A brace on the house. The same as these papists enjoy."

"I think you will be leaving, sir," said Seth.

"Is that your belief?" asked the man drinking ale.

"Makes you wonder about his other beliefs," said the man drinking porter.

They laughed. And they went on drinking. When they had finished, they put down their glasses. The man who had been drinking porter said: "I would not want another one anyway. You do not know how to keep it."

"Nor the ale," said the man who had been drinking ale.

"Then you will know not to come again," said Roberta.

"That we will," said the man who had been drinking ale. The two men looked at each other. They looked at David and Seth. They looked at Roberta.

"Scarlet Woman of Rome," said the man who had been drinking ale. They looked at each other again. They looked at David and Seth again.

"Let us tarry no longer," said the man who had been drinking ale.

"Let us leave this den of iniquity," said the man who had been drinking porter.

They walked across to the street door, went through and slammed it shut.

"Thank you, lads," said Roberta.

"We did nothing," said Seth.

"You did all that was necessary," said Roberta, "my husband is at the brewery making orders. I will tell him when he returns. I will tell him what good customers you are."

David and Seth grinned at each other sheepishly.

"You will not see those blackguards again," said Seth.

"It's a thing to be hoped," said Roberta. And she picked up the ale glass and the porter glass and wiped the surface of the bar where the two strangers had been.

Chapter 26

THEY FOUND THE MISSION EASILY ENOUGH. It had, thought Mollie, the exact squareness and lack of elegance she had expected. But she could see its attraction: solid, sparse, drab, down among the shops and taverns, the heart of commerce, the usual haunts of the usual sinners. She noted with approval the broken windows: after all, they were not stained glass, so there was no real vandalism involved. She enjoyed the notion of a church that stood for immediacy rather than propriety, but she owned she would not want it for herself and her family.

When she and Christopher went inside, the man in the waistcoat and shirtsleeves got up from his desk and came across, brushing his hand nervously through his grey receding hair. Why should he be nervous? Perhaps because he was alone in that large room. She had heard of the bustling style of worship of these low church folk and was disappointed not to see more animation in this sole representative. She thought: *I must come here again, some evening perhaps, when they have singing and clapping of the hands. If father will let me.*

Then she thought: *Now we have the omnibus, why should I tell father?*

"How may I help you?" asked the man with receding hair. To Mollie's annoyance he had addressed the question to Christopher. There was a brief silence as Christopher took the usual deep breath required to get up the courage to answer a question from an adult.

Mollie put in quickly: "We seek Mrs Barraclough, who, I believe, is in employment here."

"Ah," said the man, "Friends of Mrs Barraclough." He put his hands together and waited.

Mollie realised he wished her to identify herself. And why should she not? "I am Mollie Proudlove, the daughter of

The Reverend Eli Proudlove of St Agnes Church at Padstone."

The revelation had its effect on the man. A smile broke broadly across his face, transforming him of a sudden from detached politeness to a kind of subservience.

"Ah, Mr Proudlove," he said, "We see too little of him but he is much admired by all." Then the man looked round in a puzzled manner. "But where *is* Mr Proudlove?"

"He is not with us," said Mollie.

The man's attitude immediately changed from puzzlement to suspicion. "You have come from Padstone by yourselves?"

"We have," said Christopher, finding his voice at last.

For a moment the man's attention was switched to Christopher. Mollie again interrupted: "This is Christopher Truss, the young son of one of our employees."

Her words had the desired effect. The man's attention was back with her. "Mrs Barraclough is not here today," he said, "She has been compelled to visit sick friends and I have given her leave to do so. It is a Christian duty she is performing. Therefore I considered it a Christian duty to give her permission."

"You do correctly," said Mollie, then wondered if she had gone too far in speaking aloud her judgement. But the return of his broad smile indicated she had not. "Perhaps," she said, "you would be so kind as to give us the address of Mrs Barraclough?"

The man again hesitated. "But she is currently absent visiting…"

"Sick friends, yes," said Mollie. She forced a smile of her own to cover her impatience. "Nonetheless, I would be obliged if you could give me such information…"

Why, she thought, *was he being so difficult?* Then she realised: *He has been told to be sparing with information if inquisitive strangers should happen along.* But why? And

200

what reason could she now give for asking Mrs Barraclough's address when the lady was not presently *in situ*? Then she remembered that Mrs Barraclough managed a lodging house.

"I have business," said Mollie, "with one of Mrs Barraclough's lodgers. A Mrs..." she hesitated, then: "Shelley. Mrs Shelley."

"Alas, I do not know the names of Mrs Barraclough's residents."

She was about to say: *It is not necessary that you should know the names of Mrs Barraclough's residents...* when she stopped herself. Instead she said: "My father much admires your work here at the Mission, particularly your excursions to the navigators..."

She wondered if *excursions* was the wrong word, a word suggestive of countryside rambles rather than the work of missionaries. But it had the desired effect.

"I am most happy that our work is approved by your father. He is a much respected man..."

"And he has been speaking of late of perhaps making a visit to your services..." She saw his eyes take on a new brightness, "...and perhaps indeed to join with your expeditions into the settlements at Havelock Hill." *Expeditions!* Now *that* was the word!

Five minutes later he had written Adele Barraclough's address and the necessary directions on a sheet of paper and was asking Mollie when he might expect a visit from her father. She now allowed herself a certain vagueness; after all, she had gained the result she wanted. "But I shall speak with him this very evening," she trilled as she and Christopher left the Mission.

Only when they were outside did he realise she had never even asked the man for his name.

IN THE OFFICE BACK of Jenson's shant in Shiloh Street, Jenson himself was tallying the previous day's drink takings,

201

sat at a table, working slowly with a pencil on the back of a large envelope. The door was flung open with a crash. Jenson raised his head from the additions, gazing in surprise at the half dozen or so navvies with pick-axe handles.

"Cheat!" shouted one of them, "There's more fuckin water in your beer every day!"

"It's regular inspected," said Jenson, a thin, wiry man, not without courage, "The Revenue men come round every week."

"And you wait till we's drunk and slam up your prices!" yelled another.

"No," said Jenson. He waved the envelope. "You can see for thyssen what the revenues are!"

"We don't need to read your lies!" shouted another, though Jenson recognised the man from his striking blond moustache and knew he could not read. And then they set on the shant boss.

Jenson fought back, punching the one who called him "cheat", kicking another before they brought him down. Then he used his flailing arms only to ward off the blows, protect his head. He remained conscious for three or four minutes, then he fell into coma. The blows rained down for another ten minutes.

NAVIGATOR QUINN RIORDAN was stood at the bar in The Dragon in Granborough guzzling a quart of pale ale out of a glass jug when the Protestant navvies found him.

"Cut his ears off!" shouted one.

"Cut his head off!" shouted another.

He did not have chance to eye the opposition, to look at faces and remember them later. First they knocked the jug off the bar so it smashed. Then they grabbed him by the arms, kicked him in the stomach, laid him out on the floor, then kicked him again. He vomited. The ale came up along with his breakfast bacon and fried potato. He felt a sharp pain across his right ear and forehead. When he put a hand to his face, he could feel the hot blood. He was kicked again in the head and the mob – eight or nine, said landlord Gerry Means later – laughed and walked out slowly.

Means, a Welshman with spectacles, helped Quinn to his feet, sat him down, fed him whisky.

"It's on the house," he said.

"My ear!" shouted Quinn. He began to cry.

"Now, now," said Means, "they've not cut it clean off. Only sliced a bit away. It's only a stitching job." He produced the piece of ear in a glass and poured more whisky over it. "For keeping it pure and unspoilt," he said, "I'll get Maisy and some thread." Maisy was his wife. She came when he called.

Afterwards he said: "Right as rain, Quinn. I reckon it's your lucky day. None of the girls will ever notice. You don't want to go calling in the law now. That'll only give the house a bad name."

And Quinn, still fingering the ear, nodded.

Means settled another jug of ale on the man. His motto was: *Always look after a good customer.*

IN THE HABERDASHER'S SHOP, just along the High Street, Miss Milligan was attending a lady from Chapel with a bolt of linen for the making of a shift. The bell on the front door rang. Four navvies marched in.

"Papist bitch!" said one in a quiet, self-conscious voice. He was a man with a crooked shoulder and some people called him Hunchback. Truth to tell, he was not used to talking with respectable women and felt bashful.

"Papist bitch!" shouted a second. He was straight-backed and therefore more confident. His raised voice excited the others.

"Bitch! Bitch!" they shouted. And they grabbed her by her calico dress and tore it down the front.

"Let's see her bubbies!" one of them yelled.

Miss Milligan fainted. The lady from Chapel screamed. And Harrison, the owner of the shop, a fat girlish man with a breathy way of talking, ran in from the back, saw what was happening and started back in fright. "Now, now," he said.

"Now, now!" shouted one of the navvies, imitating Harrison's wheezing tone.

"Now, now!" The four of them shouted, sing-song, exaggerating his gasps for breath.

Then they grabbed him, they punched him, they pulled at his clothes, tore his shirt, broke his stiff collar, pushed his tie up against his nose, dragged down his trousers, upended his body so he fell to the floor. He screamed a breathy scream.

"Shut that up!" shouted one of the gang. He jumped on Harrison, jumped full on his stomach with both booted feet. He jumped again.

"Pump him! Pump him!" the others shouted.

The lady from Chapel screamed again. The jumper jumped again. Miss Milligan came round. She hastily pulled up the calico to cover her naked breast. She and the Lady from Chapel screamed in unison.

The navvies turned and ran out. They knew Harrison was dead.

THE PROVISION CART was brought up short ten yards from the Marlborough Hotel. It was stocked high with meats and greenstuff in sacks, bottles of spirits and cordials. The navvy gang surrounded it.

"Tha's come far enough," said their leader. He was a short stout man with a wall eye.

Bill Kelly, the driver, recognised him as a man he had shared a table with in the Marlborough itself perhaps a week ago. They had talked briefly about the state of the government and the unpleasantness of some of the local police, particularly in the way of demanding bribes; though he did not know the man's name. Kelly clutched the handle of his whip. "Make way," he said, "I have work to do."

"And so do we!" yelled Wall-eye and the mob on Kelly's left surged forward, grabbed him by the coat tails and pulled him down off the cart.

The horse pulling the cart reared up, but one of the navvies grabbed the bridle and patted its nose. Then the mob swarmed over the cart, pulling off the sacks and bottles, trampling over Kelly. Some of the bottles hit the cobblestones and broke.

"Help!" shouted Kelly, rolling out from under them and getting shakily to his feet, "Help! Robbery! Thievery! Help!"

One of the navvies picked up a bottle of orange cordial and hit Kelly on the back of the head. Kelly went down again and the man with the bottle of cordial began to kick him.

Then a small bald man and a tall woman ran out of the hotel carrying an iron tub between them. They were Henry and Roberta Daviot, the hotel proprietors. They stopped, they swung the tub, they threw water over the man with the bottle of cordial.

All of a sudden the mob froze. They stared at the angry couple and the metal tub and the man with the bottle of cordial, his face, hair and jacket soaked.

"That'll cool you down, Jake Burden!" said Roberta Daviot.

And at that, somebody – it might have been one of the navvies or it might have been someone in the crowd that had gathered to watch – broke into a laugh. Others joined in.

Wall-Eye shouted: "Take what you can, lads! Let's out of 'ere!" And the mob did as they were told, carried off what they could, and ran.

Later, in the shant they all shared, they celebrated with free whisky.

But they wouldn't share any of it with Jake Burden. Nobody wanted to swig the orange cordial – the only thing he had managed to bring away.

Chapter 27

THERE WAS A KNOCKING AT HIS FRONT DOOR. It stopped. It started again, this time louder and faster. He had been awake for hours anyway. Now he reached for the revolver under his bed.

Then the voice: "Allardyce! Allardyce! Get up, man!" Allardyce recognised it straightway. He grinned, put back the revolver, opened his bedroom curtains, looked out of the window.

A paddywagon! They'd brought a *paddywagon* for him! The two horses were snorting and stamping

"For God's sake!" he said to himself.

He always wore his longjohns and stockings in bed. Now he didn't bother to wash, just put on his uniform. His beard was four days anyway, so it looked intended. He went downstairs and opened the front door. "Inspector March," he said, "and transport." He nodded in friendly acknowledgment to the driver, Constable Peters. Then he motioned March to enter.

The short sturdy man with the walrus moustache did so. He carried both gloves in his left hand. He said: "There's no dignity in being a police officer, Allardyce. You know that. I know you had your horse put down..."

"I'm waiting on replacement."

"Well, that's another matter."

"It means I've not been round and about much the past few days. That's all. It means I've been conservin my energies."

"The wagon was the quickest way to get to you and the quickest way to bring you back!"

Allardyce grinned. "You're telling me *trouble*," he said. He sat on the nearest chair and pulled on his boots.

"I'm telling you *hell on earth*," said March.

MARCH AND ALLARDYCE sat in the back on the clip-clop journey to Granborough Police Station. "It's what we always feared. The navvies. No law, no sense, no morals. Sodom and Gomorrah on our doorstep. Shant Town. We should've sent the lads to burn it down before it got proper built. Now they're burning *us* down."

"Us?" Allardyce grinned. "I don't yet feel the eat, Mr March."

"But you'll soon see the scorch marks. Two nights ago a navvy got shot. A nobody called Scobie. But a navvy. That's what's important."

"In the Marlborough. I knew of that. Is e dead yet?"

"He's hardly scratched, from what I hear."

"Did one of *our* lads do it?"

March snorted in derision.

"No," said Allardyce, "I did not truly believe so. But there's some do terrible strange things when they step out of uniform. As though thinking they won't be recognised. And sometimes they're right."

"No. That's the only cheering thing about it. A papist did it. A Fenian in all probability. A card sharp called Halloran." At this, Allardyce offered his full attention. "This Halloran made off double sharp. Since then word's got round…"

"As we'd expect. As we'd be fast to know about."

"A wonder *you* didn't know it previous."

"I ad business last night. In addition to my orse being gone." In fact, he'd had two bottles of gin last night. And he knew he wasn't fooling March, nor did he need to. Still, it was important to observe protocol.

March said: "Shant Town is like Zululand. Two Roman churches in Granborough have been torched. Shops looted. Women violated, or so they tell us. At least one man killed this morning. The haberdasher in Belle Vue."

"Harrison. The nancy."

"Harrison." March sighed. "Worst of all..." He slapped his knee with his gloves. "Some of them got on to Lord Holtby's land. Attacked his gamekeeper with clubs. Killed two of his dogs with axes. Burned down a stable. Thank God it was empty, else we'd all of us be out of a job by now. His Lordship loves his horses."

"Is orses win races," said Allardyce. "Anyway, we won't be out of a job just yet, Mr March. Not while they need us to sort this one out."

"Bring in Allardyce. That's what the Chief Constable said. Says you've got experience of this sort of thing."

"Long time ago," said Allardyce, "in a foreign country. But yes, I've ad experience."

"And you're thick with The Chief."

"There's no such thing as a constable that's thick with The Chief."

"I heard you had connections in that area. Anywise, he trusts your judgement."

THE LARGEST ROOM on the first floor at the Granborough Constabulary Headquarters had been turned into a kind of operations room and March ushered Allardyce inside. There were maps newly pinned to the walls, though Allardyce thought the action more a matter of show than of competence.

De Winter, the Chief Constable, was standing with his back to them, looking out of the window, smoking a pipe. A sergeant carrying a sheaf of papers and a constable looking ill at ease stood nearby.

De Winter was a tall, thin, elderly man with a pepper-and-salt moustache, wearing full ceremonial uniform and truncheon. He turned, nodded at March, then at the others, and all three withdrew.

When the door closed, The Chief knocked out his pipe on the rim of his desk, put it in his pocket and said: "Are you on the square?"

209

"As the Great Geometer wills it. A man needs good friends…"

"… to share the weight of the world. Good." The Chief appeared to relax. He picked up the silver cigar box from his oak desk, opened it and offered it to Allardyce. "Lucifers on the desk," said The Chief.

Allardyce took a cigar, thought for a moment, then put it in his breast pocket. "For when I can afford some leisure," he said. He knew he should not smoke while the Chief did not.

"Quite right," agreed The Chief and motioned him to sit in the green leather-backed chair opposite. Allardyce knew the cigar was better than the ones he was used to, but by no means the best in The Chief's collection.

The Chief was speaking again. "That March is a damn fool. I've got Alec Crosby on leave and Jim Warburton off sick with stomach cramps, so no deputy and no chief inspector. Just March and his clodhoppers! *Stomach cramps!* I'll give him stomach cramps!"

"Yes, sir." Allardyce wondered at The Chief using the Christian names of colleagues in front of him. *Well, this might be my promotion at last*, he thought, but he did not let the hope take too much hold.

Then the door was flung open and in strode a man Allardyce knew by sight but had never spoken to. He was fat and well-dressed. "Damn it, De Winter!" he said in a voice that was girlish in its shrill anger, "My man took three hours to come round. Lucky my stallions weren't in the place when it went up. I want them hanged. I want them caught and I want them hanged!"

"Yes, my lord," said De Winter, "I propose to do just that. And I have here a man who can be trusted to carry out the task, a man who knows the world of these navigators, who has viewed their lives at close quarters. One of my most trusted men. Mr Allardyce."

Mister, thought Allardyce, *not Constable then.* "My lord," he stood up and offered his hand, which Lord Holtby took limply. Allardyce then offered the leather-backed chair, which Holtby took with more alacrity.

"Tell his Lordship of your experience, Mr Allardyce," said The Chief.

"Yes, sir," said Allardyce. He was suddenly aware of his slatternly appearance. But Lord Holtby appeared not to notice. Nor did he appear to notice the cut of Allardyce's uniform, which would have marked him down straightway as a mere constable in most men's eyes. *This man,* thought Allardyce, *does not have much business with constables. And,* thought Allardyce, *this man is a fool.*

The constable coughed politely and began the story of his Hawick adventure with a touch of embroidery here and there. He began as he had told Sergeant Joseph: "There was 30 of us..." but when he came to the part about the man with the gun, the man became a navvy not an enforcer. And when the navvy was brought down, it was by Allardyce and a companion; and with a stick, not a bullet.

"Bravo!" called Lord Holtby, "you are indeed the kind of man we need to solve this problem."

"I believe I am," said Allardyce. He did not look immediately at The Chief but he was aware of the other man's gaze. Finally, judging that he had milked the moment of its drama, Allardyce turned on his heel and faced The Chief.

"It appears to me, sir," he said, "that it is most advantageous that we should have Lord Holtby here with us today. For is not His Lordship a former officer in the 19th Foot who are at this very moment in barracks in York under the command of Colonel Redvers?"

"Indeed they are!" cried His Lordship, "Splendid idea!" His face lit up and he waved his fist enthusiastically. "Redvers served under me at Omdurman. I dare say he owes me one or two favours from that time, to say the very least."

211

"Then, sir," said Allardyce to The Chief, "shall we not telegraph Col Redvers immediately, explaining the seriousness of our situation?"

"Why yes, we shall!" cried His Lordship and The Chief acquiesced. He opened the drawer of his desk and took out a second cigar box, this one encrusted with gold leaf.

"It is fortunate indeed that we have here today a man of your calibre, Your Lordship. I have known such pleas for help to our military men fall on deaf ears or take so long in the execution that the war was over before the detachment arrived. But with your involvement, your influence…"

"A matter of hours," said Holtby, taking one of the cigars. "I assure you of that."

"In that case," said The Chief, "I think our plan must be to withdraw the bulk of our men from the centre of Granborough and create a *cordon sanitaire* round the whole of the town. The malcontents will be hemmed into the less salubrious districts and this will allow us to protect the more respectable and valuable properties towards Dovecote. This in turn will also mean greater fortification for your own estate, Lord Holtby. The outrage of last night must not be allowed to recur."

Cordon sanitaire, though Allardyce and smiled. *French, of all things!* And all it meant in this case was protecting the horses.

Chapter 28

"IT IS THE HOUSE," SAID MOLLIE, "Look! It is Snowbird."

They looked. Christopher wiped his brow. "It has been a long walk."

"But we are come to our journey's end." Mollie crossed the road, called to Snowbird, who whinnied and came prancing up to the fence. She stroked his nose once again. "So the sergeant is bound to be here. It is a sign."

"A sign for who?"

"For *whom*. A sign for *whom*. Well, for us, of course. A sign for the sergeant's friends that he is home and wanting their company."

"Then let us meet with him." Mollie noted the impatience in Christopher's voice. *Why*, she thought, *could he not look on life as an adventure?* Such an excursion as today's had whetted her appetite. She longed for more. But she knew that Christopher only longed for home, for routine, for sameness. She sighed. Then she turned and walked quickly round to the front door.

"We must knock," said Christopher.

"Then we *shall* knock," said Mollie. There was a brass knocker with a lion's head set high up on the door. When she stretched, she could not easily reach it.

"*I* will do it," said Christopher, "I am taller than you."

"I will stretch," said Mollie.

"But if you stretch, your skirts will lift and display your limbs. It is most unladylike. Better I do it."

The door opened suddenly and Sergeant Joseph was gazing down at them. "What the hell...!" he said. His right shoulder remained behind the half-open door. His left hand was pushed into his coat pocket.

"We are come with a message," said Mollie. She had decided to ignore the exclamation.

213

"From my father," said Christopher.

The sergeant scanned the road behind them. He smiled. "Well, well," he said. He opened the door to its full width. "You will come in then."

They stepped inside. The sergeant glanced along the road once more then closed the door. They followed him forward into the hall, and he motioned them to turn left into the parlour. Mollie noted the parlour walls were bare except for their rather dowdy papering, but there were hooks and nails that indicated plates or pictures had been in place until recently. She noted too that a standing mirror had been positioned in one corner so it reflected the view from the front window.

The strangeness worried her. "You have removed some pictures," she said.

"I was afraid of damage and breakages. After all, the decorations belong to Mrs Barraclough. I am merely a temporary custodian until her return."

"Are there no other custodians?" asked Mollie.

"I fear not, lassie. For Mrs Barraclough's guests are out at their labour and the house is empty but for ourselves."

"Well," she said, "Christopher and I have not come to cause damage."

"No," said the sergeant, "I am sure your motivation is entirely innocent." He indicated they should sit down and they did so. The sergeant stood in the far corner of the room, at an angle to the mirror. In such a way, thought Mollie, that he would not himself be reflected but would still be able to see the reflection from outside. A prickly feeling began to steal up her neck.

"My father," said Christopher, "wishes you to know that he will speak with you, after all, on those matters on which you previously prompted him."

"That is good to hear," said the sergeant, "Your father is a good man. But your journey has been in vain. The

214

information which he now seeks to give me is already in my possession."

"You are not pleased to see us," said Mollie. She was beginning to be angry.

"I am ever pleased to see you," said the sergeant, "If my demeanour appears uninviting, you must excuse me. It is simply that matters more pressing are currently taking up my time."

"I do *not* excuse you," she said. She was aware that Christopher was looking askance at her.

"Then I must labour under the yoke of your dissatisfaction."

At that point there was a sudden banging on the front door. Someone tall enough to reach the knocker this time. And the sergeant took his hand from his pocket. And in his hand was a large blue pistol.

CARRIBEE SAT as he had before. "God's disposition?" said Halloran, "Now what did Moleskin mean by that?"

Carribee remained silent.

"God's disposition!" said Halloran, "Now that is a strange phrasing to say the least of it. He said you had known the nature of life, the two of you, and had acted accordingly."

Carribee remained in position, staring ahead.

"And he said," said Halloran, "there may be offices for you to perform."

Carribee ignored the sound of Halloran's voice.

Halloran looked at the ceiling, looked at the walls, looked at the straw, looked at the boards of the floor and the top of the ladder. "Now what did he mean?"

Carribee said nothing.

But Halloran had begun to answer his own questions. "Did he mean offices to perform in regard to myself? Now what could those offices be? He has delivered me unto you, you black divil, and why has he done this?"

215

Carribee made no response.

Halloran said: "He has surely delivered me for my salvation, for I am his friend, I am his ally and his advisor in all matters of moment. I am family. I am as close to him as a brother."

Carribee did not answer.

Halloran said: "But how close are *you* to him? Is it closer than a brother you are? Answer me."

Again Carribee did not answer.

Again Halloran answered himself. "I think that you and I are close now, as close as Moleskin has made us. I think that you are here to protect me from the world, from the nature of life."

Silence.

"Am I right? Are you my friend as you are his?"

Silence again.

"But you cannot be my friend as you are *his*. For Moleskin is a different kind of man from me. Mebbe I killed a man the other night, mebbe I stood by while they killed the corporal, while Moleskin killed the corporal, maybe I risk being damned for it. But I am not a man like Moleskin. I am not, am I?"

More silence.

"Tell me I am *not!*" Halloran got up from where he was sitting in the straw and strode across to Carribee. "Tell me I am not, nor ever have been, for that is the truth."

He waved his hat, he smacked his hand against his leg, he raised his chin to the ceiling that blotted out the sky. "Tell me I am not due for the Hell that Moleskin surely is. Tell me there is a God will forgive me."

Carribee did not reply.

"What will become of my soul if I die? I do not wish to die. I have much to do to redeem my soul. Do you understand that, you black savage?" Halloran hit Carribee across the face with his hat.

216

Carribee did not move.

Halloran said: "I do not need your offices. I do not need you to perform for me. I will not have it. What *are* these offices? What...?" Halloran made an effort and contained himself. His voice became steadier.

"I fear those offices. I fear you do not mean my safety nor my wellbeing. I think I have been delivered here to fester. To fester and to die. What say you? What say you now?"

Carribee said nothing.

"I believe," said Halloran, "that Moleskin intends you should kill me." He sank down on his knees. "Oh God, oh God, I am come to this. Through my lust, through my greed, through my hazard on the cards..."

He began to cry. "Oh God, I cannot die now, for surely I will be damned. I must have time, dear Lord, to make good my sins. I must..." His voice first broke and then broke off.

Carribee rose to his feet. He walked slowly across the floor. He took from under the straw a coil of rope. At the end of the rope was a noose.

THE SERGEANT BURST out of the room as the bearded man in the moleskin waistcoat burst through the front door. Both men raised their guns. Both men for a moment hesitated.

Then the sergeant fell, struck by the club wielded by a second man who had come down the stairs. And, as he went down, the sergeant thought: *The window! He came through the upstairs window! I would have heard him if it had not been for Mollie and the boy!*

And, as oblivion overwhelmed, he cursed his luck and feared for the children.

MOLLIE PUSHED UP THE SASH WINDOW. Christopher was surprised it gave so easily to a girl's strength. "Get out!" she shouted, "Get out!"

217

"I will not!" yelled Christopher, "I will not!"

"It is our only hope," she yelled back. An instant's glance had told them what was happening. "Get out! Bring help!"

"What help? What…?" he stammered.

"Any help you can find!"

And then the window was full open. And then he went, half willingly, half pushed. And he thought: *Why does she not come too?* But he knew the answer. He knew it was the sergeant she loved. He hit the ground and rolled, and got to his feet and ran.

Chapter 29: Interlude

AT FIRST THERE WAS DARK like the dark on the face of the deep.

Sergeant Joseph was falling. He had been brought up to contemplate such metaphysical concepts as The Bottomless Pit, and this thing before him now seemed the very epitome of what those words might mean. At one point, when it seemed he was about to touch *terra firma*, about to find ground beneath his feet, the thought turned out to be just another illusion.

Like his mother's illusions about his father.

Instead he found himself still floating, just below the ceiling in a room he at first took to be Adele's room at the house in Dovecote. But no, there were differences: a painting of The Blessed Virgin stared at him from a bare wall; a crucifix lay on a drawing room table; a beautiful young woman who was decidedly *not* Adele sat in a chair, her lustrous brown hair falling across her face and over her bent shoulders. Her face was turned away from him because she was crying. The sobs shook her whole body. Finally, she lifted her head and her cheek was bruised and there was a fine line down the side of her forehead which oozed blood.

She spoke to him. "Your father," she said, "is not a bad man... *Non e un uomo cattivo*". She now looked *down* towards him because suddenly he had become small. She spoke to him as a woman does to a child. He *was* a child. Or rather, he inhabited the body of a child, the body of his former self.

"Mother," he said, "*mia madre...*"

"*Uno giorno caprai.*" One day you will understand.

"*Capisco!*" I *do* understand! And he did. He had always understood men like his father. The only thing he did not understand was why others did not understand.

219

He saw his father rarely. Twice a year, Colour Sergeant William Joseph would be home on leave, pay already squandered, rage already manifest. His mother locked Lorenzo in his bedroom and accepted the beatings silently. But the boy knew everything from the sight of her afterwards.

Then he would rush hysterically into one of the Edinburgh alleyways; and, after a breathless time of running, he would reach the border between the Old and New Towns – The Mound, which, he knew, had once been Nor Loch, the dump for the whole city's sewage. Now human progress dictated that the stink of a hundred years was more evenly distributed along the streets.

The scene of his vision was changing. Now he was standing on the stairs, older, calm and breathing easy, though still not as tall as his father. But the stairs made up for it.

Standing on the highest step, he could look his father in the eyes, in those blue Saxon eyes which he had not inherited; he could stare fearlessly at William Joseph, the man whose name his mother had stolen to bestow on him.

"Mrs Joseph," they called his mother, the guests in her boarding house, but it was a lie. Not Mrs Joseph, not *Signora Joseph*, but *La Signorina Schiaffino,* daughter of Schiaffino the cabinet maker, the craftsman whom William called *woodworker* as though it were an insult.

Now William was home again, drinking, shouting, using his fists as always. *"Egli porta con se la Guerra,"* said *La Signorina Sciaffino* in the language they kept from his father, the secret language that so enraged him. "I won't have him talk it!" William once said before he fell over and slept it off, "It's not a *man's* language!"

But as long as Lorenzo and his mother had their secret language, the joke would always be on William, the man who brought the war back with him.

And on the staircase now, those fists were already curled, already tensing to perform the blow, William's voice

220

was already raging, spitting out words like bullets from a Gatling gun. But Lorenzo held his ground, his higher ground, the height that made him equal. And when the blow came, it was the easiest of tricks to step back, to leave space between himself and the fist, to watch his father falter, lose balance, reach out for the bannister rail.

It was the easiest thing in the world for Lorenzo to hook his foot round his father's right leg, pull back, turn slightly, hear his father cry out, shove an open palm in his father's face and watch his father fall.

And afterwards the paying guests were suitably   but not overly – sympathetic. "But it wasnae unexpected!" They too had seen the aftermath of the beatings. They too had locked their doors when William was home. They too had looked for the day he would finally fall over and *not* sleep it off.

And to his mother Lorenzo began to make his confession: "*Ho spinto. Non ci saranno piu percosse,*" but the words did not come fast enough.

She placed a finger on his lips. She said: "*E caduto. Era ubriaco.*" And to the guests she enlarged on the thesis. "He fell. He was a good soldier and a good husband, but he drank." And they sighed and nodded and exchanged glances.

And now Lorenzo's vision changed again. And he was telling his mother that the carpentry was a craft he would always respect, but that he had enlisted to visit foreign parts, perhaps see more of that sun which his red Italian blood required and could not find enough in his watery homeland.

Though he was quick to add he would return often and joyously to see her.

And she said: "*Tu sei mi figlio bellissimo. Sempre tu sei la mia gioia.*"

And he had promised himself, right up until she died: *I will never bring the war back with me.* Even though he had already broken that promise.

And now she was long dead, he had broken that promise again. It was a different house and a different woman. But it was the same promise and he had broken it. He knew that he would be punished; but he did not yet know how brutally. Only God knew that.

But he began to pray the youngsters would not suffer also; that he would not have their lives on his conscience. "*O Dio Mio…*" he began in his strange dream. But suddenly the poetry was changed.

"*Nel mezzo del cammin di nostra vita
mi ritrovai per una selva oscura
che la dirritta via etra smarrita…*"

"*Midway upon the journey of our life
I found myself within a forest dark
for the straightforward pathway had been lost…*"

And then there was light, small shafts at first, merging slowly into the look of day. And he felt not just the throbbing in his head but the ropes that chafed his wrists and told him this was real. This was war. He had brought it back with him and would be cursed for doing so. But, as with any war, the only salvation lay in winning.

Chapter 30

ALLARDYCE went out into the paddock and inspected the three police horses: a Belgian bay gelding about ten or 11 years, some 15 hands; a chestnut roan gelding about 12 hands; and a frisky Welsh tri-coloured colt around the same height.

"Three fine horses in the yard and it was still the paddy wagon for me," he said to Constable Dougan who had accompanied him. "Well, I will take all three of these. And I will take thee and one other man on horseback. The rest can come up in the wagon the way *I* was brought over."

"We'll need the paddy anyway to bring the prisoners back," said Dougan, "If *we* come back."

"If the army is given sway in Granborough, we must hold Dovecote. We must show we've done our part."

"That's still scarce more than a dozen men. A dozen peelers against an army of navvies?" Dougan's eyebrows had climbed to his hairline. He was a middle-aged, middle height, middling fat man with a deprecating demeanour. But Allardyce had known him in tavern brawls and he usually came out a winner.

"I leave thee to make final choice of the third man."

"Then it will be Constable Broome, a young and active lad with a strong manner."

"Fine. Tha finds im and tells im. I will ave first choice of the orse."

"You will have the Belgian," said Dougan, "he is the biggest."

"How well tha knows me," said Allardyce.

IT TOOK THEM half an hour to sign the papers and saddle the horses, and another half hour to reach Dovecote. As they galloped into the main street, all appeared quiet and usual. But the horses snorted and whinnied and stamped the ground.

"It as been a brave summer," said Allardyce, "And now we're getting the result. A bad end to a good time. And the orses know that."

They made their way to the Mission, where Allardyce dismounted and found the front door padlocked. "Well, so much for the regiments of good Protestants."

"They know when to get out," said Dougan.

"They know nobody'll *stop* them getting out. It'll be a long ways different for some others."

"St Saviour," said Broome, "in Bannock Street."

THE NAVVIES WERE GATHERED at the top of Bannock Street, stretched out in a line across the horizon. They eyed the Church down below. They eyed the police – a shorter, thinner line than *they* were.

"It don't look good," said Allardyce, who was doing the looking *up* from the bottom of the hill in front of the church. He now had 15 men and he estimated the mob stood at 50 or 60 and was growing by fits and starts.

"We should reason with them," said Father Flanagan, "for they are God's creatures, after all, and have reason as we do. As all men do." He was a stocky, powerful man who, Allardyce knew, had been a farm labourer in County Mayo before he found his vocation as his mother lay dying from cholic.

"No, Father," said Allardyce, "Reason is the one weapon we do not command." The constable already knew what had to be done. It was time to retreat. It went against the grain and it would go down badly with his superiors and the townsfolk. But he could recognise a losing battle when he saw one.

"We must preserve the church," said Father Flanagan, by which, Allardyce knew, he meant the building at their back, with its stained glass and coloured statues, rather than any spiritual kingdom.

"We must preserve your *people*," said Allardyce.

The priest looked at Allardyce and a weary expression crossed his face. He nodded.

"We will take them out the back of the church, Father, and they can make their way out of Dovecote under our protection."

"Yes. Yes, you are right. The congregation is the important thing," said the priest, "Perhaps those men will leave the building alone when they realise there is nothing of value there." He paused. "I mean nothing of *earthly* value."

"It is the things *not* of earthly value they love to destroy," said the constable. What he did not say was that he counted upon at least ten minutes grace during which the smashing of pews, statues, pulpits and windows would dominate the rioters' interest and make them forget the refugees.

Suddenly the priest cried out, blood spurted from his forehead and he fell to his knees. One of the mob had thrown a stone. Within seconds, a hail of stones came down, narrowly missing the others.

Allardyce helped the priest to his feet and motioned to his men to fall back. They scurried into the church, where 20 or so parishioners had up to now sought sanctuary.

"My God!" cried a woman in a shawl, "What have they done to him?"

"E will live," said Allardyce as the priest regained his composure, wiped away the blood with the hem of his cassock and waved away the attentions of his sympathetic flock.

Well, Allardyce was thinking, *men are all true to type. A farmboy never loses sleep over spilt blood.* Allardyce made his way to the pulpit, climbed its stairs and addressed the congregation from on high.

"God knows I am not your priest," he said, "But today I will be your salvation if you will listen to me."

225

He had their attention. He began to map out his plan. They would go on foot. They would leave the paddy wagon and lead the horses.

THE NAVVIES WERE LED BY RUDD, a pock-marked ganger who shared the floor of Kate's shant. It took them a while to realise that the Catholics had gone. They went down the hill, slowly, suspiciously, stones in their hands when they did not have shovels, pickaxe handles, axes.

They came upon the front of the church and peered in the windows. Stained glass, they decided, was a hindrance to proper vision, else it would not have been a part of the Anti-Christ's abode. They smashed the windows with the stones and climbed in. They cut down the lacquered statues with their axes, hacked at the pews with their shovels, sought out the communion wine and quaffed it.

"Whores of Babylon!" yelled Rudd. He waved a wine bottle to make his point.

Two of them got to fighting over the collection box and Rudd had to chastise them with his pickaxe handle. "Are we brigands?" he asked, "Are we thieves?" He helped them up off the floor to show there were no hard feelings.

And they agreed they were most certainly not thieves. And they divvied up the coins in an honourable and open way amongst them, though there were few enough to go round.

"There," said Rudd, "that's better."

And they threw a match or two among the dry wood of the lacquered statues and fled, laughing.

226

Chapter 31

"WELL," SAID THE MAN WITH THE BEARD, "ye've come round at last." He grinned. He was big, of heavy build. A scar across his right eye where a knife had almost blinded him.

"E's come round," said the second man's voice, high-pitched, almost a giggle. Sergeant Joseph could not see the second man. He could not see Mollie.

The sergeant took a deep breath, trained his unfocused eyes on the bearded one who stood in front of him. He didn't need the clue of the waistcoat to tell him who the man was.

"You'll be Moleskin Jimmy," said the sergeant. His voice sounded weak; he had to take an almighty breath to get to the end of the sentence. And he thought: *What have they yet done to me? And to Mollie?*

He was sitting in the parlour on one of Adele's wooden chairs taken from the kitchen, his hands bound by rope to the struts in the back of it. *But not his feet. They hadn't bothered to tie his feet.* Why hadn't they killed him already?

He turned his head to look round the room and became suddenly aware of a sharp pain in his neck. He winced. Mollie was sat on one of the red upholstered chairs and the man who had to be Cockney Charlie Gallister was sat on the right arm of the chair, leaning over Mollie, imprisoning her with his left arm bent round her shoulder, and with his right hand touching the top of her bare leg, where her dress had ridden up.

She sat with her fists clenched to her face, her eyes darting round the room, from Moleskin to Charlie, to the sergeant. She gave no hint of how frightened she must be. That pleased him, though it was only as he would have expected.

"I'll get the gun," said Charlie, "I'll get is gun!" But he made no move. Instead his fingers loosely traced a pattern on Mollie's leg. She flinched. The sergeant strained at his bonds, but they did not give. Charlie laughed and touched her leg again, higher this time.

"Ye're trussed," said Moleskin, "well and truly. We took care of that. We'll not be hazarding anything more with a man like you."

And to Charlie: "*I've* got the gun. The one and only. That's all the guns we'll be needing." He waved what the sergeant recognised as a Williams & Powell revolver with a chamber that took six bullets, none of them apparently used so far.

"Two guns is better than one," said Charlie. He sounded like a child refused a sweetmeat.

"Not when *ye're* the man picking it up," said Moleskin, "No. We'll leave the other gun out of the game." And to the sergeant he said: "Now then, me bucko, it's been a while that I've wanted to meet a man like you."

The sergeant thought: *He wants to talk.* The blathering barmpot should have killed me outright and Mollie too. But that doesn't suit him. He wants to tell me about himself. So the Navy 44 was still out in the hall where it had fallen. And Mollie would know that. He felt sweat break out on his forehead.

Moleskin said: "Do ye not wonder about life, Mr Joseph? Do ye not wonder how the two of us have sprung up in different tribes, on different sides, but we are the same?"

"Israel and Ishmael," said the sergeant.

Moleskin's eyes lit up. "Oh, a man that knows the word of the Lord is a man that fears Him! I had thought ye would, Mr Joseph. For I had guessed how alike we were! We wander through this dark vale and others know not of our nature. For we are apart from them. We are the Host of the

228

Lord, the warriors of Heaven, the Angels both fallen and upheld."

"Angels," said Charlie.

"I am a soldier," said the sergeant, "therefore a warrior. But how are you a warrior, Jimmy? How are you a soldier? I had you pegged as a blackguard and a scoundrel."

This time Jimmy offered a full laugh. "Every aristocrat was a robber baron once," he said, "and it is the law of man that makes them so. But the Law of God is different."

"Does the Law of God allow the defilement of a good woman and the murder of the man who loved her?"

"She was a whore. And I had no part in the violation. And I killed the corporal only out of necessity. As the wolf kills the lamb. But you know about killing, Mr Joseph. Not only when you wear the Queen's uniform. You killed Derby George and it was a sweet event, I'll wager. As sweet for you as it was torment for him."

"It was justice."

"Justice! What is justice in this world where men lord it over the likes of us, we who are real men, who understand the way of things? No, don't talk to me of justice, Mr Joseph. The only justice is whatever we choose to seek and make happen. We carry our own justice with us."

"And why is that, Jimmy? Tell me."

"Because we are the wolves, never the sheep. We are the gangers, never the pressed men. We judge and decide and order and make happen. In a world of the foolish and the blind who believe in mercy and the mildness of the milksop, we know what it is to slay the Midianites."

He finished and subsided, as though a great work had come to its end. And it had, thought the sergeant. Moleskin Jimmy had made his statement about life, about who he was and how he was the only real thing in a world of illusion.

But there would be a final quotation. He could not end without a quotation. He was that kind of man. The sergeant knew this because he had known this kind of man before. And fought and defeated him.

A deep breath from Moleskin Jimmy. Then: "To everything there is a season, a time to love and a time to hate…"

"…a time of war and a time of peace," said the sergeant, "a time to keep and a time to cast away." And by that time he had moved his right leg just enough so his bound hands could reach the hilt of the dirk he now kept constantly in his stocking. Against such an occasion as this. Ever since the day Derby George had died.

MOLLIE HAD NOT BEEN listening to the word games of the sergeant and the bearded navvy. She had no need to exhibit her knowledge of Scripture as these two men seemed eager to do. She had her own small terrors now, less horrendous than the overarching terror that she would soon be murdered and her body wept over uselessly by her poor father.

These new terrors, more immediate, were embodied by the man whose hands were stroking and caressing the flesh at the top of her legs in a terrible, fearful way that she did not understand.

The man with the high-pitched voice was talking to her, whispering, oblivious now to the debate between the sergeant and the other man, as they were oblivious to him.

He was saying: "Now, my little one, now let us see what undergarments you do favour? Is it silk, I wonder?" His hand crept up her thigh, a finger insinuating its way beneath her petticoat, inside her white cotton bloomers. The muscles in her belly were suddenly rigid. He stroked her. He said: "No, it is not silk. A pity. I likes silk, I does."

His face was so close to hers that she could smell the whisky rankness of his breath. Her own breath was coming in starts.

230

"You do not favour stays," said the man, "though I know some young girls do so at an early age. For it keeps their waists so small a man can span them with his two hands." And he took his hands away from her and raised them in front of her face and spread his fingers and smiled lopsidedly. And he giggled.

She looked hard into his dirty, ill-shaven face and his strangely vacant eyes. Suddenly a word came into her mind. It was a word she had often heard the servants use. It was a word she had heard poor Mrs Tordoff use. Often she would refrain from using a servant's word in case her father might disapprove. But she knew this word was a proper word because she had come upon it in no less a volume than *Wuthering Heights*, with regard to its use by the servants in that book.

"You," she said to the man with the two raised hands, "are *gormless*."

And the lopsided smile disappeared. And his right hand came down on her face with a brutal force and she screamed.

MOLESKIN JIMMY JUMPED. He whirled round towards Mollie and Charlie, pointing the gun, momentarily confused. It was the first time the sergeant had seen him nonplussed.

"*What the hell...?*" shouted Jimmy.

"Get him away from the girl!" shouted the sergeant, "Get him away from the girl, you warrior of the Host of the Lord!"

Amazingly, Jimmy obeyed. He waved the gun. He said: "Charlie! I've had enough of your uncleanliness, your vile fornications. Stand up and away from her!" And Charlie did so, awkward, shame-faced, like that floundering boy who somehow still lived in his dissipated body.

And in that moment, when Jimmy's attention was turned away from him, the sergeant moved the dirk against the ropes round his wrists, carefully, carefully, but speedily and with a firmness that was etched in the muscles of his face. And the ropes fell away.

And it was Charlie, facing the sergeant, who first saw what had happened, that their enemy was free, that the tables had been turned, that the outcome was suddenly in doubt.

He squealed. He shouted: "Look! Look!" and raised a wavering arm and pointed a trembling finger at their nemesis.

And then three things happened.

First off, the sergeant made a rare mistake. He knew it was a mistake simultaneous with doing it, but could not revoke the result of his misjudgement. He threw the dirk straight at Cockney Charlie Gallister. Even as he did so, he knew very well why it had happened. The man had touched young Mollie. That was the reason. But it was the wrong reason. The man he should have feared and brought down while he had the chance was the man with the gun. Moleskin Jimmy was the joker in the pack, not Charlie.

The blade pierced Charlie in the neck and he fell back, bounced against the wall, made wet gagging sounds between his teeth while his hands struggled frantically to dislodge the blade. Then he stopped, went stiff, fell forward and hit the floor and the sergeant knew straightway he was dead.

The second thing that happened was that Mollie leapt from the chair and threw herself at Jimmy. Her wrists caught at his neck and her nails scored red weals down his cheeks. And Jimmy yelled and lashed out at her with the gun and caught her on the side of the face. And she fell.

Then the sergeant was upon him, and they fell against the armchair, glanced off, rolled across the floor, the sergeant pushing his assailant's right arm upwards and back as Jimmy fought frantically to train the gun at his head.

And at once the sergeant felt again the pain in his neck, the result of the blow Charlie Gallister had delivered on

232

the stairs. And a feeling of nausea rose inside him. And the sights around him flickered and once again his consciousness failed.

ALLARDYCE'S EXPEDITION had returned to the mission. This time he broke the padlock. The streets around were as deserted as before. He led his fugitives into the Mission, got them seated, looked for a kettle. "Bring in the horses too," he told his men.

They would not want to leave any sign outside of their present occupation, though he hoped the rioters would not bother with pursuit. It was his experience that, so often in such cases, the malcontents enjoyed most the visual results of destruction – it was the burnings and the breakings that appeased them. More often they only bothered killing when there was nothing more spectacular to accomplish.

Even so, he was quick to post lookouts. And it was only a matter of minutes before one of his constables alerted him.

Allardyce scanned the street from the Mission window. "It's only a boy," he said.

"And he's the only one out there. Are we gonna bring im in?"

Allardyce considered. If the boy was a scout for the rioters, they would be giving themselves away. On the other hand...

"I would not want im come to arm because of our inaction. Besides, he might yet be injured and require our aid." By this time the boy was no more than ten yards away and suddenly he looked familiar.

"I know that boy," said Allardyce, "By God, it is young Christopher, Joel Truss's lad!"

MOLLIE PICKED HERSELF UP. She thought: *The gun. I must get the gun.* The sergeant had dropped it in the hall when

233

the intruders attacked him. She glanced back quickly at the tussling figures of the sergeant and the moleskin man. It seemed the moleskin man was winning. And even if he were not...

What had Christopher said when she caught him smoking the cigar? "It is not for *girls!*" As though anything that existed in God's world, any pain, any joy or indulgence, could *not* be for girls!

Though some things could certainly not be for boys! One of these was the rush of blood that had come to her suddenly two months ago. Fortunately, Mrs Tordoff – obviously at the instigation of her father – had seen fit already to warn her of such an occurrence half a year previous and reassure her that it was not a symptom of consumption or any other deadly malady. The Curse of Eve, Mrs Tordoff had called it. But without any sense of dread.

Now Mrs Tordoff was dead and the moleskin man had surely been the one who killed her.

Mollie was consumed with fury. She rushed out of the room. The Colt 44 lay by the staircase, large and steely and blue. But not as ungainly as the airgun had been. She picked it up. It was *not* too heavy. Not too heavy for a girl. She clasped it was well as she could in both hands. She turned and fell against the door of the parlour, forcing it open again.

The sergeant, it seemed, had succeeded in wresting the gun from the moleskin man's grasp. It had somehow been flung across the room to land by the window. But the moleskin man was pummelling the sergeant and the sergeant suddenly lost his grip, and the moleskin man was on his feet and turning and running and bending and picking up the gun with a deft sweep of his arm and aiming it straight at the sergeant.

And Mollie's own gun was heavy now and she had begun to perspire. Perhaps she should wipe her brow. She felt suddenly vulnerable. I *am* a girl after all, she thought. And she

234

thought: *If I am a girl, should I really be doing a thing like this?*

And she thought: *Well, I am proud of my cleverness. Let us see if I can be clever at this.*

The moments became something else: not quite hours, but extended and elastic. She had lost her sense of time. She could hear her heart beat. No, more than hear it – feel it. She became suddenly calm. She said to herself: *I will shoot. I have the chance to shoot and I will do so.* And then she saw that the moleskin man was cocking the pistol in his hands. With great effort, using both her thumbs, Mollie cocked the Colt 44. She manoeuvred the gun as best she could – it was not, after all, as heavy as the airgun. She took aim and gritted her teeth and pulled the trigger.

There was a jolt that shuddered her from head to foot.

And the moleskin man screamed as the bullet hit him in the chest. He fell against the wall, then steadied himself, turned his body, and – with a look of utter disbelief upon his face – turned his gun on Mollie.

But that moment of turning had been enough for her to use both thumbs again, to cock the pistol one more time and aim at the moleskin man's face, now filling with hatred. And she took aim and clenched her teeth and pulled the trigger a second time. And the head of the moleskin man exploded and the body of the moleskin man fell back, slid down the wall, arms flailing. And the gun in his hand came up – as though of its own accord – and flame spurted from its barrel followed by a sound as loud as thunder, as loud as her own gun had sounded.

And the sound filled her head and seemed to fill the world.

And the bullet hit her. And it was *her* turn to scream. She screamed with the shock of it though there was yet no pain. She could see the bone burst through her skin and the blood spurt out of her. It was then the pain joined with the horror of it.

And perhaps, she thought, as she fell into a swoon, it is a good and necessary thing to bear pain and horror on occasion. Well, it would be hard, terribly hard, to die. But she had one satisfaction at least. No. Two.

First, the shot was good. This time the partridge would not fly away. This time the partridge was killed. No doubt of that.

And secondly, God be praised, her Sergeant Joseph was saved.

THE SERGEANT WAS already on his feet as Allardyce and Dougan crashed into the room.

"It's not a constable we need," said the sergeant, "it's a surgeon."

"It's only the arm," said Allardyce.

"Then it is the arm we must save," said the sergeant. And he picked her up and carried her to the door.

Chapter 32

THE 19TH FOOT WERE STRETCHED OUT ACROSS THE TOP of Granborough's Main Street. Down below, the navvies shouted and swore and threw bricks and stones and one or two waved pistols.

The troops had made good time – a commandeered train from York to Selby, then a forced march across the countryside. "We will not let the daylight come again before we meet these insurgents," said Colonel Redvers.

He dispatched his two best captains   Lewis and Rees – to command the prongs of his pincer movement. So they had come into Granborough in early evening, one line from the west, one from the north east, and quickly secured the outskirts of the town.

"Not much resistance so far, sir," said Rees, "the locals are more welcoming than is usual."

"And so they should be," said the Colonel. "We are saving their women from defilement and their businesses from destruction. But we have not yet met with the navvies."

But they met with the navvies soon enough.

Now the sun had begun its long setting, the navvies were tired. Pleasantly tired, for it had been a good day's work. But tired nonetheless. They stood outside the taverns that they had invaded some hours previous and sang songs and shouted their insults.

"There are more than a hundred by my calculation. This will be the main force of them and we must engage them before darkness," the Colonel reiterated to Lewis and Rees, "Or they will slip away."

"We are lucky," said Rees, "that we have the summer light."

"We must engage them in the next quarter hour," said the Colonel, "or the summer light will be gone and so will they."

And so they engaged the navvies.

The Colonel reckoned on the advantage of the heights to aid victory. Main Street was like a valley in the centre of the town, and the navvies – instinctively but foolishly – had settled in a solid formation at the lowest level. Attack for them meant uphill, escape in the opposite direction also meant uphill, though a few might dribble away in the side streets.

"I had hoped to surround them," said the Colonel, "but I believe we have enough purchase on them now. We must be swift and we must be brutal."

And so they were.

At first, on their way down the hill, they tripped and blundered as they avoided the stone-throwing and avoided also slipping on the loose stones already thrown. Halfway down the hill, Lewis gave the order to stand and fire. They did so. Even though their position commanded little accuracy, the tight bunching of the target meant some would undoubtedly be hit. Rees, using field glasses, saw at least eight men fall.

The soldiers advanced a further 50 yards down, the stone-throwing becoming more accurate now, with one or two troopers falling. A shot rang out from the other side.

"Halt!" shouted Lewis, "Volleys!" And their own firepower rang out again. And – at Rees's rule-of-thumb reckoning – some 20 of the navvies were hit.

"We can have a massacre here," said Lewis. He repeated this, shouting to the Colonel some few yards higher up. The Colonel sauntered down to him.

"If need be," said the Colonel, "for I have the fullest support from the highest echelon."

"Holtby," said Lewis.

"The idiot has his uses."

They proceeded further down the hill, gaining momentum. They saw the navvies break ranks and turn to run.

"Halt!" shouted Lewis. He waited for the fleeing navvies on the other side of the hill to be level with his own men, then shouted: "Volleys!" and the volleys came yet again and a large number of the navvies fell. "Good," said Lewis, mainly to himself. Then he waved to the Colonel and the Colonel waved back.

The navvies down below were of a sudden scurrying all over, making for the side streets. "Fire at will!" shouted Lewis. And they did, firing into the valley below them, watching with joy the flailing arms and crumpled legs, hearing with a fierce pleasure the screams and cries.

And when the first troops reached the bottom, there was little resistance. Most of those navvies still unhurt were on their knees, hands in the air, begging for mercy, sometimes in the name of Jesus Himself whom they had so much forgotten earlier. The wounded lay and moaned as wounded would.

Rees, ever the man for a headcount, said: "Colonel, I believe we have captured some 80, wounded more than 30 and killed maybe half a dozen. We need to bring in the surgeons."

"Right," said the Colonel, "but they will tend our own wounded first. Even to the slightest scratch." It was constant thinking on the welfare of his men that had made him the excellent commander he was.

"And shall we then take Shant Town?" asked Lewis.

"Indeed we shall. For there will be assizes and hangings after this and we will need to gather the miscreants. But we will not burn any dwelling if we can avoid. For this is the pledge I have given Lord Holtby. It is our guarantee of protection if the radicals should attempt to bring us before the judiciary."

"Of course," said Lewis.

THE EXHAUSTED NAVVIES looked up from their drinking and their loud talk. They looked up in surprise as Carribee came down the ladder from his loft. He was fully dressed in clothes he had never before given them the chance to see: a ragged red military jacket with gold epaulettes, the front unbuttoned, a jacket that had once belonged to a Grenadier; ballooning pantaloons that might have been copied from a woodcut illustration to the Arabian Nights, though he knew none of the men who watched him had ever read the Arabian Nights; and stern, studded, brown navvy boots. He carried a grey knapsack hung over one shoulder. He reached the bottom of the ladder, his feet squelched in the mud and shit of their home and he turned.

Carribee stood, still slightly stooped from his descent. And then he spoke. He said: "I leave here. I leave here now." And he saw their surprise turn to amazement.

One of the men – his name Carribee remembered as Butler or Bulmer – said: "He spoke." He said it in a breathless tone of voice that might not have been out of place after the healing of a cripple at a Baptist meeting.

Carribee looked round him. He smiled. One of the men – Carribee did not know his name but always thought of him as Bad Knee because his legs were twisted by some long-ago accident – said: "Have a drink with us, mate." And he offered the half-empty bottle of rum from which he had been swigging.

Carribee knew this kind of invitation always led to a challenge. If he declined, it would shortly be followed by such a comment as: "So we're not good enough to drink with ye?" If he accepted, it would lead to more awkward questions with the same result.

Carribee spoke gently. He said: "No."

Bad Knee stretched to his full height and his lips began the move that would end in a snarl. But Butler or Bulmer said: "Watch it, Dixon. Don't be a damn fool." And Bad Knee – Carribee would always think of him by that name

240

– hesitated, adjusted his lips, took a step backwards and started guzzling away at the rum again.

Apart from the guzzling noise, there was silence.

"My friend is dead," said Carribee. He let his gaze wander the room. "My friend Moleskin is dead."

"How would you know?" asked Butler or Bulmer.

"Because he has not returned," said Carribee, "So our business is finished." And he added: "Also I hear soldiers in the streets and I know this is no longer any place for me."

And he sighed. And he stood to his full height. And he walked with broad strides, but not quickly, towards the door. In a moment or two he was gone into the morning.

He knew they would quickly climb the ladder, enter his loft, landing like vultures for pickings. And they would find, hanging from the roof beams, the body of Handsome Halloran, handsome no more.

IT WAS THE FIRST DAY FOR WEEKS there had been any rain. Now it hammered down. Kate and Betty did not welcome it.

"All very well for some," said Kate, "for farmers and suchlike. For them Nettles and his daughter. But no good for navvies."

"And nuthink good for us," said Betty, clamping her remaining teeth on her pipe, "gangs laid off, men stinking round the shant all day, can't get drunk, can't get whores, can't even play cards 'cos they've nowt to lose and there's nowt to win."

"Not to mention the good men been killed..." said Kate.

"Many of em good payers," said Betty.

"We're in a bad way, pet," said Kate, "And not just us..." She was thinking of her nephew and how his business had suffered in the wake of so much upheaval. Some of his girls had refused to pay the usual; others had sloped off to

241

London, or wherever, looking for a better berth, without so much as a *by your leave*, and leaving a month's rent owing. She sighed.

They were in the bar of the Marlborough, sitting in a corner, hugging tankards of ale, the only customers.

"But it'll change fast enough," said Betty.

"You reckon?" said Kate.

"His Lordship's bringin in new men, I hear. Well, he's bound to... Got contracts and such. Got to honour contracts. Got to build t' bloody railroad."

Kate took a swig of her drink. "Them soldiers was a brilliant sight, quite shinin' I thought them."

"Was you here? Was you at Main Street when it happened? The Battle of Granborough Main?"

"Lookin out. Lookin out of a window or two. Lookin out from this very room to be onest."

"Don't look like they did a lot of damage." Betty was glancing round the room, searching the usual crannies, finding how little had changed.

"No, I reckon as ow they'd got *fatigued* by the time they got here. They was tekkin free drink o'course. What with Master and Madam Daviot slopin off like thieves in the night before they come. But they was past their worst by that time. One or two even brought me a drink." Kate smiled at the memory.

"Daviot. I've always thought that a funny name. Unpleasant. A worryin name. I'm thinkin it might be French." Betty huddled close to Kate, head-to-head. "Did you see it all then?"

"All them soldier boys. And their uniforms. And their shot. Admirin, that's what I was. Makes a change from navvies."

"Oh, navvies got it downstairs, they do, no doubt about that..."

"When they're not dead drunk..."

242

"But they look such shit, most of em, whereas your soldier..."

"Yer brave soldier boy..."

"Nuthink like a red jacket to warm the cockles..."

They both laughed then. "Some we'll miss," said Kate, "navvies, I mean. And a few others."

"Handsome Halloran. Hanged hisself over a gamblin debt. So they say."

"Shame about the tooth."

"Oh, I *liked* that tooth. I like a man with a bit of character."

"And your Moleskin..."

"Not *my* Moleskin. Any rumours to the contrary, any tales of Moleskin and me in business together is just lies. He's a man I stayed well away from, you know, unless it were time to get rent."

"And right to do so. But it's strange to think him gone. Killed by a sodomite is what I heard."

"Well, nothing about that man would surprise me. But he had a way with him, I'll admit. Never saw him afeared of nuthink. And no man lived but wasn't afeared of im!"

"A man that other men are afeared of! That's good, that is."

"Oh yes. That's the very best, that is."

"I'll tell you summat that'll surprise you. Moleskin's dog."

"Oh, that devil! That fearsome beast..."

"No, he's not. I've still got im. What home did the poor mite have after Moleskin was gone? And he's good to have around if any of the lads tries something naughty. Oh, he's fierce alright. But e's lovin too."

"Well," said Kate, "who'd've thought it?"

And then the sun came out again.

And neither one of them mentioned Cockney Charlie.

Chapter 33

MOLLIE'S LEFT ARM WAS ITCHING quite terribly. The point at issue lay just below the bandage where her fingers could not reach. "Wait for a moment," she said to Christopher. She threw off the sling – it was just an old scarf her father had found in a drawer – and looked round the room.

"I want a pencil," she said, "Find me one."

Christopher handed her a pencil. She pushed it down beneath the dressing and scratched away. "Ahhhhh!" she said ecstatically.

"Should you really be doing that?" asked Christopher, "did the doctors say it was right?"

"They said I should do it just as often as I liked. Every time the wound itched, I should scratch it."

"No, they didn't," said Christopher.

"No, they didn't," admitted Mollie. She was starting to think that Christopher was becoming more intelligent with the passing of time. For a start, he had recently got into the habit of contradicting her. And to her surprise, she quite enjoyed it, though she didn't often let him get away with it. It must be a sign that he was growing up, she thought. She also noted he had got significantly taller in the past few weeks.

They were sitting in his bedroom, lying across his bed, on a wet day in late August, trying to remember how to prove the Pythagorean theorem. It was a new idea of Miss Brockelbank that the children should know some basic geometry. Again to Mollie's surprise, Christopher had proved himself far more susceptible to the mysteries of Pythagoras than she had. To put it bluntly, he was miles better at the subject.

Well, *she* was still better at poetry and history. And geography and the novels of Walter Scott. So God in His mysterious way had clearly intended to balance their relationship.

"Now," she said, "let me look at the diagram again." He showed her his own pencilled diagram, the fat squares sat on the sides of the triangle like angular toads, and all those lines AB, BC, CD and so on, cutting across everything like the strands of a spider's web. She sighed. "Do I understand I am supposed to copy this?"

"I'll do it for you," he said and he took back the pencil, picked up his ruler and the little board they had taken to using as a kind of movable desk, and began to draw on a clean sheet of paper.

Mollie turned and gazed out of the window. The rain had given over and there was a hint of a rainbow across the field, starting behind the dry stone wall – the *wet* stone wall as it was now.

"You're not paying attention," said Christopher.

"No, I'm not." It didn't hurt to prick the bubble of his conceit now and again, to show who was really in charge. Even so, she needed to be able to draw that diagram when Miss Brockelbank tested them next Tuesday. So she made the effort to look interested as she lay on the bed next to him and gazed over his shoulder. At one point she put her hand on his arm and he hesitated for a moment.

Then: "Let ABC be a right-angled triangle," said Christopher, "having the angle BAC right-angled."

"Right," said Mollie.

"Right-*angled*," corrected Christopher.

"Yes," said Mollie.

"I say that the square on BC is equal to the squares on BA and AC."

Mollie said nothing.

"For let there be described on BC the square BDEC and on BA, AC the square GBHC."

She hid a yawn with her hand.

"Through A, let AL be drawn parallel to either BD or CE and let AD, FC be joined…"

245

She knew the next part had to do with angles.

"Then, since each of the angles BAC, BAG is right-angled, it follows that with a straight line BA..."

And then the clock on the chest of drawers struck the hour.

"Oh dear," said Mollie. She raised a finger to her lips, "I fear it is already time for me to return home."

"It is still quite early," said Christopher.

"We are having early tea," said Mollie.

"You could have tea with *us*."

"But I have promised father."

"Then I will walk you."

"No," she said, "another day perhaps. But you may fetch my coat."

He went off to find the coat while she went into the living room where Mr Truss was polishing the airgun with an old rag. His movements were slow with the peculiar deliberateness that she usually noticed only in men of great age.

"How goes the schoolwork?" he asked, though he did not raise his eyes from the task in hand and his speech was as slow as his polishing. "I believe the science of geometry is of great usefulness in the plotting of trajectory and the use of artillery."

"I too have heard that." Mollie smiled and gazed at him. She knew his situation was a direct result of his wounding, with perhaps the added effect of the morphine. But alongside her pity for Mr Truss was a feeling of *joy* – yes, she had to admit the word. She was delighted that she herself had made such a fine recovery from her own wound. Was that selfish? Was that heartless? Was it a sin to feel such pleasure?

Christopher returned with her brown tartan gaberdine, the one with the hood, and helped her on with it. "We can do more tomorrow if you wish," he said.

"I will think about that," she said. Then: "Goodbye, Christopher, Goodbye, Mr Truss."

They offered a chorus of farewells and Christopher let her out through the front door. When she looked back, she saw him waving from the window and she smiled to herself but did not return the wave. Instead, she turned once more towards the vicarage and quickened her pace.

At that point she realised she had left the sling-scarf in Christopher's bedroom. Should she go back? She thought the better of it. In any case, he might decide, on discovering the scarf, to bring it over to the vicarage...

It was when she reached the dry stone wall – the point where she had seen the foot of the rainbow – that she was suddenly aware of the sound of the horse along the road that ran parallel. And she knew a moment before she turned that it was Snowbird. Now he pulled in at the side of the wall and whinnied and she went across and touched his nose and stroked his main. And she looked up at the rider.

"Sergeant Joseph," she said, "I wondered when I should see you again."

THE SERGEANT HAD NOT been quite sure of his intention in riding out that September day. It had partly to do with exercising Snowbird, partly with reminding himself of the wet Yorkshire countryside one more time before seeing his world utterly displaced by desert, scrubland and jungle.

If it also had to do with seeing for the final time certain people, he had not fully decided who those people might be, but he had known Mollie would be one of them. First of all, he had to know how the arm had set, for it continued to nag him that he should have been braver in her rescue, should have seen off the danger with more alacrity.

He had been making his way towards the vicarage when he came upon her in the field. It was opportune to speak to her then. He was not loth to renew acquaintance with Mr

247

Proudlove, whom he had liked from the start, but he did not regard this as a primary goal. His business with the vicar, as with Joel Truss and Constable Allardyce, was effectively ended; but with Mollie he felt no closing. Something about the girl had enticed him from the start and he could not exclude her from his affections. Now, it seemed, he had been given his chance for a final meeting.

"Young Miss Proudlove," he said, "I have come to offer a soldier's goodbye."

"And what is special about a soldier's goodbye?"

"Only that a soldier is never sure of his return." And he dismounted and walked alongside of her, the wall separating them. When they came to the end of the wall, he opened the gate and walked Snowbird onto the grass. The horse began straightway to graze and Mollie patted his neck and flanks.

"Well," she said, "and what does my sergeant say when he says goodbye?"

"Your sergeant has his own special words for he has been honoured with the gift of tongues. The words are these:
Nel mezzo del cammin di nostra vita
mi ritrovai per una selva oscura
che la dirritta via etra smarrita.
Ahi quanto a dir qual era e cosa dura
esta selva selvaggia e aspra e forte
che nel pensier rinova la paura!"

And Mollie said:
"Tant'e amara che poco e piu morte;
ma per trattar del ben ch'i'vi trovai,
diro de l'altre cose ch'i'v'ho scorte...
Oh, sergeant, these are fine words indeed!"

He laughed. "You have learned Italian since I last saw you."

248

"Only a smidgin. Only a few lines' worth. I am still very ignorant." And she added: "I no longer have to rely entirely on Mr Longfellow."

"Even so," he said, "it is a fine translation!"

"It is something I have often studied since and something I shall never forget. Far better than Mr Browning and *Porphyria's Lover!*"

"Oh yes! Far better, Miss Proudlove!"

"You did not let them strangle *me* with my hair, Sergeant."

"But I let them injure you, Miss Proudlove. And that to my eternal shame."

"Well, you see how recovered I am. So let us celebrate the good rather than speak of the evil."

There was a brief silence between them. Then she said: "You did not leave me in the forest dark when the straightforward pathway had been lost." She sighed. "Life is not all like Mr Browning is it? Yet it is not all like Mr Shelley either."

"Nor even like *Dante Alighieri.*"

She turned to Snowbird. "I should like to ride him. I have done so once; but then I was a child and I sat safe in the arms of the sergeant. Now I should prefer to sit alone on him."

"You are *still* a child."

"In some ways, yes I am. I own that is true. I go to the schoolroom and I giggle when the boys act rudely. Today I have studied Pythagoras and have failed to understand it. And I have teased poor Christopher beyond what would be decent if I were *not* a child. But in other ways..." She hesitated. "Will you help me up, sergeant? I know I can trust your strong arm."

He helped her into the saddle. Snowbird stayed still while she mounted, then raised his head and snorted. "It is good," she said, "that I have my raincoat with its long skirts so I will not be immodest, now I am no longer *altogether* a

249

child. Now you must let go the rein and give it into my hand."

He did so. She pulled the horse round to the left, away from the wall, and completed a circle. "You see how I hold him, sergeant, how my arm is grown strong again."

"I see you still wear the dressing like a wounded soldier."

"But today I threw away the silly sling."

"That is progress."

"Dr Arbuthnot will think so." Snowbird made a second circle as she directed him. "What," she said, "will become of Mrs Barraclough, now you are returning to your regiment?"

"Adele has made her own life here as I have made mine far away. She will be well, I know that. She will find... others."

"Do you mean other *men*, sergeant?"

"I am sorry, Miss Proudlove. I had not meant it to sound unseemly."

"I am sure you did not." She made a further circle. "And while you are away, sergeant, shall I write to you?"

He remained silent.

She brought Snowbird to a halt. "That must mean I should not."

"There is no future in writing to soldiers, Miss Proudlove. You will find there are plenty of fine young men within your county."

"And supposing I do not choose to remain in my county?"

"Then there will be find young men wherever you go. For, as I told you when we first met, you are fair in the tint of your hair and fair in the eyes of men."

She stopped the horse and climbed down. His hands touched her shoulders to steady her.

"Oh sergeant, we have seen so much, you and I!" Her eyes were wet.

He touched her lips with his finger then mounted Snowbird. He touched the brim of his hat. "Good day to you, Miss Proudlove."

"Good day to you, Sergeant Joseph."

He did not look back.

AND LATER, AS HE RODE INTO DOVECOTE, as Adele came out of the house to greet him and he began in his mind to fashion the final words he would say to her, he was suddenly reminded of another woman, only glimpsed in a sepia photograph, a woman who had played such a major role in his life and whom he had never actually met. And he thought: *No future in writing to soldiers. No future at all.*

Epilogue: Busumbi, Southern Africa, 1868

THE CORPORAL STOOD STOCK STILL with the smoking rifle in his hand. He could feel his heart beat-beating. He could hear nothing of the life around him, only the sound of the shot reverberating. His shoulder still felt the recoil.

He said to the sergeant: "What have I done?"

The sergeant said something but it was inaudible. Later the sergeant would say to him, repeating word for word what he'd said at that moment: "What have you done? You've saved my life, Phil!"

Now the corporal looked round at the others, men he'd shared his life with, men he'd have *given* his life at any time to protect. They were cheering, surely, though he couldn't hear them. They looked as if they were cheering. They supported him. They thought he'd done right. For a moment it lifted him. He smiled. He raised the rifle above his head to acknowledge their approval. They waved their arms. Yes, he had done right. He knew it then. Later he would doubt again. But for the moment he felt he had done right. He laughed.

Now his hearing returned. Not a pipsqueak at a time – but suddenly, a great rush of sound. The sergeant was bleeding, dabbing at his stomach with someone's tunic; and Dr Walters, the surgeon, rushed up to him, pulled the tunic away, opened a black bag and poured some brown liquid from a green bottle over the wound.

The sergeant cried: "Dear God, Mr Walters! The cure hurts more than the damage!"

"A little hurt will save you from infection!" said the surgeon. He was a short, plump, grey-haired man with a permanent stoop who showed little fear in action and no respect for any layman's medical opinion. Rumour had it he had once been a major but had been demoted for drunkenness to second lieutenant. Certainly it was noted he never now touched alcohol.

"Infection!" shouted Pvt Horswell, a foolish and reckless man. "And the sergeant and the corporal have saved us *all* from infection!" And another cheer went up, and the corporal joined in.

And then the soldiers standing around him moved aside, made way for the lieutenant.

"Briscoe!" snapped the lieutenant. And: "Joseph!" He did not use their rank to address them as he usually did. The corporal stood sharply to attention; and in doing so, dropped his rifle. He felt foolish of a sudden.

The sergeant made no move; the surgeon continued to dab the wound. "A stitch or two," he said.

"More than two," said the sergeant.

"You can count them while I do it," said the surgeon. He turned to the lieutenant. "Sir," he said, "this man needs immediate attention."

"And the Zulu?" asked the lieutenant. It was the first time anyone had mentioned Bekhi.

"I believe he is dead," said the surgeon, "but I will ascertain." He walked across to the body, bent over the face, lifted the eyelids, picked up an arm to feel the pulse, then stood again and returned to the lieutenant. "Yes," he said, "the man is with his Maker."

"Before his final judgement," said the sergeant.

"Now," said the surgeon, "I must deal with the stitching, if you will excuse us, sir."

The lieutenant said nothing. The surgeon turned away, escorting the sergeant towards a large rock where he manoeuvred his patient into a position half-sitting half-lying, took a needle and thread from his bag and began the operation.

"Could I not have whisky?" asked the sergeant in a loud voice. The men standing around laughed again.

253

"Whisky is for celebration," said the surgeon.

"Give him the whisky!" shouted Horswell. More laughter.

The lieutenant turned to the corporal. "Briscoe, what happened here?"

The corporal looked hard at the lieutenant and then – almost as if he were an actor seeking a prompt – across to the sergeant, now pulling extravagant faces and letting out high-pitched wails to entertain the men as the needle burrowed in and out of the gash in his stomach.

The corporal had often wondered what made the sergeant the kind of man he was. The sergeant had the gift of command. That was the simplest and best way to state it. He could inspire the men, rouse them to action; he could be a bully or a father confessor. He was feared and he was loved.

I assuredly love him, thought the corporal. But how could this be so? Was it something in his face, his voice, his bearing? All these things and yet... Others seemed to have such individual gifts but could never use them as effectively. The sergeant was the man the corporal wished himself to be.

"Briscoe!" shouted the lieutenant. He was red in the face now.

The corporal studied that face. He saw a boyishness that in some way reflected his own. He saw a certain dogged quality, a willingness to go the distance when the going was straightforward. But he also saw the thing he dreaded in himself – he saw fear.

"Sir!" he said, coming to attention again.

"Tell me what has happened here."

"I have shot the Zulu, sir." This in his loud, staccato parade ground voice.

"And why have you shot the Zulu?"

"He stabbed the sergeant, sir."

"And why did he stab the sergeant?"

The corporal wanted to say: *Because he was a traitor, sir. Because he has killed his fellow scout and was leading us into ambush. Everybody knows that, sir. Everybody except you.* But he could not. *Fear, he thought, I feel the fear.*

Finally he said: "We must ask the sergeant, sir." This time he spoke in his natural voice. He thought: *I will not show the fear.*

"This is extraordinary," said the lieutenant.

"Yes, sir."

"Get your tunic, corporal. And then we will talk again." The lieutenant walked over to where the surgeon was finishing his needlework. He began talking to the sergeant. The sergeant was answering him with the casualness that a wounded man was perhaps allowed when talking to an officer in the field. At this distance his words were indistinct.

The lieutenant and the surgeon then walked away, towards that area where the lieutenant had laid his bedroll. The sergeant came back to the corporal.

"I am to get my tunic," said the sergeant, "I am to be properly dressed."

They retrieved their tunics and began walking over to where the lieutenant and the surgeon were talking. That conversation, thought the corporal, looked somewhat heated. They passed a detail of two soldiers digging a grave for the Zulu. The soldiers stopped digging momentarily to acknowledge them.

The lieutenant and the surgeon stopped their conversation. The lieutenant motioned for them to sit on the ground. "Again I order you," said the lieutenant, "to tell me all that happened in this matter."

The sergeant said: "We had grown suspicious of the Zulu, sir. We believe he had killed his uncle, the brave Ayanda, and had made agreement with our enemies."

"What reason have you to think this?"

255

"I personally have served with Ayanda on a dozen campaigns and I do not believe he would refuse to return to camp at this juncture. Such a move would countermand your orders, sir, and that is something Ayanda would never contemplate."

"You must let *me* be the judge of that," said the lieutenant. The surgeon leaned forward as if to say something but the lieutenant silenced him with a wave of his arm.

"I know," said the sergeant, "that Beikhi had argued for a rapid advance to the top of the escarpment. I believe such an action will lead us into ambush."

"If there is such an ambush," said the lieutenant, "you will have only yourself to blame. That shot will have alerted our enemies even if they had not previously known of our whereabouts." He sighed. "But we know we are close to our quarry and it would be foolish to allow ourselves to be stayed now. Rather rely on our superior firepower and courage."

"Sir..." began the sergeant.

"Enough," said the lieutenant.

The sergeant raised an arm. He had in his hand the long curved knife that he must have taken from the Zulu. He slashed at the lieutenant's throat and rolled aside as the blood spurted out.

The corporal did not move at all, and so it happened that he felt his trousers splashed with the hideous warm liquid. "*Aaghhh!*" he shouted.

The lieutenant rose momentarily to his feet and clutched his throat but no sound came from him. He fell in a heap at the corporal's feet.

The sergeant jumped up. He turned to the circle of men standing round them. "Look!" he shouted, waving the knife, "the evil Zulu has done for Lieutenant Castleden!" He turned to the surgeon. "Mr Walters, you have saved many a life in this campaign. I trust your silence in this matter will be responsible for saving many others."

The corporal was violently sick over the lieutenant's bedroll. It was the first time in five years of military service that he had allowed himself to vomit in front of his fellows.

Before he washed his trousers in the stream that ran at the bottom of the camp, he took from his pocket the sepia photograph. "Oh my love," he said, "I will be with you soon and the army will see no more of me."

Fiction in Nettle Books

Heaven Scent
John Winter

A comic novel set in the swinging sixties. Charlie wanted to be part of the sexual revolution but it sort of passed him by. Now he and fellow reporters on a seaside weekly paper have something to take their minds off summers of love – when the sleepy resort is rocked by mystery explosions. Is it the Isle of Wight Republican Army?

ISBN:978-0-9561513-6-0 **£10**

Homer's ODC
Michael Yates

Raymond is a shy young man with two A levels. He wishes he'd gone to Uni. But his father wants him to take over the family business. And his father is a gangster. Barry wants to be a poet. But he's also – in his own words – a user of the mental health services. A shot rings out. It's the shot that brings Ray and Barry together – and sets off a sequence of violent events that ends in grim murder and even grimmer poetry.

ISBN:978-0-9561513-7-7 **£10**

Pomfret
Edited by Brian Lewis

Ten stories about historical Yorkshire town Pontefract by Yorkshire writers including Colin Hollis, Howard Frost, Linda Jones, Robin Gledhill, Ann Rhodes, Walter Storey, John A Goodrich and Susan McCartney. Illustrated by Yorkshire artists including Jane Walsh, Barbara Smith and Dianne Ibbertson.

ISBN: 978-0-9561513-8-4   **£8**

Non-fiction in Nettle Books

Flying with a Broken Wing
Sat Mehta

A boy's story of growing up in India's turbulent times. Sat Mehta was five years old when he and his family became destitute refugees, his uncle murdered during partition riots. Then Sat suffered a broken arm, complications set in and amputation seemed inevitable. Then a famous English surgeon agreed to operate...

ISBN:978-0-9561513-2-2   **£10**

www.ingramcontent.com/pod-product-compliance
Lightning Source LLC
Chambersburg PA
CBHW071136260626
47162CB00003B/814